Essence of Galenia

Book Three

◆

Into the Valley

By

Laura L. Comfort

Essence of Galenia: Into the Valley

By Laura L. Comfort

ISBN: 978-0-9920792-6-0

"When we believe in lies, we cannot see the truth, so we make thousands of assumptions and we take them as truth. One of the biggest assumptions we make is that the lies we believe are the truth."

— Don Miguel Ruiz

Lexis,
I hope you enjoy
reading this as much as
I enjoyed writing it.

For Sydney and Keaton

◆

Thank you for sharing this adventure with me and

welcoming these characters into our lives!

Table of Contents

Prologue

RUMOURS WERE FLYING.

As the summer approached, so too did the semester change, which meant senior students would be moving onto the Percipio and new students would be arriving from Kokoroe. This, however, was not the talk of the tower. Regardless of the Master's hope for secrecy, word had spread that the fabled Yaru did indeed exist and one had infiltrated the Citadel. The details of his capture and release were still unknown, but the rumours had everyone in a frenzy. Everyone that was, except Kazi.

Kazi was dejected; he had stolen away to a deserted bedroom on the tenth floor to mope. It was the floor reserved for the Tahtays, the Masters and visiting persons of importance. It also happened to be where the Yaru had materialized. The room he chose was the recently vacated one of his closest friend.

The freckled-faced youth looked passed his reflection to stare out the window at the retreating backs of Hanna and Nandin. Watching his friend disappear into the woods with a stranger felt wrong. Karn, Dylan and Tasha would be following her and it tore him up that he wasn't allowed to join them. He knew he had little to offer if it came down to a rescue mission and his stealth techniques left much to be desired, but it didn't make staying behind any easier.

He contemplated trying to sneak out of the castle and meet up with the team in the woods — once he was there surely they wouldn't send him away. He couldn't help but feel that it may be the last time he would see Hanna, and watching through the window as she walked willingly into enemy territory just seemed too cowardly for a best friend.

"Kazi, I would like a word."

Kazi turned to see Master Juro standing in the doorway with his usual stoic expression. His pencil-like silver beard and long grey hair marked him as someone of years. The unique pearl-like robe signified that he was a Juro of distinction.

So intent on his dilemma, Kazi didn't hear Master Juro enter and was taken by surprise. He wondered if he was about to get in trouble for being in Hanna's room as he was technically not supposed to be on this floor. He stumbled as he took a few steps forward and bowed. It never ceased to amaze him that someone barely half his height could still be so intimidating.

"I hoped you would accompany me to the Sanctuary," Master Juro continued unceremoniously.

Momentarily stunned, Kazi tried to rationalize why Master Juro, the leader of all the Juro and one of the most powerful individuals on Galenia, would want Kazi to join him to the most prestigious destination there was. Nothing came to mind.

"Why me?" he blurted out.

"Karn is under the impression you may attempt to follow them and, although your intentions would be admirable, it would rather defeat the purpose of leaving you behind."

Kazi cussed under his breath, then looked up hastily, concerned he may have offended Master Juro.

A thin smile crossed Master Juro's face.

"It may not have been the immediate course of action you were hoping for; however, I will be rendezvousing with Karn and Hanna in the mountains," he explained.

Kazi's eyes lit up. "Really?"

"If all goes according to plan."

2

Not wishing to dissuade Master Juro from his offer, Kazi still felt the need to ask, "Why would I be able to go with you and not Karn...and what's the point of going to the Sanctuary? Isn't that in the opposite direction?"

"I have a few companions I need to recruit to our cause before we join them. The reason I'm allowing you to accompany me is a matter of your safety. I plan to have the majority of the Vaktare as an escort. That should be enough swords to keep you protected."

"I should think so!" Kazi replied, his usual grin returning as he thought of the privilege of travelling with Master Juro and the specially trained warrior Jagare.

"Is that a yes?"

"Yes sir! Thank you, sir!"

"Good. I will let Master Jagare know you are excused for the next term. Be ready to leave within the hour. Inform the stable hands we need five horses saddled and ready to go."

"I will," Kazi bowed low and extra long to show his appreciation. "Is there anything else we need?" he asked as he straightened, but discovered Master Juro was already gone.

CHAPTER ONE

Camp it Up

HANNA CRIED OUT.

Frustrated by gaining yet another bruise, she leaned over to rub her leg where a branch had smacked it.

"Tell me again why we have to ride through the wilderness instead of taking the road?" she asked Nandin.

The two of them travelled through the woods south of the Citadel for over an hour making their way to Thickwood Forest. Although the brush wasn't as dense as in the forest, they still rode their horses single-file and with no actual path; their haphazard trail often took them closer to the trees and bushes than was desirable.

Karn and his team were taking the road south before heading into the forest to go to the clearing where the Yarus' camp had been and where Hanna, as Darra, had first met Nandin. When they arrived they would seek out trail signs left by Nandin in order to follow them the rest of the way through the forest and across the Valley of a Thousand Rivers.

"It's like I told Karn," he explained as he ducked under a low branch, "no Yaru would be taking the road this close to the Citadel, especially after the attack at base camp. It's the same reason I told them we couldn't be seen with them — if there are any Yaru in the area they might attack your friends before I can explain that I'm not a hostage."

"I'm still surprised Karn went along with it. He's taking a chance trusting that you'll leave trail signs for him."

Nandin chuckled. "He doesn't trust me at all, but he does trust you. I'm sure he's confident that you'll keep me honest. Besides, he probably has someone following us."

She glanced over her shoulder checking if she could see anyone behind her; nothing appeared out of the ordinary.

"In that case, aren't you worried that whoever's following us might be attacked?"

"Not particularly. I warned them not to follow. If they do and the Yaru attack, it's their own fault."

"That seems a bit harsh. I took you for someone who was opposed to violence."

"I am, but being tied to a chair and used as a punching bag has left me a little less than sympathetic at the moment."

Hanna opened her mouth to respond; yet no words came to mind. Finding Nandin being beaten in the dungeons of the Citadel made her angry and she reacted rather recklessly when she joined him in the cell and locked the Vaktare out. Thinking back on the scene left a bad taste in her mouth and a knot in her gut. She didn't know the people she was helping were capable of such brutality. It made her feel naïve and a bit skeptical of what she had come to accept as truth. In all the stories she'd heard about Mateo and the Kameil, no one bothered to divulge how outcasts were punished if they returned. After witnessing what they did to Nandin, the Vaktare killing the Kameil at the camp, and the stories Cassey had told her about hanging people, she no longer believed in the us-verses-them scenario. Both sides had done things she didn't agree with.

Her mission was to help stop the tears from destroying Galenia and she knew that was the right thing to do regardless of anyone's political agendas or views. Of course, what she wanted most of all, was to go home.

5

As Nandin wound his way through the woods, he was unaware of the current moral dilemma Hanna was facing. He was feeling rather triumphant. Not only had he infiltrated the Citadel and was bringing Hanna back to the valley as he had planned, but he was doing so with both Master Juro and Master Jagare's approval. In addition, they had provided them with horses and had given them provisions for the journey. Mateo was sure to be impressed by these accomplishments.

Nandin had every intention of honouring his agreement to see Hanna safely out of the valley — if that was what she wished. He was optimistic that once she arrived there she'd want to stay. Why wouldn't she? The valley was peaceful, the people were kind, and the castle was an amazing, beautiful place to live. Even though Mateo was unlikely to know anything concerning the tears, he was probably the only one who could do anything to fix them and was the most likely person to get her home. Obviously the Juro didn't know how, which is why they sent Hanna, or Darra as she had pretended to be, to spy on the Yaru in the first place.

It was a long day trekking through the woods. Hanna was so tired that she kept dozing off in the saddle. They stopped briefly throughout the day to grab a bite to eat and to water the horses. When Nandin finally chose to make camp, Hanna could barely stand. He insisted that she rest while he saw to the horses, got a fire going and began preparing dinner.

"How do you do it, Nandin?" she asked. "You haven't had any more sleep than I have and you have far more injuries." She indicated the multiple cuts and bruises evident on his face that were the result of being beaten by an over zealous Vaktare who had managed to get quite a few hits in before Hanna had interrupted the interrogation.

He glanced over at the bruise still apparent on Hanna's face and shook his head. "I'm still upset with Blades for punching you; it wasn't called for. The guy has anger issues," he grumbled as he added meat to the pan and placed it over the fire. "But to answer your question, being Yaru gives me an edge. I have increased stamina and my wounds heal faster — if they didn't my face would have been swollen for at least a week and I probably would be sporting two black eyes."

When he looked up he saw she was beginning to drift off. "Hanna, stay awake a bit longer. Can you watch the food while I get the wraps set up?"

Dazed she replied, "We're having wraps?"

"The pico wraps...you know, for sleeping in the trees?"

"Oh right, the hammocks." She sat up and stretched. "Yes, I can watch the food. Thanks for doing that."

He jumped up and set to work. As they travelled, he realized he didn't really know much about her. Everything he thought he knew pertained to Darra; Hanna explained Darra *had* existed, but was killed by a wolcott along with her family. Hanna had used her identity as it was a convenient and believable cover to get her into the Yaru camp. The more he inquired the more it become clear he didn't know much about Darra either as their conversations had mostly concerned Mateo and the valley. He had thought her questions were merely out of curiosity and a desire to gauge whether or not she could trust him; now knowing that she was probing for information he wished he had said a little less, not because he wanted to keep things from her, but from the Masters whom she spied for.

He was disappointed that she was so tired as he hoped that over dinner they could get to know each other better. It was a six-day journey to the valley though, so he figured he'd have plenty of opportunities to learn more about her. After their ordeal at the

Citadel he hoped she would be more forthcoming about who she actually was.

* * *

When they made camp the first night, Kazi was surprised that the Vaktare who accompanied them were not only there to provide protection, but to continue with his education. He was excited at first when they drilled him: calling out pushups, sit-ups and getting him to do laps up and down the road. It made him feel like, once again, he was part of a team as they joined him in his exercise. Next they tested his skills with the sword, followed by his abilities with the bow...even Kazi knew both were lacking.

"In the case of an attack, you need to be able to defend yourself until someone can assist you," one of his Vaktare said.

Kazi's shoulders slumped at his need for help; the man simply patted him on the back.

"Jivan were not built for this, you mustn't be too hard on yourself. Even a Jagare of your age is not expected to deal with the dangers you may encounter. Your friendship with Hanna is the only reason you are permitted on this expedition, but being strong of heart will not protect you from beasts or Yaru should either wish to cause you harm. Make it your goal to learn how to survive; leave the assaults to those that have the training and the skills to do so."

Kazi straightened up and nodded. He had no delusions that he could be the slayer of beasts or Yaru, but if he could protect himself he may even be able to protect others too, and that would be useful.

It was determined that a staff was the best weapon for him to wield. Effective in blocking blows from swords and claws alike, it would also help him keep attackers at a distance. They started off practicing techniques using long sticks. Kazi felt relatively slow and clumsy.

He was drenched in sweat and starving by the time they called it quits. Happily, he joined the group by the fire which was particularly bright after training in the approaching gloom of the night. The Jagare had taken turns giving him instructions allowing the others to set up tents and assist Master Juro with the fire and the meal. Kazi was grateful when he was handed a canteen of water along with a bowl of stew and warm bread, freshly baked in the fire.

As he finished sopping up the last of the gravy with his bread, Master Juro turned to him.

"I wonder young Kazi, if you have enough energy to play a tune for us? I noticed you brought your viol along with you," he said pointing to the six-stringed instrument and bow that was conveniently sitting beside him.

Kazi grinned, "Absolutely! But...I don't know anything fancy. I'm not sure my songs will be to your liking."

"We are sitting in the woods, on the side of a road resting in front of a campfire; I am sure your songs will be quite fitting."

Kazi thought it a shame he didn't have the opportunity to get to know Master Juro better while he was at Kokoroe. It seemed he wasn't as stodgy as Kazi had originally thought.

CHAPTER TWO

Trust in Deed

SENDA APPEARED.

Without a wagon to pull, the journey south was much quicker than when he had headed that way with Karn during Hanna's, or Darra's, first mission. Kazi was disappointed to learn that they wouldn't be entering the city. His travels with his father never included a stop beyond the massive walls of Senda. It was disappointing to come, once again, so close yet still remain outside. His curiosity would have to wait.

Knowing that his destination was the Sanctuary, though, appeased him. It was the hub of Galenia. All of the twenty-four main towns or cities, as well as all three schools, had representatives there. Two delegates were selected from their home community to stay at the Sanctuary for two years, after which time they were replaced by new representatives. The former would return home, but could put their names in for the next selection process.

Kazi wasn't sure what all was discussed, but he knew they dealt with population concerns, the status of the nesting grounds and made decisions about the Kameil problem.

"Master Juro, will I be able to go into the Sanctuary?" He hoped he would — staying outside in the stables tending the horses would be a great disappointment.

"I am sure that can be arranged," Master Juro replied.

"Will we get to stay overnight or do we have to sleep

outside?"

Master Juro eyed Kazi. He could understand why Hanna had befriended the boy, they seemed to have the same persistent curiosity.

"They have guest quarters in addition to the delegates lodging. The commute from Senda is not quick; it would be inconvenient to stay there."

"That's good, we're in a hurry after all. I sure hope we won't have to wait long before the council meets." He was glad he was invited to join Master Juro; he just didn't want to be held up too long by political protocol. What would the point be of going to the mountains if Hanna was already on her way back from her mission?

"I sent a message ahead requesting council, as is my custom when I come to the Sanctuary." He nodded to his closest guard. "I believe Kazi, you are due for another run?"

After their first day of travel, the Vaktare insisted that every now and then Kazi dismount from his horse and jog. Their reason was to improve his stamina and keep him in shape. Noticing the slight smile on Master Juro's face, Kazi wondered if it had more to do with preventing him from asking any more questions. If Master Juro would be more forthcoming with the details, or made some sort of small talk, it would have made for a more interesting ride. Sitting next to the taciturn, tight-lipped Juro, time just dragged. He was glad to be running again; the Vaktare proved to be better company.

* * *

After a decent sleep the previous night and a fairly relaxing day riding through the forest, Hanna was looking forward to an evening chat along with another dinner prepared by Nandin; his cooking was delicious.

As he gathered kindling and began getting the fire started, she opted to unsaddle and water the horses and set up the pico wraps. By the time she was done, the aroma from the meal he was preparing had her drooling. Eagerly she settled down beside him and took the offered plate.

"So tell me," he said, "what do I actually know about you? From what I learned at the camp, minus what I now know to be true, your name is Hanna, you're fourteen years old and not from Galenia."

"I'm fifteen actually."

He rolled his eyes — she had even lied about her age. "Did you tell us anything that was true?"

"Yes, of course. Everything I said about Darra was true, I just wasn't Darra."

"Were you really going to Senda?"

"Sort of...we were trying to make it look that way. I was actually attempting to get invited into your camp. But my reasons for going to Senda were true. It was all on a hunch; the Masters don't actually know that there are Kameil there."

"You mean they didn't know. Since you found out that there are — "

She shook her head. "No, they still don't know; I didn't tell them."

"Why not? Wasn't that your mission? To find out information and pass it on?"

She sighed feeling conflicted. "Yes, that's what I was suppose to do. And I'm sure they'd be less than pleased if they find out I didn't tell them everything."

Nandin tilted his head as he looked at her. He wasn't angry

that she had infiltrated his camp in an attempt to learn secrets — recently he had snuck into Senda and done the same thing. The fact that she kept some of those secrets intrigued him.

"My mission was to learn what Mateo was up to and to find out about the tears. They didn't give me instructions for anything other than that. Besides, their treatment of the Kameil has never really felt right to me and I don't want to be responsible for anyone being hung."

He smiled. Hanna was on his side even though she might not have accepted it yet. It escaped his notice that she was following her own code and not one determined by the Masters or Mateo.

"I'm still surprised that they recruited you considering you're not one of the three main races. I would have thought you'd be exiled for being different."

"The fact that I'm different doesn't bother you?" she asked.

He shrugged. "Why should it? I'm a Yaru surrounded by Kameil and I follow Mateo who doesn't really fit either description. It's my duty to seek out those who are different and offer them our protection. But you are a bit of a puzzle. How did you end up becoming Darra?"

It was easy to talk to Nandin. She couldn't quite put her finger on it, but for some reason she felt she could trust him. Out of the two of them, she was the one who had done all the lying. Even if he wasn't all that he seemed, she no longer felt the need to deceive him and was a little relieved to share her story — at this point it could only help her. If she was able to convince him she wasn't from Galenia and she really did come through some sort of portal, he was more likely to believe that the tears existed and were causing destruction. And if he believed her, he would plead her case to Mateo and hopefully both sides would work together to fix the problem...and send her home.

When she mentioned the tears, he pulled out a map he had been given from Master Juro that was marked with the locations of the known tear sites — it had taken some convincing to get it. He argued that Mateo would want to see the damage caused by the tears before he believed it was happening. Then he could learn how to fix them or prevent more damage in the future.

Hanna pointed out where she had entered Galenia and the tear site outside Kokoroe. When she finally got to the part where she was attacked by a wolcott, he was impressed by the description of her Essence shield.

"What's it like manipulating the Essence?"

The question surprised her as it wasn't something people typically asked — the Juro knew how it felt and the others were impressed by it, but even Kazi hadn't asked her what it felt like. The only time she had ever described it was to Master Juro when she went to Crystal Valley. He had asked in order to assess how far along she was in her ability to detect it.

"It feels like what you'd imagine clouds should feel like. Soft, fluffy, but not really solid."

"Do you find it difficult to use it?"

"It depends, I created that shield without even knowing how, moving objects takes lots of concentration and then there are things I can't do yet like floating or controlling fire with any sort of accuracy."

"Mateo doesn't use it much...I've always wondered why."

"It can be exhausting — after that wolcott attack I even passed out; of course I also went into shock from the whole situation, but even little things can make me feel drained. Master Juro often told me: 'Manipulating Essence can have repercussions — do not use it for what you can do without it' which was his cryptic way of saying magic has a price; don't use it if you don't need to."

Nandin nodded his understanding. He studied her for a moment, looking for indications of deceit. One of the reasons he had been promoted to Commander was his ability to read people. He knew what to say to motivate them and he had a way of gaining their trust. When she had come to him as Darra he thought he understood who she was and what she was thinking; finding out it had all been a lie, made him question his judgment. As he watched her tuck her hair behind her ear and return his gaze, he was inclined to believe what she told him. It seemed naive to think she was being honest with him now, yet he felt she was.

CHAPTER THREE

In the Dark

HANNA JOLTED.

She had been sleeping peacefully when some sixth sense awoken her. She tried to sit up, but couldn't. After the initial moment of panic, she realized she was in her pico wrap hanging from a tree. The sleeping bag-type hammock was closed shut like a cocoon. It required her to keep calm in order to undo the fastenings.

As she fumbled with the ties, she tried to discern what it was that caused her to wake up. There was no wind, nor any great owls hooting nearby. As she listened, it became evident that the usual insect buzzing and rhythmic chirping of the night were faded off in the distance rather than surrounding her. It must have been the relative silence that had woken her. Once the wrap was open, the fragrance of the forest filled her, and with it the smell of smoke.

Leaning ever so slightly out of her bedding she gazed at the ground below. Through the thin veil of smoke, a small red and orange glow danced. She knew it was nothing to be concerned with as she watched the shadow of a figure hunched over in front of the small fire. He sat there unmoving, his head in his hands.

Careful not to make too much noise, Hanna removed herself from the warmth of her wrap and carefully descended from the tree using her rope pulley.

She jumped as muscular hands grabbed her waist to lower her the last few feet to the ground. Nandin's assistance caught her off guard. She should have known he'd have noticed her climbing down the tree; even so she wouldn't have expected for him to suddenly appear to lift her to the ground — it felt a bit too familiar a gesture for someone she barely knew.

"Problems?" he asked as he helped her undo the safety rope. She wrestled free of the harness, and made her way to the fire.

"I was going to ask you the same thing."

Nandin shrugged as he resumed his seat on the ground.

"Can't sleep."

She laughed. "I figured that much out myself. What I was trying to get at was why."

"Lots on my mind I guess."

Oh brother. Nandin's vague answers were getting her nowhere quickly. She waited. It was unlike Hanna to hold her tongue, but Nandin had the look of someone who was just told there was no Santa Claus. When he wasn't more forthcoming she questioned him again.

"Care to expand on that?" she replied. "You seemed pretty chipper earlier; what's changed?"

He took a deep breath. "I just…I just don't know what to think anymore. When I…abandoned my village a year ago it wasn't because I disagreed with how things were done; I really hadn't given much thought to the treatment of the Kameil or anyone else for that matter. I was too busy feeling sorry for myself. I was eighteen and already tired of the life I was living. The life Mateo offered gave me purpose and…I don't know, I felt like I was doing some good. Discovering the Kameil community I realized how society had turned their backs on these people who really needed help. Jon and I felt that one day we'd be able to prove the Kameil deserved equal rights and shouldn't be cast out and neglected, although now I'm not so sure."

"How can you say that? Don't you think everyone should be treated the same?"

"Of course. I'm saying I'm not sure it *can* happen. Look what they did to me Hanna," he said as he touched his bruised face. "They're not interested in change. If it wasn't for you, they never would have let me leave...I probably would have been hung before I could even plead my case. And they were the *Masters*, not some leader of a village frightened by a raid."

He sighed as he leaned back on a fallen tree. "Like everyone else I looked up to those people, but I didn't know they were like that."

"Neither did I. I knew they were scared and were desperate for answers; I never would have guessed Master Juro would order you to be beaten like that."

"He didn't exactly order it. That Vaktare, Erac, seemed to feel the need to punish me for some of his men getting killed in the clearing — Master Juro told him to stop, of course he still left him in the cell with me; and when I refused to answer their questions he allowed Erac to continue "persuading me". If those are the kind of people the Masters employ how can I ever trust them?"

"I think you've overlooked something Nandin."

He turned to her unsure what she meant. "What?"

"Do you think Blades is your kind of person?"

"He's trying to do the right thing...sometimes he gets a bit carried away."

"Well maybe it's the same with Erac. Maybe Mateo is a great guy who's trying to help all types of people, but from what I gathered it seems to me his Yaru are often criminals that have been banished. If those are the kind of people that he employs how could *I* ever trust him."

"The Yaru aren't criminals!" he argued. "We were regular

18

people who believed in his cause. And if that's really how you feel, what makes you think you can trust me?"

"You said that people make their way to the valley and if they are candidates he makes them Yaru."

"Right."

"And haven't those people been banished? Isn't that why they seek out Mateo in the first place?"

"Well yes, sometimes, but that's not always the case."

"Which is why I'm inclined to trust you. I'm no Yaru expert or anything, but I have met a few and I'd say that not all Yaru are created equal...Blades has that criminal vibe to him."

"Thanks — I think. But this is besides the point. My Yaru aren't beating people up to get information."

"Are you sure about that?" she asked. "It's not like you follow them all around. You saw what Blades did to me. I doubt that was the first time he punched someone."

He leaned forward and poked at the fire as he realized he'd never really thought about that before. "That's not the only thing bugging me," he said before he lost his train of thought. "The Masters started planning an attack on the valley without even thinking about speaking with Mateo. Already they're discussing the need to fill in the quarry...and for what? Over some dead trees? They're willing to fight and kill people to protect nature?" He shook his head in agitation. "And to think, they learned so much about the valley and it's all because of me — I've betrayed Mateo."

She hesitated before attempting to reason with him. In reality, he had told them very little; it was because of Hanna that they knew so much. At the moment she wasn't sure how she even felt about that. What she did know was how she felt about the tears.

"The damage caused by the tears is more than just the death of a few trees…all life in the area is dead or dying. If something like that keeps spreading, how will anyone survive? You won't be able to grow food, without plants the animals would die…everything's connected Nandin. This could have a devastating effect on everyone if it keeps up."

"Of course it would — if it is really that serious. But we're talking about just a few tears here."

"That's how these things always start. It happens all the time back home. There are tons of endangered species — animals that have been wiped from existence. If Mateo is doing this we have to get him to stop before it goes too far. My planet is constantly in danger because people don't think or care of the consequences, especially if they're not around to face them."

"I suppose. But what gets me is that they were so quick to blame Mateo just because they don't know why it's happening."

"They've ruled out everything they can think of — except what Mateo's doing."

The fire crackled and sent sparks up into the darkness. Nandin watch them as he replied, "I think blaming Mateo is just an excuse. He understands the Essence in a way no else does; they need his help, but they're not willing to admit it. And I would bet he's the only one who can get you back home."

Hanna stared at the fire not saying anything. The notion that Mateo was her only chance at getting home filled her with dread. The entire time she had been on Galenia she had witnessed the fear his name instilled. He was the Bogeyman; he was terror and this was the person she had to depend on to get her home?

"What is it?" he asked noticing the tension in her face.

"Mateo has a bad rep…I really have no desire to meet him. After all, it was me that told his secrets, not you," she said recalling how she overheard Nandin talk about liquid Essence while lying outside his tent in the Yaru camp.

Nandin flashed her a winning smile. "The stories about Mateo are greatly exaggerated. Besides, I promised to protect you...as the Commander I have a lot of say. If you just want to check out the quarry and be on your way then so be it."

"What if I discover that there is Qual in the quarry? If I tell that to Master Juro they'll no longer just be considering filling it in; they'll plan on it."

"Well then I'll need to convince Mateo something has to be done. I'm sure he will do what's needed and we can prevent an attack altogether."

"I hope you're right Nandin. The whole reason I volunteered to go with you was to prevent bloodshed, I really don't want to be the cause of more."

As the embers died down, they agreed it was time they both tried to get some sleep. Hanna climbed back up her tree and settled into her pico wrap, but she couldn't quiet her mind. It was easy to reassure Nandin that taking her to the valley so she could learn what was occurring at the quarry and then help her to pass that information onto Master Juro was in everyone's best interest. She told herself for months that gathering that intelligence would not only save Galenia, it would help her find her way home. But the events of late had cast doubt in her mind.

When she joined the Yaru and Kameil camp less than a week earlier, she saw a different side to the story than she had been told. She met scared, troubled people struggling to survive and brave souls who strove to protect them. She had witnessed the cold contempt of the Vaktare forces as they ripped through the camp and killed indiscriminately. The nightmare of seeing her newfound friend Cassey and her daughter being killed caused a pain in her heart.

Later she learned that the leader of the Vaktare was dismissed for issuing the kill order as it was not the order he was to give and, although she was relieved that the Masters didn't approve of the murder of innocents, their treatment of Nandin revealed a dark side she didn't believe they had. Master Juro's words of being one with nature and connecting with the world were somewhat hollow to her now. They watched as the Vaktare tied Nandin to a chair and beat him for refusing to talk. She didn't even get a chance to explain her side of the situation.

She thought she knew these people. She thought they were peaceful. Life at Kokoroe had been serene and calm. The glare in Master Juro's eyes that night left her doubting everything she had come to believe about him. He had seemed above emotion — untainted by the temperamental influence it had on a person's judgement. Now she understood that wasn't the case. His shell cracked and anger seeped through.

Yet for all she had witnessed and learned in the passed few days, she realized that nothing had changed. Her mentors proved to be more human than she had imagined, flawed just as she, but her mission was still the same. The tears were damaging the world and had to be stopped. And she still needed to find her way home. Now with Nandin's help, an unexpected ally, there was hope she could solve those problems and, if all went well on this mission, no one would get hurt.

CHAPTER FOUR

State of Mind

THE WHISPERING DIMINISHED.

Kazi stood quietly and almost still against the wall, gazing in wonder at the circular meeting room as the delegates took their seats. The domed ceiling gave the space a sense of opulence and made him feel small. Pennants of a variety of colours hung around the room depicting the symbols of the all towns and cities on Galenia adding to the sense of importance about the place; it really was the heart of society. The delegates were seated in two circles, one inside the other, all facing inwards. The Juro sat on in the inner ring and beside them were staffs set into the floor. The slightly raised outer ring of seats were occupied by the Jivan and Jagare.

The chairs high backs were carved with symbols along with a number so even when someone was seated the carvings could be seen. Another interesting item that was attached to each chair was a pole. Kazi was unsure what the poles were for.

Against the far wall on a raised dais stood a lone figure. The well-dressed, barrel-chested individual was scanning the room, seeming to take in all the details. His survey paused as he made eye contact with Kazi and the lady standing next to him.

When he looked away Kazi whispered, "Who is he?"

"That would be the Steward. It is his job to keep the meeting running smoothly."

"I thought that was your job."

"No, I am the Corretay," the Jivan said, a touch of arrogance in her tone. "I am honoured with the task of passing messages between the delegates and tracking attendance."

Kazi thought the task of passing notes was hardly a noteworthy task, but said nothing as she continued to inform him of the details involved.

"When they raise the appropriate colour of flag, I approach," the Corretay went on to explain. "Each delegate has four flags that can be raised. The orange flag indicates that they have a message, the white one symbolizes their agreement with the discussion or a 'yes' vote, black is to vote no or to disagree with what is being said and the blue flag is when the delegate has something they wish to say. It is the Steward's job to call out the name and location of the next speaker. Master Juro, for example, is sitting in the chair labeled NW-3, northwest-three, because Kokoroe is the third most northwest location on the map and therefore, his seat is placed in the northwest of the inner circle so everyone knows where to find him."

"I see," Kazi replied. When he first walked in the room, it all seemed so glamourous and interesting. After standing against the wall waiting for the delegates to enter and stuck listening to the Corretay lecture him about everything: from the way the dome was built to the luxury of the pillars made of a rare, polished stone, he had about enough of the place.

His attention was drawn to the centre of the circles where three individuals sat at a table with pieces of parchment and quills, two of them were Jivan and one was Juro. They were busy writing notes and he wondered what their role in all this was. Noticing Kazi's gaze, the Corretay continued the never-ending lecture.

"Those are the Keepers of the Council. They record what is discussed during the meeting as well as the decisions that are made. Now, if you'll excuse me, the flags are going up," she said as if Kazi had been detaining her.

She walked around the outer and then inner circles, gathering notes from each delegate who had raised an orange flag. Once she finished collecting them, she took them to the Steward before heading back to her post against the wall next to where Kazi stood.

"What were on the notes?" Kazi asked quietly.

"I do not know the details," she said as if the point was obvious and he should have known, "They usually just have a rating as to the importance of the matter they choose to discuss so that the Steward knows who to call on to start the session. Of course, today it's rather clear who it will be."

"I'm guessing that would be Master Juro?"

The Corretay cast a sideways glance at Kazi.

"Obviously Master Juro."

"Right."

"Master Juro rarely leaves Kokoroe," she went on to explain, oblivious of the fact that Kazi wasn't that interested. "When he does, it is due to a matter of great importance. More often than not, when he brings something to the Council, it is the item that is deliberated on for that day. I assumed, being his travel companion, you would have known this."

Kazi wasn't easily annoyed, but the Corretay was starting to get on his nerves. Being silent didn't prevent her from speaking — she would assume he didn't know anything, on the other hand, asking questions gave her a chance to ridicule Kazi's ignorance. He figured he'd rather ask questions; at least she would tell him something he actually *wanted* to know.

"Why are the staffs standing in the floor like that?"

"You will see soon enough. Now quiet; it's about to start."

Kazi bit his tongue — it was going to be a long day.

The Steward spoke in a loud voice that could be heard throughout the room.

"Good morning. Keepers of the Council, please begin your accounts. I, Steward of the Sanctuary, do hereby begin the council session on this, the twelfth day of the six month of the year eleven o' five. Are all the delegates ready to begin?"

"Aye," replied fifty-two voices in chorus.

"Does the Corretay declare an absence of any delegates?"

The Corretay took a step away from the wall.

"No absences to report," she answered loudly.

"Are there any Messengers in attendance?"

Kazi smiled; he knew Messengers were given places of honour in the council chambers. They brought important communications with them and were always heard first as they rarely stayed in any one location for long. Being in this most prestigious place, he felt proud to be the son of a Messenger.

"No Messengers for today's session," the Corretay said and stepped back.

"Then let the session commence. Our first speaker will be Master Juro, of the northwest-three quadrant, Kokoroe." The Corretay eyed Kazi with a smug I-told-you-so look on her face; Kazi pretended not to notice and concentrated on Master Juro instead.

"Thank you Steward," Master Juro said. Kazi thought he was surprisingly loud for someone who was usually so soft spoken. "Some time ago, I brought forth an issue concerning tears that had been occurring across Galenia. I am afraid these tears have proven to be catastrophic. I have reason to believe that the few we have uncovered are only the beginning."

Master Juro paused as he noticed a blue flag being raised.

The Steward announced. "Leader Sansha of the southeast-one quadrant, the Percipio, would like to speak to this issue."

As one, all the Juro's chairs spun to face the new speaker.

Kazi couldn't resist asking. "How did they do that?"

In hushed tones, the Corretay replied, "Their chairs sit on platforms on top of a wheel so they can turn. Since they sit on the inside circle they would have their backs to the Jivan and Jagare if they couldn't pivot, this way they can see whoever speaks. They use the Essence from their staffs to pull or push themselves as needed. Now hush."

Watching the session soon became as dull as Kazi had expected as the morning wore on. Patiently, Master Juro would listen to the questions and doubts the delegates had before moving on to presenting his case. It surprised Kazi that it wasn't an easy thing to do. Many of the Juro didn't accept Master Juro's explanation of the Qual or even of its existence. He was able to convince them that it didn't matter exactly what Mateo was mining, but still need to be stopped, as it was most likely the cause of the tears. Again, Kazi was taken aback, but this time it was at how readily everyone accepted that Mateo was to blame and needed to be dealt with.

Kazi wondered if they would ever do more than talk when finally, a Jivan asked what Master Juro proposed to do.

"There is only one way to stop the quarry; we will have to go there ourselves."

Flags moved up and down as they either agreed or disagreed with Master Juro. Most of the Juro seemed to be in agreement, although, several blue flags were also raised. Before the Steward could interrupt, Master Juro pressed on.

"I have already sent a special team ahead to find us a safe passage into the mountains. Master Jagare's Vaktare forces are awaiting our arrival to escort us. Two dozen senior Juro have been summoned from Kokoroe to join me. What I am requesting is the additional support of the Leader Juro — those in attendance and the ones that can be spared from the cities. Will you offer your support? What say you?"

Kazi was shocked at Master Juro's proposal. All he had been told was that they needed to report Master Juro's concerns and he wanted to pick up a few companions while he was here. What he was proposing had never been done. He brightened at the thought; a massive Juro force like that was sure to help Hanna escape from the valley if Nandin failed. It would be a rescue mission on the grandest scale.

The flags had all been lowered as Master Juro made his final proposal. Slowly, the white flags of the Juro began to rise, as did the others.

The Steward spoke again.

"Let the record show, the council has approved the request of Master Juro of the northwest-three quadrant for the support of the Juro delegates to join him on his expedition to the eastern mountains. It is also required that the delegates from the cities are to dispatch letters requesting the additional aide from the Leader Juro of those cities. With this decision made, I, the Steward of the Sanctuary, dismiss these proceedings. Further discussions as to the particulars of this expedition are to occur outside these proceedings and are up to the discretion of Master Juro. Any delegates who disapprove of this decision will raise their black flag and it will be noted by the Keepers of the Council."

The flags went down and the delegates began to leave. The Corretay leaned close to Kazi.

"Now we wait," she said. "Master Juro will likely call a follow-up meeting and then let you know where he wishes you to be."

"Won't they just continue meeting here?"

"No, this room is strictly for the council session. There are rooms on the lower floors where other meetings occur. Ah, here comes Master Juro now."

"Master Corretay, would you be so kind as to show Kazi back to our quarters? It may be some time before I can join him there."

The Corretay bowed and turned to Kazi. "Come along then."

Kazi wished he was back in the woods heading east; it would be much more exciting than visiting the Sanctuary and he was anxious to get this rescue mission up and running.

CHAPTER FIVE

Cap in Hand

NANDIN DISMOUNTED.

The gentle breeze kept the approaching heat at bay. It wasn't yet midday on the sixth day when he halted their ride and began unsaddling his horse. Hanna rode up next to him curious as to what he was doing.

"Why are we stopping? Is something wrong?"

"This is the best place to wait for Karn. Once we cross the last river and go over the ridge we'll be in plain sight of the valley."

"I didn't know we were planning on meeting up with Karn. Aren't you worried about being seen with the wrong people?" she said a hint of mockery in her voice.

He offered his hand to encourage her to dismount and then returned to rubbing down his own horse.

"If there were any Yaru in the forest, we would have met up with them by the time we started crossing the rivers. We don't keep any sentries out here and if someone comes this way from the valley we'll see them before they see us."

"What would happen if they see Karn and the others?"

"They would investigate. Usually the only people out this far are heading into the valley. The last thing we want is a Yaru escort for your friends — they'd be taken straight to Mateo, which defeats the whole plan of keeping them hidden."

"And if Mateo met them…would he think they were outcasts?"

"I doubt it. He seems to know when people are lying. More than one Yaru or Kameil has been busted trying to get away with something," Nandin chuckled as he recalled his friends receiving quarry duty for their misbehaviour.

Even though Nandin seemed unconcerned, the idea of her friends being 'taken straight to Mateo' left her queazy. He never said what Mateo would do to them; she had a feeling he didn't actually know. She wondered if being Commander gave him enough say to protect them if necessary — it wasn't something she planned to put to the test.

They had entered the river valley first thing that morning. A few bridges spanned the deeper and faster flowing rivers, but more often they twisted and wound their way to cross calmer streams. Life was abundant in the valley; the trees grew tall and wide, fruit-baring bushes were everywhere and they had spied several animals bounding through the brush or taking their fill from the water beds.

A cacophony of noise filled the air; above the bubbling and splashing of the hundreds of rivers (or thousands, if the valley was named literally) there was a thunderous crashing sound. Nandin explained it was the Great White Wall, where all the rivers joined together at the edge of the mountains to form a waterfall so vast it was considered the edge of the world; to go over would be to fall off the face of Galenia.

They waited beside one of the calmer rivers with plenty of tall grass along the bank for the horses to graze on. Since there were no fallen logs or large stones to sit on he pulled a blanket out of his pack and laid it out. After they met up with Karn, he hoped to push through to the valley without any more stops, so he grabbed some food for an early meal.

Hanna finished removing the saddle, rubbed down her horse

and joined him.

"This is a nice little picnic you've got going," she said as she sat down. "I could just stretch out in this sunbeam and have a nap."

"Go ahead, I'm sure we'll be waiting for an hour or so before they get here."

"Why is it that we're waiting for them?"

"This is where we part and go our separate ways. We'll be going across the river heading straight east to Mateo's valley, but Karn needs to get into the mountains — without being seen by the sentries on the wall. It'll be easier for me to point him in the right direction rather than devising a trail marker to say 'cross that river, go around the bend and head for this bunch of trees which mark the mountain pass'."

He offered her a plate of dried meats and leftover bread he had made that morning. There was also a bunch of fresh berries that they collected when they stopped to camp. It was in those moments that the importance of her mission seemed surreal. Wandering through the bushes gathering fruit as they talked, reminded her of calm summer days back home. It was only when Nandin whistled and clucked that she was again filled with a keen sense of dread and snapped back to reality. He explained the noise was a way to frighten off any beast that may be wandering nearby.

"Something on your mind?" he asked, noticing she was studying him.

They had been alone for almost a week. Every chance they got they would talk, sharing their concerns over the current situation, debating issues of the treatment of the Kameil and the validity of Mateo's 'Yaru' solution. More than once she felt Nandin had taken a lot on faith and his need to believe in Mateo had made him too trusting in her opinion, but overall she had to admit she liked him. He was noble, sincere. He had moments of dark brooding over his inner turmoil, which compelled her to try and make him laugh in order to shake him from his doldrums.

The time she had spent at Kokoroe taught her not to get too attached to people. She didn't belong here and the closer she got to others the harder it was to leave them or watch them go. After Kazi left to go to the Citadel she worked harder at keeping her distance. She was so happy to reunite with Kazi, but it made it that much worse when it came time to say good-bye again.

And yet, here was Nandin. A Yaru. An enemy — at least, he was according to the Masters. So much of what he stood for made sense to her. She couldn't help but admire him. He had helped a lot of people and it was clear he truly believed it was right thing to do. And there was this way his eyes crinkled when he smiled…

"Helloooo…Hanna, do you hear me?"

"Sorry," she said as she sipped her water. She felt the heat rise in her face and was suddenly embarrassed that she had been starring. "To answer you're question, yes, there's lots on my mind, but nothing you haven't already heard me say." She silently berated herself; this was no time to get a schoolgirl crush. "I think I'm going to take that nap."

She laid down trying to push thoughts of Nandin out of her mind. She recalled the times she had spent with her friends back home in an attempt to distract herself, but they held less and less hold on her heart the longer she was on Galenia. As she enjoyed the warm sun on her back, it was thoughts of Nandin that lingered as she finally dozed off.

* * *

She had no idea how much time had passed when she woke to

the sound of hushed voices. It pleased her to discover that, at some point, Nandin covered her with a blanket as a cool breeze had picked up. As her eyes flickered open she quickly pulled the blanket over her head.

"Too bright, too bright!"

"I don't think you're too bright, particularly since you're heedlessly napping so close to Mateo's valley."

"What difference does that make, Dylan?" she asked as she sat up, careful to shade her eyes as she slid out from under the blanket. "I'm not exactly attempting to hide…that is my destination after all."

He plopped himself down beside her. "True enough. Sort of a crazy situation you got yourself into here."

"Don't I know it."

Tasha stepped closer and tentatively kneeled on the edge of the blanket less than at ease to do so. "Is something the matter Hanna? Why are you shielding your eyes?"

"Cause it's bright. I sure wish I had my sunglasses."

"What are sunglasses?"

"You wear them over your eyes to block out the light."

"But then…how could you see?"

Hanna chuckled. "They don't block it out completely, you can see through them." Seeing Tasha's confused expression she explained further. "They're glass — dark coloured glass." It was an odd realization that she had never seen anyone on Galenia wearing glasses; sunglasses were a novelty they had yet to discover. "I would settle for a baseball hat, that would help too."

"Base ball hat?" Dylan said. "That's odd having a ball as a hat."

"Sorry, I did it again," at times it was all too easy to slip into sayings and terms unique to her home. "A baseball hat has a stiff brim to shade your eyes. I know you have hats here, but they typically have brims that go all around and are sort of floppy."

Without explanation Dylan popped up and began tramping around the bushes and cutting at the long grass. Hanna didn't bother trying to figure out what he was up to and instead turned her attention to Tasha.

"Where are Karn and Nandin? And didn't you have a few of the Vaktare with you?"

"Nandin took Karn and one of the Vaktare ahead to show him where we need to go. Another Vaktare took our horses into the woods when we found you since we can't take them any further and the last Vaktare is lying low by the ridge keeping watch in case anyone leaves the valley and heads this way. Dylan and I were left to watch over you."

"Gee thanks. You got the good gig — it comes with food." She opened the container of fresh berries and offered them to her friend. Tasha smiled and gingerly picked one out of the bucket.

"Careful Tasha, you wouldn't want to overdo it."

When Tasha raised her eyebrows and looked at the berry; Hanna couldn't help but laugh. Sarcasm was often lost on her taciturn, Jagare friend.

Hanna scoffed at the mess Dylan created on the blanket as he dropped his collection of cuttings and settled down once again.

"Do you know how to braid?" he asked unconcerned with the mess he'd made.

"Yeeeesss…why?"

He gave her a handful of the long grass after tying a knot at one end. "Here, braid these…and then do some more."

"Okay. Arts and crafts in the middle of nowhere outside enemy gates — Kazi would love this."

When Nandin and Karn returned awhile later, Hanna set to

saddling her horse.

"What is that?" Nandin asked pointing at Hanna's head.

"Dylan and I made it. It's a baseball cap made out of grass mostly."

"Made out of grass…instead of balls?"

"Don't be silly, instead of fabric."

"And you're wearing it because…?" he asked leaving the explanation of the name of the hat for another time.

"It keeps the sun out of my eyes."

After speaking with Tasha, Karn made his way past the horses towards Hanna.

"What are you wearing?" he questioned an odd expression on his face as he starred at her.

Hanna sighed, Nandin answered before she could speak. "It's a grass hat. It's to keep the sun out of her eyes."

"It looks ridiculous," Karn replied.

"Dylan made it," she said.

"That would explain it."

"Hey, I heard that!" Dylan called out.

Nandin shook his head. "Remind your team to keep their voices down when you leave here. It's doubtful you'll encounter anyone in the mountains except Jon, but I wouldn't push my luck."

Karn glared at Dylan. "He shouldn't be yelling out here either; he's usually much quieter than that."

Dylan made his way towards them and placed a hand on Hanna's shoulder. "I blame Hanna, she's a bad influence…napping, making hats — you'd think she was on vacation rather than a mission."

"And speaking of which," Nandin said, "it's time we got going." He lifted his saddle onto his horse and quickly tightened the straps.

"Hanna, may I speak with you a moment before you go?" Karn said.

She nodded and followed him away from the group. By his tone of voice she knew he was all business.

"Are you sure you want to go through with this? It's not too late. You could come with us into the mountains. Nandin showed me where the trail starts — I'm sure Dylan can figure out the rest of the way to the top; perhaps we could get a view into the valley and that would be sufficient."

"Thanks for the offer Karn, but I need to get close to the quarry...I don't actually know how to find out if there's Qual there, I just know I can't do it from a distance." Seeing his doubts and concern, she placed a hand on his arm. "I trust Nandin. He'll get me out, I know he will." She hoped she sounded more believable than she felt, but she had every intention on seeing this plan through.

He gave her a hug. "You're the bravest kid I've ever met. Just don't take any chances in there."

"Kid? Really?"

"I mean it Hanna, be safe. And if you can't figure out what's going on, don't waste your time, just get out."

"Yes big brother."

He took off her cap and ruffled her hair. "I'm serious...this hat looks ridiculous."

She punched him on the arm. "Hey, this is an original piece of art, although, I'd give it up if I had a pair of shades," she said snatching it back and adjusting it in place.

"Shades?"

"Sunglasses...ask Tasha." She turned and headed to her horse before he could insist on an explanation. In her opinion, Dylan did a great job considering the limited time and resources he had. It was better than any souvenir she could have bought; she hoped she could get it home in one piece.

CHAPTER SIX

Kindness of Strangers

THE WALL WAS INTIMIDATING.

Hanna stopped as they crested the ridge and the fortifications of Mateo's valley came into view. Mistaking her look of fear for one of amazement, Nandin urged her on.

"It's pretty impressive isn't it? And you can really hear White Wall now."

"Wh…what?" Hanna stammered.

"Remember, the Great Wall that is the waterfall at the edge of the world?"

"Oh…right. It's the wall between the mountains I'm concerned with. How the heck am I ever going to get out of there? Maybe this isn't a brilliant idea after all. That's totally a prison."

"No it's not. Trust me, it will be fine. No one will even notice you leave through the mountains."

"They'll sure see me coming into the valley. Anyone standing on that wall has a clear view; there's nothing blocking us between here and there."

Nandin continued to coax her forwards. The plains in front of the valley allowed them to ride side by side for a change. "There's nothing to worry about. I'm a Yaru remember? No one's even going to think twice about us coming in. We are always bringing people with us. Trust me, it'll be fine."

"I do trust you, it's Mateo's I'm worried about.   What

if...what if he wants to keep me there?"

"Mateo doesn't take prisoners. People come and go out of the valley all the time. I'm sure if you told him you wanted to leave, he wouldn't stop you."

"I'd prefer to get out without having to meet him...if that's even possible."

"Of course. I'll get you in and out as quickly as I can. Once you've had your trip to the quarry, Jon will take you into the mountains to meet up with Karn...once Karn arrives that is."

"And how long will that be do you suppose?"

"It's going to take Karn at least a day from where we left him to get to the northern mountain pass. Should only be a couple days before Jon finds them. But don't worry, he will find them."

Nandin took the lead down into the valley and headed towards the wall. Hanna urged her horse forward to catch up, hoping Nandin knew what he was doing.

"By the way, if you don't want to draw attention to yourself, I'd lose the grass cap."

Without argument she removed the hat and hung it over the horn on her saddle; the last thing she wanted was to be noticed. The sudden image of a crowd of people watching her as she entered the valley gave her goose bumps — she wished she could use the Essence to turn invisible.

They crossed the vast grassland and approached the massive wall. A sentry called down a greeting to Nandin and the iron gate was opened for them. Hanna marvelled at her surroundings as she rode beside Nandin into the valley.

"There are so many!" she whispered while gazing at the Kameil around her.

"I know. Incredible isn't it?"

He led her through the market and wound his way through the

house-lined streets as she watched the Kameil happily going about their day. It wasn't long before they dismounted and tied the horses up to one of the few hitching posts along the street. Once Hanna was ready, he headed towards a house a few doors down, eagerly walked up to it and knocked. A moment later the door opened and young women wearing a simple cotton dress, quickly stepped out and stood on her tiptoes to embrace him. Hanna thought she looked frail; yet, it didn't prevent her from being attractive. In fact, the light red hair that framed her pale, delicate face made her quite pretty. Hanna was caught off guard by her desire to pull Nandin away. She was suddenly aware of how plain and tomboyish she must have looked with her hair pulled back and sporting her hunting gear — she was glad she'd taken off the grass hat. She forced herself to smile when this attractive stranger traced the remnants of a cut on Nandin's forehead with her fingers.

"Oh Nandin, I'm so relieved to see you! I was so worried when I heard where you were going. And with good reason I can see. Jon will be here shortly; he planned on stopping by early today. Please come in, come in." As she waved them in she turned to Hanna. "This must be Darra. I'm glad to see that you are safe. I met the Kameil that just joined us from Senda — they told me everything that happened."

Hanna was startled when Sarah gave her a hug and shook her head sadly as she gently touched the purple bruise Hanna still had under her eye.

"Sarah, this is Hanna," Nandin said as he closed the door. "Darra was just a temporary name. And this is Jon's betrothed," he said winking at Sarah. At that bit of news, Hanna's moment of insecurity subsided.

"Hanna is it? I have to say, I'm surprised that you stopped in here. I would have guessed you'd be taking the Seer straight to Mateo. I sense a story coming on. Please, sit," she said pulling out chairs around a table in the middle of the main room. "You both must be tired from your travels. Can I get you some tea and perhaps something to eat?"

"Oh, yes please," Hanna replied as she gaze around at the simple surroundings that was Sarah's home. The stone walls were softened by handmade quilts that were hung randomly around the room. Aside from the table, there was a small area that was set up as a sitting room. Only one window let light into the space.

As Sarah disappeared through an open doorway to gather some food and drinks for her guests, Hanna leaned over and spoke softly to Nandin.

"How does Sarah know I'm the Seer?"

"When you passed Blades on the road to the Citadel he told us that you looked at him the way Mateo did when he was trying to see our Essence. After what we went through, that's not a look you forget. You obviously aren't a Juro, but the Sight is a unique skill. If you actually did see his Essence then that would make you a Seer."

"Yeah, I get it." Hanna sighed. Even in the valley she couldn't escape that nickname. "It just seems odd because that's what everyone else calls me too."

"Well there you go. Guess we're right."

"And now you know I can move the Essence; does my title upgrade to Mover?"

Nandin laughed. "I think I'll stick with Hanna, if it's okay with you."

"Please do."

Sarah returned carrying a tray with a tea serving and a plate of treats and carefully placed it on the table.

"So what brings you to my door?" she asked sweetly.

"Hanna is curious about the valley — I'll explain more when Jon arrives, but for now I have a favour to ask."

"Ask away!"

"She's nervous about meeting Mateo — "

"Most people are when they first get here," Sarah nodded knowingly.

"Yes," Nandin continued, " so I wondered if you would mind letting her stay here a few nights."

"That would be wonderful!"

"Will it be okay with your folks?"

"Of course, of course. I can set up an extra bed in my room — it won't be a problem. Hanna, let me show you around. Bring your bag and I'll give you a place to put your things."

Nandin nodded that she should go with Sarah. Hanna smiled, picked up her bag and followed. She couldn't say for sure, but if she were to guess, she'd place Sarah in her early-twenties. It surprised her she was so eager to have a stranger share her room. Her hospitality and cheerfulness reminded Hanna of Cardea and she suddenly felt nostalgic for those first few weeks she had spent on Galenia when things were still new and trouble-free — that is once she recovered from almost dying due to lack of Essence. Passing through the market reminded her of the simple town of Kayu where people seemed to enjoy their lives. Meeting the happy-go-lucky Sarah added another reason to believe that people liked it here. It was not what she had expected to encounter. Could this truly be Mateo's valley?

Sarah quickly emptied one of her dresser drawers for Hanna to use despite Hanna's insistence that she didn't need one.

"Oh Hanna, I've been an only child all my life; I'm delighted to share my space with you. It'll be like having a sister!"

When Hanna was settled, they returned to the main room. Their hostess poured each of them tea and offered them cream and sugar and the sweet tarts that she had made that morning. Finally satisfied that her guests were content, she went to sit down when there was a light tapping on the door; it opened before she reached it. Jon took a step towards her, wrapped an arm around her, and dipped her as he gave her a kiss.

Nandin cleared his throat.

"Good afternoon Jon."

He almost dropped Sarah on the floor when Nandin spoke, but caught her and returned her to standing. Hanna was amused that the strapping young man blushed at being caught kissing his bride-to-be.

"Nandin, you're alright! What are you doing here?" Taking in the bruise and cut on his face he added, "What happened to you?"

Sarah grabbed Jon by the hand and led him over to her guests. "I'm sure they will tell us. Let's sit."

She poured another cup of tea as Nandin explained everything that happened since they left the clearing. Hanna studied their reactions as she tried to determine what kind of people they were and how much she could trust them.

Jon raised his eyebrows in amazement when Nandin described how he scaled the walls of the Citadel to get to Hanna; Sarah's dreamy expression was a clear indication of her optimistic views.

"How romantic!" Sarah said. "He climbed all that way to rescue you."

"Oh yes, he was a real Romeo — saving me at knife point. I'm not sure attempted kidnapping is what I'd call romantic."

Before Nandin could defend himself, Jon requested the story be continued. He hung on their every word and even laughed when Nandin confessed that Hanna had knocked him out in one hit.

"Had he actually said something when he climbed in my window I would have been less freaked out and wouldn't have whacked him like that — most likely."

"If you hadn't proceeded to drag me across the room and tie me to a chair, Master Juro wouldn't have burst in and carted me off to the dungeons."

"He didn't!" Sarah cried out.

"He did," Nandin replied in all seriousness, but a hint of bravado crept into his voice and he couldn't help but make light of the situation he'd been in. "He had me beaten for all my trouble...the least he could of done was let me have a chance to recover from my climb and the concussion Hanna gave me before he started the interrogation,"

"No, no," Jon said, "it's best to interrogate when the prisoner's already in a weakened position."

Everyone stopped and stared at him.

"What? It's the same with hunting, if your prey is wounded it's a lot easier to take it down."

"Jon, are you seriously agreeing with their treatment of Nandin?" Sarah asked incredulously.

"Of course not...well...actually yes, I am. If someone snuck into your bedroom and had you at knife point I wouldn't hesitate taking a few swings at him."

Hanna and Nandin exchanged looks then both burst out laughing. "I never looked at it that way," Nandin said. "I suppose if it that happened to Hanna at Mateo's castle I'd have done the same thing. In fact, now I think about it, I got off lightly."

"That's because I intervened."

Sarah clapped her hands together. "Did you really?"

They went on to explain what Nandin was questioned about and how Hanna couldn't stand by while they pummelled him. Jon crossed his arms and shook his head when he heard how she had stood up to them.

"That was disrespectful," he criticized. "I can't believe you did that."

"Seriously Jon?" Nandin scoffed. "You're Yaru now, not Jagare, remember? You're supposed to be on my side. You could at least pretend that your friend getting tortured was upsetting to you...I am you're friend, right?"

"Of course," Jon said waving the comment aside. "But just because I'm Yaru doesn't mean I suddenly hate the Masters. That wasn't why I came here. They are honourable men and deserve our respect."

Hanna spoke up, "Well, I wasn't about to let them keep hurting him, what was the point? He didn't know the answers to their questions...there was no need for it. Besides, I already found out everything he knew."

"It wasn't your place to interject," he scolded sounding so much like Biatach she could have laughed.

"You think that's bad," Nandin grinned as he spoke, "wait until you hear how she refused to leave and actually slept in the cell with me all night."

"You slept in the dungeon with him?" Sarah gawked. "Oh Jon, Nandin's got himself a guardian angel!"

Jon said nothing, but just continued to scowl his disapproval. When they got to the heart of the issue of why Hanna had been sent to spy on the Yaru in the first place, Master Juro's concerns and theory that Mateo's quarry was the suspected cause of the tears that were causing damage to Galenia, Hanna was surprised how quickly Jon accepted it as fact.

"I knew it," he said. "I knew what Mateo was doing would have some dire consequences. It just didn't seem right."

Sarah placed a hand on Jon's arm as she leaned forward to talk in conspiring tones "What I want to know is: however did you escape? I thought for sure once they caught a Yaru, they'd never let him go."

"I have Hanna to thank for that as well. She insisted on coming to the valley — they had no choice but to trust me with her safety."

Jon graced Hanna with a hint of a smile, the only sign that he was actually pleased that Nandin made it out alive. "So what's the plan? What do Master Jagare and Master Juro want us to do?"

It bothered Nandin how Jon was so eager to follow the Masters' orders and showed no concern about betraying Mateo. He had assumed that, after all this time, Jon would feel some allegiance. Still, who was he to criticize when he was the one bringing the plan to Jon in the first place? And wasn't that one of the reasons he could trust him?

"We need to get Hanna into the quarry so she can see exactly what's going on and how close Mateo is to releasing the Qual, if that's what it is. Then she needs to get the information back to her friends who hope to meet up with her in the mountains. I've instructed them to go north through the river valley so they aren't seen from the wall, and then enter the mountain pass in the forest. I told them to stay put once they get there or they'd easily get turned around…I hoped you'd be willing to find them and lead Hanna to them when she's ready. They wanted to come into the valley with her, but I thought it was better for them to stay at a safe distance. The rest of the Yaru would not take kindly to Vaktare coming here."

"Certainly I'll find them and no one will even know they were there. I can make sure of that. The Yaru are up at the castle so they're not a concern; I'll tell the Kameil to leave off checking the traps for a few days."

"Good. I need to go to Mateo and see if I can convince him to stop the mining until we get this whole thing sorted out."

"How do you plan on doing that? If you tell him what Master Juro said I doubt he'd believe it. And what do you plan on telling him about Hanna? He's aware you went after her. You don't plan on just handing her over to him, do you?"

"She'd prefer not to meet Mateo so I've asked Sarah to let her stay here…and she graciously agreed. This way you could get her to the quarry and out of the valley in short order. As for Mateo, I'm sure he will want to find out more about these tears before any more damage is done. He'll stop the quarry, I have no doubt."

"That makes one of us," Jon said. "Why are you so sure he'd stop the quarry? I bet he'll do the opposite just to spite Master Juro."

"Jon, his goal is to help people, not destroy the world. He'll listen."

Jon nodded. "I hope so. But it's the right decision to leave Hanna here."

"Would you be able to take her to the quarry?"

He nodded. "You'll be safe with me, Hanna."

"Thanks Jon," Hanna said.

Jon rubbed his chin. "It's us who should be thanking you. You took a big chance coming here…now let's get on with it."

"Do you have time now? How long have you been in the valley?" Nandin asked.

"I came here straight from the farmer's pass. I'll be fine in the valley for awhile yet."

"Good. I'll go speak with Mateo now…come find me when

you're done."

Hanna placed a hand on Nandin's arm as they stood. "Will I see you again?" she asked suddenly concerned.

"Absolutely. I trust Jon, but I will be joining him to escort you to your friends...I promised to keep you safe and take you back and I plan to see it through."

As Nandin started to leave, Jon grabbed him by the arm.

"Watch your back, Nandin. Blades was none-to-happy with what went on in the clearing."

"Getting attacked by the Vaktare didn't make any of us happy."

"It's not that — aside from the injuries he sustained from an arrow that grazed his shoulder and the burn that Hanna gave him — she humiliated him. The men are making matters worse by giving him a hard time about being bested by a girl half his size. Also, you wouldn't let him go after her to redeem himself. I think he feels he has a score to settle. Like I said: watch your back."

"Noted. I will keep it in mind."

CHAPTER SEVEN

Of the Essence

THE HOOVES ECHOED.

Nandin had the satisfying sense of returning home as he urged his horse forward over the cobblestoned bridge while tugging on the lead rope that was attached to Hanna's unmanned horse — there was no point in leaving it at Sarah's as there was no stable there and she wouldn't be able to take it on the narrow paths of the mountain. So much had happened since he'd last left the castle to infiltrate the city of Senda. He had yet to report on that mission and now he brought the additional news of his success at gaining access to the Citadel. When he passed through the gate and entered the castle grounds, he saw Hatooin rushing from the keep to meet him.

"Master Mateo is in the library," Hatooin said breathlessly, "he is most anxious for your return."

Nandin handed over the reigns of the horses and entered the keep, making straight for the library. With mounting excitement he leapt up the stairs two at a time until he reached the appointed floor. When he entered the library, Mateo rose from his desk to cross the room and embrace him.

"Nandin, I'm so glad to see that you've returned. The men explained what happened at the clearing. What were you thinking going after that girl alone? And with her being surrounded by those fighting men...the Vaktare? Are your injuries from the attack at the camp? No one mentioned you'd been hurt." Although his words were of concern his face revealed the pride he felt as he gently touched the cut over Nandin's eye.

"I felt responsible for the girl," Nandin replied. "I had been meeting with her for days and then she just slipped through my fingers. I needed the other Yaru to see to the safety of the Kameil and I didn't want to weaken their numbers to go chasing after her. Besides, it was less risky for one of us to try to break from the group unseen. My wounds came later when I got caught sneaking into the Citadel."

He went on to explain that he took a shortcut through the woods to get to the Citadel and that he watched and waited for some sign of Hanna — known as Darra by those from the camp. When he discovered she was in staying in a room on one of the top floors, he waited until dark to climb the walls.

"You climbed up the side of the Citadel?"

"Yes sir."

"Nandin that's…impressive. Did anyone see you?"

"No sir. Unfortunately when I attempted to quietly wake Hanna she reacted by knocking me out. Master Juro heard the commotion and I was taken to the dungeon."

Nandin noticed Mateo tensed when he mentioned the dungeons so he refrained from going into too much detail. Unlike when he told the story to Jon and Sarah, the retelling to Mateo took on a much more somber feeling; without Hanna sharing the tale, all humour was lacking. Mateo motioned for Nandin to take a seat as he listened.

"Hanna stepped in before things went too far…she insisted on staying in the cell with me all night to discourage them from questioning me further. "

"She sounds like a remarkable girl; when can I meet her?"

Nandin sighed; he knew it would come to this. "They've been filling her head with the usual myths. She's afraid to meet you."

"I thought you would have been able to persuade her otherwise," he mused. "Is it true she has the Sight?"

"She has the Sight and then some."

"How is this possible? Is Master Juro doing experiments?"

Nandin shook his head. "No, she's not from Galenia. She came through a tear...she said it was like some sort of portal. Apparently she's from a whole different world."

"You said that was what they were questioning you about; what is a tear?"

At first Mateo seemed merely curious and a little intrigued. As Nandin explained Master Juro's theory that the Qual was a liquid at the core of the planet, Mateo's eyes lit up, excited to hear his own theory being described to him, but when he heard that they had learned about the quarry and the liquid he was mining, a darkness came over him. He clenched his fists and finally stood. Nandin continued explaining and shared Master Juro's suspicion that Mateo was the cause of the tears and they sent Hanna to determine whether or not there was Qual in the quarry — if it was they planned to fill in the quarry to prevent the liquid from escaping.

Mateo began to pace, and his voice shook with anger as he ranted. "This is quite the scheme they've got going, using this girl to spy on us. Even now she's somewhere in the valley collecting more information to send back to Master Juro! They've created this whole doomsday story to stop my quarry. It is most likely an elaborate ploy to prevent me from creating more Yaru...or curing the Kameil. And now they plan to bury my LIFE'S WORK!" He paused mid-step and snapped at Nandin, "How could you be so foolish telling them about liquid Essence?"

Nandin was turning red, partly from his shame and embarrassment that he'd let secrets slip, but mostly due to Mateo's accusation. He stood to face Mateo. "I didn't tell *anyone* about liquid Essence, not even when they tried to beat it from me!"

"Then how — "

"Hanna overheard me speaking with Sim."

Mateo inhaled deeply trying to calm the storm that was rising inside. He place a hand on Nandin's shoulder. "I shouldn't have doubted you. Do you believe this tale you've been told?"

"I don't know how much I believe; I'm just trying to get to the bottom of it all. Did you know about the tears?"

Mateo shook his head and resumed pacing.

"You've given me much to think about. We still have more to discuss, but leave this with me for now; we'll carry on in the morning."

Nandin nodded and quickly left the library. Mateo was obviously furious and his own thoughts were in turmoil. The fact that Mateo was more upset about his quarry than the possible destruction of the world had him questioning his loyalty. Perhaps Mateo wasn't the man he had come to believe him to be.

* * *

Mateo paced around his study.

"They know EVERYTHING!" he ranted.

"Does that matter?" Hatooin asked hesitantly. "I mean, what can they do about it? It's not like they can get into the valley and stop you."

Mateo stopped pacing and glared at Hatooin. After a moment his expression softened and he slumped into his chair. He valued

Hatooin's opinion, as he tended to noticed things that Mateo overlooked. Often he requested Hatooin to listen in on conversations, not only so he didn't have to repeat it, but also for a different perspective.

"I suppose you're right," he said. "What difference does it make if they know about the Yaru or liquid Essence? It's not like they will steal the idea and make Yaru of their own. Or maybe they will...enhance those Vaktare of theirs."

"Do you believe what Nandin said about the tears?" Hatooin asked as he sat in front of Mateo's desk.

"Nandin believes what he was told. But that doesn't mean he was told the truth. They think they have every reason to try to stop what I'm doing and Nandin conveniently fell into their laps."

"His willingness to believe their story most likely allowed him his freedom," Hatooin reasoned.

"Most likely. I'm sure his high morals helped too. If he had killed the Vaktare in the forest, I doubt the girl would have vouched for him."

"It is too bad he's not a little less honourable — since he's proved he can get into the Citadel, it's feasible he could get to those crystals in the caves you told me about."

Mateo's head snapped up. "I hadn't thought of that, but you're right, he's found a way in. He was caught because he tried to get Hanna. I bet Nean could get in undetected and to the caves...if we do get to the Qual, as they call it, the extra crystals could be used to make more liquid essence."

"And what do you make of this girl?" Hatooin asked.

"She's still a piece of the puzzle I can't quite figure out. Obviously they sent her to gather intelligence, but how can she have the Sight when she's not Juro? I doubt very much she's not from Galenia still..." Mateo slammed his fist on his desk. "Damn it, why didn't he bring her to me!"

"Surely you can convince him to?"

"I'm sure I can, I just hate that I have to. I can tell this whole thing has cast doubt upon him...I can't have that. I need my Commander to be steadfast; otherwise he's no good to me."

"May I make a suggestion?"

"Go ahead."

"Gather the Yaru together for a celebration tonight."

"And what would we be celebrating?"

"Everyone's successful missions and Nandin's skill at getting into the Citadel to rescue the Seer. How he bravely held up under torture and then was able to persuade both Master Juro and Master Jagare to let him go. The men will love it — he'll be a hero. Even someone like Nandin would allow his pride to influence his decisions."

Mateo smiled. This is why Hatooin was valuable; he understood how to manipulate people and he had no scruples about it.

* * *

Hanna gawked at the sight before her. The pit was enormous, the quarry impressive, but it was the castle built on the floating rock that questioned her reality. Transfixed by its wonder, she was rooted to the spot trying to fathom why it didn't fall.

Jon gave her some time to take it all in then noticed she had begun to sway.

"Hanna, are you okay?" he asked.

When she turned to look at him, she almost fell. He grabbed her arm to steady her.

"I guess I'm a little dizzy. Gee Jon, did you notice how rosy everything is?"

"Rosy?"

"You know…pink."

Jon smacked his palm to his forehead.

"I completely forgot! Hanna, what are you using for Essence? Did you take capsules?"

"What? Oh, no silly, I have the pouch of mini-bits of Essence." She clumsily attempted to lift up her pouch, but only managed to grab her shirt. "I usesht it when I went to the clearing lash time," she explained.

"You better hand it to me. Nandin should have thought to tell you to remove it when you first entered the valley. You're suffering from an overdose of Essence."

Hanna teetered as Jon led her away from the quarry. He slipped his arm around her waist to support her as they went. She gave him a dazed smile, tripping as she went. When he lifted the pouch from around her neck she giggled — for some reason she found that ever so funny.

"Where we goin, Johnny? Ishn't the quarry tha-a-way?" she asked flinging her arm out behind her.

"We need to get you back to Sarah's to rest and get the excess Essence out of your system."

Hanna raised her hand as if she had an argument to make, but at that moment her head flopped down and sleep suddenly overtook her.

CHAPTER EIGHT

On a Pedestal

THE DOOR CRASHED OPEN.

Nandin had just finished getting cleaned up when Nean barged into the room uninvited to escort Nandin to dinner. At first Nandin opted out, but when Nean explained that Mateo had a big announcement to make, he was eager to participate. He was doubtful that Mateo had decided to stop the quarry after their brief, but heated discussion, yet he still hoped there was a chance.

"You're a little banged up," Nean said grinning at the remains of a cut and the yellowish bruises covering his friend's face, "looks like you've had some fun."

Nandin shook his head. "You need to see a healer."

"Me? Whatever for? I'm injury-free."

"I don't know about that, seems to me there might be something wrong in your head. Being tied to a chair and whacked about is not what I'd call fun."

"That depends whose doing the whacking. Who tied you up?"

"Hanna did the first time…that's Darra's real name."

"Really?" he said pausing mid-step, "And she beat you too?"

"I'm afraid what you might say when I admit she did knock me out," he held up his hands to stop Nean from commenting, "let me add that it was the Vaktare that did the damage that's still evident on my face." Nandin frowned. "I've been back to the valley for less than half a day and this is the third time I've told this story...maybe I should wait until we're all eating dinner so I only have to repeat it once more."

"Finish telling me first."

"Nope. You can wait."

"What? Come on...tell me!"

"Hey, I don't even know if Mateo wants me talking about this yet. I probably should ask him first. He's mad enough at me as it is."

"He's mad at you? You found Hanna and were beaten up by the Vaktare and he's mad at you? What did you do? Trade his secrets for your freedom?"

When Nandin grimaced at Nean's words, Nean grabbed him by the arm to stop him.

"You've got to be kidding me! You sold out?"

"No!" he wrestled his arm free as he raced down the stairs two at a time. "It's because I didn't that I got hit...but I'm not saying anymore!"

Nean chased him all the way to the dining room unable to catch up or convince him to speak another word. As Nandin burst into the crowded room, he desperately sought out a place to sit that might be in relative shadow where he could hide his injuries from most of the men and avoid their questions.

"Nandin!" Mateo called out as he saw him weaving his way through the Yaru keeping his head low and shielding his face as he went.

The men parted to let him through and all eyes turned to him. Considering Mateo was on a raised platform at the head table where all the captains and he sat during special occasions, there was no way he could prevent being noticed, so he stood tall and acknowledge the Yaru as he passed by. Hearing the whispers that followed him, he hoped Mateo was prepared for everyone discovering what had happened, as there was no way he could leave without the rumours spreading.

Nandin took his usual seat beside Mateo. He couldn't help but feel a bit ashamed to be sitting there. Nean's words about selling out had hit a nerve. Guilt had been tugging at him ever since he'd left the Citadel, and even though he had been deceived into trusting Darra and giving away secrets, he still felt responsible.

Mateo greeted him then stood up, waiting to get everyone's attention. When the room quieted and the Yaru had all taken their seats, Mateo spoke in a voice that resonated around the room.

"Thank you all for joining me tonight. With the Commander returning home we are now all officially in attendance and there are a few things I would like to say. This past month you've been busy working on your various assignments: our Huntmaster has kept the farmlands free of attack and has been doing an outstanding job recruiting some of the Kameil to assist him on the hunt. Thank you Jon." All the men joined him in raising their mugs and they shouted their agreement. When they settled he continued, "Sim's team has been scouring the countryside for our much needed Essence resources, Plyral and his men have rescued many Kameil families and Thanlin and Blades took their teams to take care of a bunch of Addicts that were causing havoc."

Following the accomplishment of each captain Mateo raised his glass to toast the men. "I would also like to congratulate all those that enlisted new potentials and, as you can see, our brotherhood has grown — you are most welcome additions!" The men pounded the table, delighted at Mateo's public acknowledgment of all their hard work.

"Some of you may have heard that Captain Nean, his team and Commander Nandin infiltrated the city of Senda and sought out the Kameil that were hidden there. It was a dangerous, yet successful mission. Thanks to their efforts, we not only saved several Kameil families, we have established a valuable connection with those that remained in the city. What can I say other than I am impressed?"

Mateo waited for the men to settle down again after they broke out in applause. It was not his custom to be so forthright with the work the Yaru did, but he knew the men talked and to some extent were already aware of all the things he mentioned. The details of the missions were still not disclosed nor would they be by either himself or those that knew them.

"As I'm sure you are all aware, since most of you were involved, our camp in Thickwood Forest was attacked, and although some of the Kameil were lost to us, I am proud to say the Yaru repelled the invasion admirably. Those families that made it to the valley are forever in your debt. What some of you may not know was the reason behind the attack."

"A frightened, young girl came to us, seeking our help. She was a very unique individual, a Kameil with the Sight. A specialized force of warrior Jagare known as the Vaktare entered the camp to capture her," Mateo glanced at Nandin out of the side of his eye. He wondered how his perversion of the truth was sitting with his Commander — he could trust that the rest of his Yaru captains who knew the truth would follow his lead, but Nandin had an honest streak about him and had yet learned the value of half-truths.

Nandin leaned on the arm of his chair, a stony expression on his face. He wasn't sure where Mateo was going with this, but he was pragmatic enough to understand that if he told the Yaru Hanna was working for Master Juro, she would very quickly be deemed as the enemy. He'd prefer the Yaru knew the real story, but with Hanna in the valley he had no desire to put her at greater risk. Referring to her as Kameil might offer her some protection, but it was a lie. Still, it was an easier, quicker explanation that the Yaru could accept.

"While most of you saw to the safe return of the Kameil," Mateo continued, "our Commander took it upon himself to rescue the Seer." The room went quiet. No one other than the Captains knew where Nandin had gone. After the attack they were all eager to get back to the valley; going after the girl protected by Vaktare was a risky undertaking, to do it alone was courageous, and a little insane.

"Now I'm sure he can tell this story better than I so I won't bore you with details. What I will share is that the Vaktare took the Seer back to the Citadel and secured her in a room on the top floor — to be close to the Masters presumably. This castle fortress though did not stop our Commander. He climbed the outside wall and snuck into her room. If the girl hadn't panicked, Master Juro wouldn't have even know he was there — "

"Master Jagare you mean?" Nean boldly interrupted.

Mateo shook his head. "It just so happens Master Juro was at the Citadel. At this point I'm sure you've figured out that this is how our intrepid hero acquired these nasty injuries — being taken to the dungeon by the Vaktare and two of the Galenian Masters is hazardous to a Yaru's health."

There was a murmur of astonishment from the men. Unable to refrain, someone called out, "How did he survive?"

"The Commander is skilled in diplomacy — he *talked* himself out of the situation. Not only did he manage to rescue the girl, but he brought back vital information."

"And horses," Nandin said attempting to hide his smile.

Mateo clapped him on the shoulder.

"You are a champion, Commander. To Nandin!" Mateo said

raising his glass once more.

"To Nandin!" the Yaru echoed as they stood and raised their glasses.

Nandin smiled modestly at the praise as he looked around the room at the men. He noticed even Blades was on his feet — he wasn't smiling, but he was standing...that had to count for something.

* * *

Nandin was completely blindsided by Mateo's speech and the adulation of his brothers that followed. During the meal while everyone was seated and engaged in their own side conversations, Mateo had leaned over to speak to Nandin quietly. He welcomed Nandin to share the details of his adventures with the others except anything that pertained to the tears or the Qual.

When the opportunity presented itself, Nandin quietly questioned Mateo's jaded version of the situation. Mateo replied that not all the Yaru needed to be privy of the whole situation, but the captains would be informed of the truth.

"And how am I to explain what it was that I said that won me his freedom?" he asked.

Mateo smirked. "Make something up or say nothing at all."

Never having mastered the art of deceit, nor ever wishing to engage in it, he opted to avoid saying anything. He wasn't sure how he'd hold up to Nean's interrogation, but thankfully, when the night came to a close and they all made their way back to their rooms, Mateo had requested to speak with the Captains. The other Yaru accepted that their Commander had privileged information and were content enough that he divulged details about his capture and what quickly became an over-exaggerated perception of his torture.

One by one the men disappeared into their rooms. Jon joined Nandin before he too went to bed.

"That was interesting," Jon said when they were alone. "Why do you suppose he made all those claims about Hanna?"

"I'd like to believe his intentions were honourable and he was attempting to protect her."

"How so?"

"We were attacked in our own camp for the first time ever. People died and we were forced to flee the forest. Imagine how the Yaru would feel if they learned that not only did Hanna lead the Vaktare there, she was working for them. That instead of coming to us for help, she came as an agent of the Masters — the same Masters who then tortured their intrepid Commander."

Jon raised his eyebrows. "Most of that makes sense, but torture? Intrepid Commander? Getting a little carried away, aren't we?"

Nandin sighed as he sat on his bed and pulled off his boots, tossing them aside. "I know. Which is why I can't help but think it was less about protecting Hanna and more about Mateo making me into a martyr. He got everyone worked up and since I'm not suppose to tell them about the tears, they think I'm also holding back on the extent of my interrogation. Trust me, I don't feel like the hero everyone's making me out to be...I haven't had the time to figure out why he did that. But I'll worry about it later. Tell me how it went with Hanna?"

When Jon explained their lack of success at the quarry, both of them took turns berating themselves for forgetting about Hanna's possibility of overdosing from Essence. Nandin was especially distraught that he forgot, considering he had remembered to ask Jon how long he'd been in the valley concerned of the same fate that had befallen Hanna if he lingered too long.

He admitted that his conversation with Mateo wasn't as favourable as it sounded during dinner. That in truth, Mateo was less than pleased with what he'd heard and they were to talk more about it the following day. He wasn't sure what had caused Mateo's complete turn-around in attitude. It made him uneasy.

"Maybe he's worried that now you've learned that he's doing something dangerous you'll switch sides, maybe become a double agent."

"That's ridiculous Jon. After what they did to me, why would I ever want to work for them?"

"Because they're right. Mateo's putting the world at risk by causing these tears and he has to be stopped."

"Geez Jon! We don't know that. I hate that you're so quick to believe Master Juro's theory. Could you at least hold off casting stones at Mateo until there's proof? Hanna hasn't even confirmed that there *is* Qual at the bottom of the pit. "

"Didn't you just tell me Mateo got upset when you spoke with him alone and now he's acting completely differently? Surely that counts for something."

"A change in attitude is a far cry from proof. I know you want to believe Mateo's a villain, but look at his actions. Remember all the people he's saved? He's curing your Sarah; he saved her family and so many others. Come on, he's *helping* people for crying out loud!"

Jon mumbled as he made his way to the door. "Yeah, yeah, you keep reminding me. I just can't help it…there's something not right about him. I can feel it. Trust me, one day you'll see, behind all those silky words and lofty ideals there's a dark agenda. We know he wants to make a perfect race; that's why he really made the Yaru."

"We know that do we?"

"Of course we do; he said so the first time we met him. He wants everyone to be equal, no race better than the next and he was proof that the combination of all the races was possible."

"You're paranoid."

"We'll see," Jon said as he left the room, "we'll see."

CHAPTER NINE

All Things Considered

HANNA STRETCHED.

She smacked her lips together as she sat up, rubbing the sleep out of her eyes. Stifling a yawn she smiled at Sarah who was knitting in a chair opposite her.

"Hey Sarah."

Sarah returned her smile. "How are you feeling?" she asked.

"Good thanks." Suddenly, she looked around her as if noticing her surroundings for the first time. "What am I doing back here? I thought Jon was taking me to the quarry?"

"He did, well close to the quarry, but then you fell ill so he brought you back."

"I was ill? I remember seeing a floating castle and then...then things got woozy."

Sarah nodded, her hair slipping over her shoulder as she spoke. "Yes. It was from too much Essence."

Hanna's hand went straight to her pouch, but her pouch wasn't there. Seeing the panic on her face, Sarah set aside her knitting and crossed the room to retrieve an urn that was placed unobtrusively in the corner. She removed the lid and reached inside, her arm almost disappearing from view before she pulled out a small item in wrappings.

"It's here. Go ahead, take a look."

Hanna pulled the wrappings off her pouch and opened it to

peak inside and make sure all her rocks with flecks of Essence were still there. When she let out a sigh of relief she began to place the leather string over her head.

"You'd better not," Sarah said, "there's too much Essence in the valley. You'll only pass out again. It will be safe here." She patted the urn and held out her hand.

Reluctantly, Hanna wrapped her pouch and handed it over.

"Why is there so much Essence?"

"According to Mateo, it's released when they dig in the quarry."

Hanna took a moment to look around. "Now that you mention it, I do see that the Essence is more concentrated in here than most places I've been to, but it's not overly obvious."

"I suspect that it becomes thicker the closer you get to the quarry."

"I wonder why I never noticed it?"

Once Sarah replaced the urn she sat next to Hanna on the sofa. It was wide and long without a back. The wooden frame was topped with a thick mattress and made a suitable bed. They were sitting in the front room that she had been in when she arrived with Nandin. The sofa, a table and one other comfortable looking chair that held Sarah's knitting, were the only furniture in the room. The window was open to let in a breeze, yet the room was still a bit too warm.

"Maybe the change was just very gradual." Sarah suggested. "Besides, there are plenty of other things to look at the first time you walk through the valley."

Hanna had to agree. "Where did Jon go?"

"To the castle. He's been down here awhile, but can't stay in the valley too long either. He's a pretty big guy though so he can last a bit longer," she said with a wink.

"Really? So if I was bigger I could handle more Essence?"

Sarah shrugged. "I have no idea. I just made that up. But I do know he can be down here for a couple hours before he's affected. But it depends how close he is to the quarry."

"Oh. So now what? Should I just go check it out myself?"

Sarah shook her head. "No, that probably wouldn't be a good idea. Jon said he'd come back in the morning."

Hanna stretched then leaned against the arm of the sofa, tucking her legs up under her.

"Okay, good. I'm pretty wiped anyway. Thanks for letting me hang here; it's really great of you."

"It's no problem, I'm glad for the company actually. With my wedding coming up I've been given early leave from the bake house. Mateo has a bunch of people up at the castle making all the preparations so I don't have much to do."

"A wedding sounds fun…how will that work exactly? If Jon can't stay in the valley for too long how could he live here with you once you're married?"

"Oh we wouldn't live here, this is my parent's place. Besides, I'm moving into the castle. Mateo is preparing a special suite for us." Her face lit up as she spoke; obviously excited about the new path her life was about to take. "Speaking of my parents," she continued, "they'll be home soon. Do you have enough energy to give me a hand with dinner?"

"Of course."

Sarah led the way into another room. It had a tall worktable with a few small baskets of veggies, a sink with a drain, but no taps and a bucket full of water. A couple of small rabbits hung above the counter. Sarah plucked one down and with a sharp knife began to skin it. Seeing Hanna turn pale, she recalled the first time she saw her mother skin an animal — she refused to go in the kitchen for days after that experience.

"Would you peel some potatoes for me?" she asked hoping the detraction would be helpful.

Relieved, Hanna picked up the basket and the proffered knife and placed them in the sink, turning her back on Sarah gutting the rabbit.

"So how is it that Jon, or any of the Yaru for that matter, live in the castle with all the Essence floating around?"

"That's one of the reasons the castle was built where it was. There's less Essence higher up, plus the castle is surrounded with high walls that help keep it out."

"I guess that makes sense, but then, how will you be able to live there? Being Kameil, you need the Essence right?"

"Mateo has offered to cure me."

"What do you mean?"

"He's going to give me a dose of liquid Essence. After that I won't need any other source. I'll be able to go anywhere on Galenia without ever having to worry about dying from a lack of Essence!"

Even though they were back-to-back Hanna knew that Sarah was beaming.

"What about your family? Will he be treating them too?"

Sarah sighed. "Maybe one day. Right now there is precious little of the liquid. I'm really lucky to be getting it. Jon and I can actually live in the same place — it would have been difficult to be married and only spend a few hours together every night."

Hanna hated to point out the downside to Sarah's plan, but she felt compelled to make sure Sarah had thought the whole thing through.

"I'm sure you'll miss your parents and friends."

"Of course not. I'll stop in whenever I'm down in the valley and they'll come to the end of the week feast as usual."

"Where's that?"

"At the castle. Mateo has a feast every week and different Kameil are invited to come, but once I'm living there, my folks will always be welcome."

"How — " Hanna started to say, but Sarah anticipated her question.

"He supplies everyone with Essence pills for the night. It's great fun too! There's always music and dancing. That's where I met Jon. You wouldn't know it to look at him, but he's ever so graceful on his feet. I remember the first time we danced…"

As she peeled the potatoes and listened to Sarah's story, Hanna reflected on how different Sarah and Jon seemed to be. Jon was so serious and skeptical of Mateo where as Sarah was so bubbly and seemed grateful, even trusting, of him. Hanna conceded, from everything she had learned and seen of the Kameil, Sarah's situation was about to be much improved, if not entirely ideal.

"Are you worried about getting the treatment?" Hanna asked.

"Not at all. There are lots of Kameil who live and work in the castle and they've all had it. It's not supposed to be as intense as what the Yaru go through. We just get one injection and that's it."

As she threw the rabbit skin in the garbage and cleaned off the counter she grabbed some carrots and began to dice them. "Maybe if you stay in the valley he will treat you too. Then you'd never have to worry about your pouch."

Hanna could see why the idea had merit, and maybe if she planned on staying on Galenia forever it would be worth contemplating, but she wanted to go home. Who knows what would happen if she was filled with Essence and then went back to Earth? But it was more than that. Liquid Essence didn't belong to Mateo — it wasn't his to give away. If Master Juro's suspicions were right, what Mateo was doing was destroying the planet. Killing their world for her ease of mind just didn't seem ethical.

CHAPTER TEN

Think it Through

KAZI REFLECTED.

He had been thinking a lot about his dad lately. The more time he spent travelling with the Vaktare, the more he realized how extraordinary he was. His job as a Messenger took him all across Galenia as he delivered important scrolls and parcels to everyone: from the common villagers to the most important members of society. But what impressed Kazi the most was that his dad did it alone. He was a Jivan: no Jagare strength to take on beasts if he was attacked and no Essence abilities to help him escape. He survived on his wits — his ability to know how to keep himself safe. He slept in trees if required, set traps and knew the best places to make camp. Better yet, he knew the places to avoid.

Messengers were well known and respected. Every town had special Inns, or at the very least rooms, set aside for them, they received gifts all the time for their services, and they had a place in the meetings at the Sanctuary for when they carried important information to share.

Kazi had no intention of becoming a Messenger like his father, but he did want to be someone who counted. He wanted to be brave, and smart and noticed like his father. And it was along this line of thinking that led him deep into the woods to spy on the

Vaktare's hunt.

Initially he had followed with no real expectations; he wasn't stealthy enough to keep up so it was likely by the time he had gotten close, the whole thing would be over. When he heard a beast crashing through the underbrush he did what any sane person in his position would do: he hid. Once it was clear the beast had gone, he came out and continued to track the Vaktare. It was much easier than he thought it would be. Whatever the creature they were hunting was, it had cut a swath through the thick underbrush as it had hurried away.

As he followed the path, he reasoned that he had no delusions about becoming a hunter; he just wanted to watch and hopefully pick up some useful tricks. Besides, he was bored. As much as he appreciated the privilege of hanging out with the Juro, Kazi was back to his initial assessment that the leaders were all depressingly serious and ultimately, rather dull. Kazi was desperate for a bit of excitement.

The trail ended at a clearing. Careful to keep himself hidden, he peered through the bushes. He spied a ferodel on the far side, pacing back and forth on its hind legs. The front legs were short and used for pulling fruit off of trees, digging holes as it searched for rodents and tearing apart its prey. Typically they were not known for attacking people, but when they did the damage they could inflict was significant. Kazi's pulse quickened as he took in the long, razor sharp claws and it's pointed teeth as it snarled; he thought perhaps he shouldn't have come. He cast his gaze around the space looking for the Vaktare. Fear gripped him when he saw that the Jagare, Zane, had fallen and was lying on the ground cradling his leg.

The beast eyed the helpless man as it paced, moving closer and closer. Suddenly, the ferodel charged. Kazi didn't think twice:

he took up his staff and leapt into the clearing. He swung his weapon with confidence and yelled at the creature as he bashed it on the nose. It shrieked in pain and fear, spun around and disappeared into the woods.

Kazi whooped in delight at his defeat of the beast, but jumped in surprise at the sudden appearance of Zane at his shoulder. He looked the Jagare up and down.

"Well...there goes dinner," Zane mumbled.

"You're not hurt?" Kazi said puzzled by this realization.

"Of course not."

"But you were lying on the ground...I don't get it."

"That's because you weren't part of the plan," he replied cuffing the youth upside the head. "The ferodel was relatively young. One sight of us and it took off. I was trying to convince it I was an easy target and get it to chase me so I could lead it into a trap."

"Oh," Kazi lowered his head. Instead of heroically saving the day it turned out that he had inadvertently ruined it. "I thought you were in trouble," he said under his breath.

"Thanks for attempting to save me. You do realize if that had been a full-grown ferodel you could have been killed. What made you think you could take on a beast with nothing but a staff?"

The other Vaktare pushed their way into the clearing, weapons drawn and casting about for danger.

"Where did it go?" one of the Vaktare snapped as she approached.

"Halfway around the world by now I'd wager. Young Kazi here whacked it on the nose and scared it away...it appears my acting skills were so convincing he was concerned for my safety."

As the Vaktare glared disapprovingly at him, Kazi desperately sought a way to redeem himself. "I could have helped if I had known what the plan was."

"How's that?"

"I could have been the bait."

The Vaktare chuckled. "And what would you have done if you couldn't gain your feet before it was on you?"

Kazi confidently lifted up his staff. "I'd have hit it with this," he said, a smile across his face.

Zane shook his head. "Give it here."

"What? Why?"

"Obviously having a weapon has made you cocky. I just told you that if it was full grown you'd be killed, but that didn't even affect you. I think if you are empty-handed you won't be so foolish."

"But…but if you were really hurt you could have been killed! Was I supposed to just sit here and watch?"

"Kazi, if I was truly hurt I wouldn't have been lying there like that. I would have had my weapon in hand ready to defend myself or dragged my sorry butt up a tree. At the very least I'd have been screaming my head off so my comrades would intercede before I was clawed to death. We're a team out here, not one man for himself. Consider that your lesson for the day. Now," he extended his hand, "give me your staff."

Reluctantly, Kazi handed over his only weapon. He felt vulnerable without it and understood that was exactly how his trainers wanted him to feel. It was clear to the Vaktare he was crestfallen. It had not been their intention to humiliate or disappoint him, they just wanted to keep him alive.

"Kazi, you're Jivan…a thinker. Why not work on establishing those gifts rather than trying to be something you're not?" Zane said.

"And how am I to do that?"

"You could try to come up with a plan to get us into the valley to fill in that quarry if it comes to it."

"Or maybe compose an epic song to commemorate our victory!" another offered.

Kazi's grin returned. Battle planning and song writing appealed to him. He doubted he'd be able to come up with a great plan, but he was willing to give it a shot. He'd just make sure he wrote it down in limerick, that way if it was a lousy plan it would still be the suggested epic song.

The Vaktare laughed at Kazi's instant switch in demeanour. Each of them would have been mortified if asked to relinquish their weapons; the sting would have been filed away and brought out in moments when anger and adrenaline were needed. Witnessing the acceptance and goodwill that Kazi exhibited was an unforeseen lesson to them. It left Kazi completely baffled when Zane patted him on the back and chuckled, "You're a bigger man than me Kazi Krigare's son, a bigger man than me."

CHAPTER ELEVEN

Guilt by Association

NANDIN FRETTED.

He had woken in a cold sweat that morning after disturbing nightmares of people screaming and the clashing of swords. No one had spoken to him about the Kameil that had died in the clearing — last night he was a hero who had done no wrong. As he dressed and gathered his notes, he realized the guilt he'd been carrying since meeting Hanna needed to be dealt with.

Mateo's initial anger was well founded, not only for risking the cure for the Kameil, but for the lives that had been lost on Nandin's watch. At the camp, he had been so enthralled in his discussions with Hanna that he had neglected his Commander duties. How was it the camp was attacked without warning? And he had plenty of Yaru who could have prevented any Kameil from dying if he hadn't ordered them after Hanna. It had been a time to show his leadership ability and he had failed completely. He was a fool if he thought bringing Master Juro's theories to Mateo was enough to earn his redemption.

True, if the quarry did cause harm to Galenia, Mateo needed to know about it and cease digging, but without the liquid, no cure could be made and the Kameil would remain sick. There had to be another option. If only he could convince Mateo to try to find it.

Nean's question of him being a sell-out also weighed heavily on his mind for he felt that, although not exactly an accurate account of what occurred, his compromise was a betrayal. Between his failure at the camp and the information he had leaked, he felt like he was undeserving of the reverence he received from Mateo's speech.

By the time Hatooin arrived to summon him to Mateo's study, Nandin concluded he had to find a way to get off the pedestal he had been put on and take some responsibility for his failures. Allowing Hanna to take the blame for spilling Mateo's secrets and not admitting that it was still he who had spoken them in the first place seemed cowardly. And being made a martyr left a bad taste in his mouth.

Upon hearing Mateo's permission to enter the study, Nandin went in, approached with determination and then knelt down in front of the desk. "Mateo, please forgive me. I failed in my duties," Nandin said, expressing his regret. "Our camp had been compromised, people died and your secrets were revealed to the Masters. The Yaru need to be made aware of my failures; I shall step down as your Commander."

"Have a seat Commander, I have no desire to remove you from your charge. After the defeat they suffered at the camp, the Yaru needed a morale booster. Your heroic deeds did just that; don't take it away from them now." Mateo sighed. "I thought you understood I absolved you of any fault last night? Did I seem insincere?"

Nandin slumped into the chair across from Mateo dropping his pack of notes on the floor. "It was an amazing honour that you bestowed upon me in front of the men, but you and I both know I let you down."

Mateo shook his head. "How could any of us have known

they'd have a Kameil-like spy in their midst? We all became somewhat negligent; I for one never would have thought the camp would be attacked. Historically the Masters preferred me rounding up the Kameil and taking them away. To kill and reclaim them was unprecedented. As for our secrets: you've proven to be skilled at speaking to people and bringing them to our cause. I never questioned how you did this or what you said. The truth of the matter is, it was your diplomacy that won your release from the Citadel — if you hadn't I never would have known of their concerns or their plans. For this I am most grateful to you."

He studied his mentor's face and found no deceit. Nandin's successes outweighed his failures and Mateo believed he was still worthy of the role of Commander. So intent on the conversation, Nandin hadn't even noticed that Hatooin had returned until he placed a steaming cup of tea in front of him. Mateo waited until Hatooin exited the room to resume speaking.

"Tell me about these so-called tears."

"They don't understand what they are and asked what I knew about them or what caused them. Of course, I don't know anything about them."

Nandin paused to collect his thoughts.

"Hanna said random areas were completely without Essence — like it was ripped right out of the whole area causing everything to die."

"Interesting. Where did these tears occur?"

"All over the place…here," he picked up a scroll and unrolled a map, spreading it across the desk. "I convinced Master Juro to give me this map of the known occurrences. Hanna came through this one here by Kayu and she saw this one up here by Kokoroe," he explained as he pointed. "Master Juro thinks that if the Qual was being drained in the valley it might result in it being depleted in other places. He said without Qual, Essence can't bind to living things which would then cause them to die."

"I know this to be true, it is why the Kameil can't retain their Essence as they have no Qual, but I was unaware that Qual being released here would drain it elsewhere. I've never heard of these tears before — none of our people have witnessed them. Master Juro could just be making that part up...but you think he's right, don't you?"

"I'm not really sure what to think, but Hanna's argument is pretty convincing — she sure sounds like she came from another world. I figure that if anyone could solve the mystery as to what's going on it would be you. Master Juro said all the Essence is gone from the area. There's no one who knows more about Essence than you, which means you're also Hanna's best chance at getting back home."

"You mentioned before that Hanna claims not to be from Galenia. That she came through these tears. Explain."

Nandin shrugged. "I'm not sure I can. Hanna said one minute she was on her world and the next she was here. I didn't really believe it at first. It was obvious she wasn't normal, having the abilities of all the races, but a different world?"

"Wait. She has *all* the Juro abilities? And Jagare?"

"Yes. And probably Jivan too, she is a thinker after all. Over the last few days she's told me about all these strange things from her home. I didn't know what she was talking about most of the time. It sure didn't sound like anything on Galenia."

Mateo slid forward on his seat ever so slightly. Calmly, he said, "That tale is far-fetched. I'm not convinced. I'm sorry Nandin; it sounds like a fabrication. Perhaps they did their own experiments on this poor girl and it resulted in these tears. And do you think they would admit that to anyone? Of course not — not when they have me to blame," he paused as he thought it through. "They would need a plausible story as to where Hanna came from — even the average citizen wouldn't believe she was born that way."

Nandin shook his head. "It's not like that."

"How do you know?"

"I just...do. I know it in my gut. Talking with Hanna is... convincing."

Mateo sat back suppressing a smile and sighed. "If only you could convince her to come here. I would be able to tell by just looking at her if she was from Galenia."

Nandin shifted, feeling uncomfortable at the prospect of bringing Hanna to the castle. Although Mateo was in better spirits, his initial anger had left its impression. Hanna was an agent of Master Juro; would Mateo do to her what the Vaktare had done to Nandin? Was Mateo capable of such brutality?

Mateo walked around the desk and placed a hand on his shoulder. "What's the problem son?" Mateo asked softly, sensing Nandin's hesitation.

"They had me beaten..." he left the thought unfinished.

Mateo frowned. "You think I might do the same to her? Take out my revenge for what they did to you?" Nandin just looked at him unable to voice his concern. "Vengeance is not my way. I'm more interested in getting to the truth."

"And after you speak with Hanna, what will you do?"

"Stop the quarry, of course. If Hanna is what she says, then it's worth investigating the rest. It is not my plan to rip the world apart."

That's what Nandin needed to hear. His goal was to stop the digging until they found out what was really going on. All he had to do was let Mateo speak with Hanna for that to happen. Nandin knew she hoped to leave the valley without encountering Mateo. He had known Mateo wanted to meet the Seer and, although he never came out and said she wouldn't have to come face to face with Mateo, he had implied as much. But if a simple meet and greet was enough to stop the quarry, then so be it. It would just be a quick stop and then he would take her out of the valley.

"I'll talk to her...she'll understand it's for the best."

Mateo smiled at Nandin's confidence. "Now that she's seen what it's like inside the valley, I'm sure she'll be less afraid to meet me."

"It's more that she's afraid you won't let her leave. I explained that people come and go out of the valley as they please all the time."

Mateo rubbed his chin as he leaned back on his desk. "But she didn't believe you?"

"She did, but she's worried you might not let her go since she was working with Master Juro."

"Yet she came to the valley anyway. Even if she doesn't come to the castle I could still stop her from leaving. I would just instruct the guards at the gate not to let her go...but I have no intention in doing that. "

Everyone who had taken part in the discussion at the Citadel had been concerned about that very fact. Even Nandin was willing to admit that if Mateo didn't want someone to leave he could stop them from going out the front gate, which is why he planned on taking her into the mountains. He couldn't let Mateo know that though, so he continued to act as if the gates were the only way out.

"So you'll let Hanna leave?"

"Of course. It is not I who closes gates to those that come in need. Our walls protect us from their persecution, they were not meant to use as a prison."

"That's what I said!"

Nandin relaxed. He was absolved of his failings. Mateo was willing to stop the quarry until he knew what was really going on. Mateo would do the right thing; he was a man worthy to follow.

Mateo smiled. "Shall I arrange for a private dinner? Just the three of us?"

Nandin stood and extended his hand. "Just the three of us."

CHAPTER TWELVE

Pit of Despair

HANNA BECAME KAMEIL.

Sarah had kindly supplied her with a fresh set of Kameil-style clothes for her excursion to the quarry. She had to roll the pants up as well as her shirt sleeves, but the belt held it all in place and the dull grey and brown fabric would help her blend in with the Kameil that worked the quarry. She felt if she appeared as one of them there was less of a chance anyone would question her being there or try to stop her. Drawing attention to herself might make it difficult to escape; it was better if she took no chances. In hindsight she should have done it the previous time she had gone to the quarry. Since she never actually made it, it didn't really matter.

As she stood on the doorstop waiting for Jon's arrival, she shifted her gaze until she saw the Essence in the air. There was definitely more in the valley than anywhere else.

"Good morning, Hanna," Jon said as he approached. "Feeling better I hope?"

"Yes thanks. Are you still okay to go?"

"Fine, fine. I'm just going to stop inside and say hello to Sarah."

It wasn't long before they were once again making their way back to the quarry. This time, Hanna attuned herself to the Essence. She observed that it intensified in colour as the concentration of Essence became thicker the closer they got to the quarry. Breathing became easier. As the Essence pressed against her, it was everything she could do to not reach out and touch it.

When the floating castle came into sight, she glanced at it skeptically, not really trusting her eyes, but proceeded to follow the workers towards the pit without mentioning it.

"No wonder I overdosed," she whispered to Jon, "there's so much Essence here."

Jon raised his eyebrows at her observation as they continued; he was not used to anyone being able to observe the Essence. When they reached the edge of the pit he stopped.

"Do you need to go further?"

Hanna gazed down into the enormous hole. It was big enough that she thought the floating castle itself would barely fill the space. A rough road was carved along the walls, spiralling to the bottom. Already there were workers leading a mule and an empty cart around the path. As she watched, she tried to see if she could get any sense as to what may lie under the surface.

"I'm not picking up anything from here. Would it be out of the ordinary if you took me down there?"

"New Kameil to the valley usually get a tour of the quarry. Some go down into the pit, some don't."

She indicated they should continue. As they wound their way into the pit, Hanna dragged her hand along the wall.

"Interesting," she mumbled.

"What is it?"

"These rocks…they're different than most. The Essence has just settled on them like dust, which is probably why it fills the air when they hammer away at them."

"The Essence doesn't normally sit like this in regular stone?"

"No, the Essence is part of it…it doesn't just sit on top…*oh!*"

"What?"

"Master Juro said that liquid, the Qual, binds Essence to everything it's in. The valley is filled with all this stone and I'm guessing it doesn't contain any Qual. That's why the Essence just floats here — there's not much for it to attach to."

They continued walking in silence, Hanna still touching the wall as they went. When they finally reached the base, Jon offered to help the Kameil load their wagon. He explained that Hanna was new to the valley, and was curious about the quarry; she insisted on following the road all the way to the bottom of the pit. The men nodded knowingly, as Hanna picked her way over the large rocks.

When they finished loading the last of the stones, they thanked Jon and began making the long trek back up the road; Jon made his way over to where Hanna was sitting.

"Well? Anything?"

She held up a stone she had found that was flat on one side. Using a smaller stone she had carved a picture onto it.

"You know how I said that the Essence sits on these stones like dust? Well, because of that I can feel them, I can feel the Essence." She pointed to her picture. "This shows the bottom of the pit and where I coloured in is where I can feel the Essence. See these gaps?" When he nodded she said, "There's no Essence there."

"What does that mean?"

"According to Master Juro, everything on Galenia has Essence, everything that is but pure, liquid Qual."

"So that means...?"

"That means if they dig a bit further they'll tap into a very big supply of it — it'll just fill up this pit. One big Qual lake."

"Are you sure? How can you tell how much there is?"

"I suppose I can't. But Jon...it's this huge void. I can feel so much! When I put my hand against this boulder I know that if I wanted I could just pull the Essence right out of it. And the Essence in the walls just goes on and on, but here, on the ground, it's not that deep. It feels like...like a hole. Like space."

Jon grabbed her elbow and helped her stand as another group of Kameil with a wagon and mule made their way toward them.

"You've seen enough then?" he said.

"Yes...can I keep this rock?" she held out the one with her drawing.

"Sure, you can keep a souvenir," he said loudly as he took the stone from her covering the drawing with his hand. "Good morning," he said to the workers as they got out their tools.

The men acknowledged him, each with varying degrees of disdain on their faces. Hanna carefully climbed over the boulders back to the road, suddenly wanting to be anywhere but in the pit. When they were out of earshot she felt the need to voice her concerns.

"Jon, when they reach the Qual, whoever is down here might not make it out. It could be a slow trickle, but it could erupt like a volcano. It depends on the pressure behind it. I just know that this is a very, very dangerous place to be."

Jon quickened his pace at the thought. Even though she was practically running to keep up, Hanna didn't mind. When they emerged, Jon motioned around the worksite.

"Would you like to see more of what goes on here?" he said for the benefit of those listening in.

As he spoke, a few Kameil glanced over. Hanna noticed they gave Jon similar looks that the last group of men in the pit gave him.

"No, I'm pretty tired now. Let's head back," she said also for the eavesdroppers.

When they were once more walking the deserted roads of the city, Hanna asked, "What was up with that?"

"What do you mean?"

"Those people, they looked like they hated you or something."

"Oh, that. Lots of the Kameil who work the quarry don't like it there. It's hard, dangerous work."

"And they're forced to do it?"

"Yes and no. Mateo has a rule that those who wish to live in the valley must contribute to the quarry for a certain number of hours a week. Even the children will help out with some of the lighter jobs."

"Why? I mean there's enough of them, couldn't they just say no?"

"Well, it's partly for their own good. As you saw, that's where the most Essence is. A few hours a week at the quarry will provide the Kameil with the amount of Essence they need to stay healthy. The ones who are putting in their few hours, like that first group we met, typically don't have a problem with it. It's the lifers that tend to dislike Mateo…and the Yaru."

"Lifers?"

"That's what they call themselves — those that have to work the quarry full-time."

"And they're forced to work there for their whole life?"

"No, but there are enough accidents that they end up working until their life is over — from their prospective that is. The big accidents can be lethal, but the minor ones can cause injuries that can cripple, leaving the victim unable to do much else. In their eyes, their life is over."

"That's tragic. Why would anyone choose to work full-time then?"

"Sometimes they do it because they need the work. There are only so many tradesmen the valley requires. For the rest, I've heard rumours that it's a type of punishment Mateo has. As a Yaru, no one will tell me the details, they don't trust me since I'm 'one of Mateo's men'."

"Mateo didn't tell you?"

"No. Being Yaru doesn't make me privy to everything Mateo knows."

"What about Sarah? She's Kameil; shouldn't she know what's happening to other Kameil?"

"She came to the valley only a short while before I did. She's not that connected to the lifers. They don't talk much." He paused to look around ensuring they were alone. "There is another rumour I heard though. The Kameil know that Mateo's found a cure and they've put two and two together to determine that this liquid has something to do with it. They have a suspicion that Mateo could have cured them instead of making Yaru. You can imagine how that made them feel. Mateo may have convinced a lot of people that the Yaru are necessary, but if it you could choose between making someone with enhanced skills or be cured of sickness, which would you prefer?"

"So are they right? Could he have cured them instead of making Yaru?"

"That's my guess, but Mateo is less than forthcoming with those details too."

CHAPTER THIRTEEN

Be Not Afraid

SOMETHING WAS UP.

As they entered Sarah's house, they found Nandin waiting for them. He sat at the table: legs stretched out and nursing a cup of tea while Sarah hurried to the kitchen to retrieve more cups. As they approached, Hanna studied him. His expression seemed off, like he was trying too hard to be at ease.

"So, how'd it go?" Nandin asked calmly as they joined him.

Hanna sighed as she slid into a chair and spun the rock around on the table. "It's about as bad as it could be. There's Qual down there alright and it could erupt at any time."

"Then I guess it's really important that they stop digging."

"That and add a few tons of rock to the pit."

She went on to explain what she discovered and her fear of what it meant. "Did you have any luck persuading Mateo to stop the quarry?"

"Almost."

Jon leaned forward. "What does that mean?"

"It means, Mateo needs a bit more convincing."

"How so?"

"He requires first-hand information. I didn't see these tear sights myself, so my knowledge isn't that reliable. I only know what I was told. Hanna's a witness and could probably answer whatever questions he had."

Jon's expression darkened. "Nandin, you didn't tell Mateo Hanna was in the valley did you?"

"I never said I wouldn't tell him she was here," he argued.

"But you put her at risk!"

"No Jon," Hanna intervened, "it was only a matter of time before Mateo knew I was here. After all, I came through the front gate. I'm sure someone would have told him Nandin didn't return alone."

Nandin cocked his head, "You're not worried about meeting him?"

"Ha!" Hanna laughed, but there was no humour in it. "Of course I'm worried, in fact, I have this sudden urge to run away, but I didn't come all this way to just look at the pit."

"You didn't?" Nandin said taken aback. "I thought the plan was to get you in and out as fast as possible. Didn't you tell Karn — "

"I know," she interrupted. "It's what I kept telling myself, otherwise I may not have had the courage to come here. But I've been thinking about what you said — Mateo's my best chance at getting home. I spent nine months at Kokoroe learning all about the Essence and defensive fighting skills, which is all very cool, don't get me wrong, but no one there was willing to do anything about making a portal or whatever to send me home. For them, that would be against nature." Seeing the shocked expressions on those around her she felt she needed to explain further. "Listen, I'm all for stopping the destruction that's happening here and I don't want to be the cause of more. I've done everything they asked to help solve that problem, but...I want to go home."

"Hanna," Jon said softly, "even if Mateo could find a way to send you home, what makes you think he'd let you go?"

"Why wouldn't he?" she asked, although she knew she should

be skeptical.

"Mateo has a way of keeping people here," he continued. "I had every intention of discovering all that I could and then return to the Sanctuary to report what I'd learned. But I'm needed here…protecting the farms, feeding the Kameil — it takes more time than I have. I can't just leave. But more to the point, I'm not sure Mateo would let me."

"What?" Nandin blurted out. "Of course you can leave. I do it all the time!"

"I know Nandin," Jon said, "But I can't be the only person to ever come here to get information. And yet, no one has succeeded in doing so. Aside from the Kameil and the Yaru, no one has ever even met Mateo."

Nandin clenched his jaw; Jon could be so infuriating. "Listen Hanna, I promised you before, when you want to leave I'll get you out. If that means today, then we'll go now. If it's in a week, I'll take you then. But it's true, Mateo is your best shot at getting home and you are our best chance at stopping the quarry. You just have to meet him for that."

"Why is that exactly?" Jon asked.

"I told him everything, but his response was that Master Juro made up the whole story to prevent him from making more Yaru. And he thinks Hanna is the result of some experiment."

"Seriously?" Hanna scoffed.

"Come on Hanna, if I came to Earth and someone told you I was from another world, would you believe them?"

"Well…no."

Jon shook his head. "I think he just wants to meet the Seer."

"Listen Jon, we are trying to save the world here. Mateo said he would stop the digging if he talked to Hanna. Actually, he said he only needed to look at her to determine if she was from Galenia or not."

"And why would that matter?" Jon argued.

"He doesn't trust Master Juro or Master Jagare at all. He has a lot of reasons to doubt them, yet he's willing to consider their story — if she proves to be what she claims. He'll halt the quarry until we've looked further into the tears." He turned his attention to Hanna. "He promised that you could leave whenever you want to. He said the valley wasn't a prison, just like I did."

Jon rolled his eyes. "Of course he did Nandin, what did you expect him to say? 'Bring Hanna to me so I can lock her in a tower and experiment on her?' He told you exactly what you wanted to hear."

"You're being paranoid."

"Paranoid?" he hollered.

Nandin held up his hands in defence. "Ok, ok…perhaps you have reasons to doubt him."

"Jon enough," Hanna said. "I know it's risky, but this is something I have to do."

"Fine. Then I'm coming with you."

"No," she said firmly. Before he could argue she continued. "I need you to find my friends in the woods. They need to know what I've learned and I'm hoping you can show them a safe place to wait for me." An unpleasant thought suddenly struck her, "You didn't tell Mateo about them, did you Nandin?"

"Give me some credit, if he knew they were there he'd send the Yaru to retrieve them and that completely defeats the purpose — "

"Yes, it does, but you don't seem to like keeping secrets."

"True. And even the ones I want to keep seem to have a way of getting out," he said looking at her knowingly. "I do keep my promises though and I said I would see you safely to your friends.

I realize you have little reason to trust me, but if I had no intention on getting you out, I wouldn't have bothered leading Karn through the river valley, nor would I have waited to show him to the mountain pass. I also wouldn't have left you at Sarah's or had Jon shown you to the quarry. What would be the point?"

Hanna held up her hands. Aside from her gut feeling that Nandin was trustworthy, his arguments were valid. "I got it, I got it. Now I just need to write a message to send with Jon…that is if you'll take it," she said looking to him expectantly.

Sarah placed her hand on Jon's cheek.

"My family didn't trust Mateo either when we first came to the valley, but we took a chance and it's the best decision we ever made. Our life is so much better here." It was hardly the first time that she'd had this discussion with him. She knew he was angry with Mateo and had reasons not to trust him. He often needed the patient reminders of all the good Mateo had done. "I'll go to the castle with them; if there's trouble I'll come find you."

He took her hand away and kissed it as he reluctantly he agreed.

"I'll get you some paper," she said to Hanna.

Sarah disappeared from the room and quickly returned with pencil and paper that she place on the table. Hanna moved her rock souvenir to the side and began writing her note. "I'll need one of you to proofread this as I'm still not great at writing in Galenian," she said as she wrote. "Worse case scenario: if Mateo doesn't let me leave, then at least Master Juro will know what's going on here. I can rely on you, right Jon?"

Jon pushed back his chair and knelt beside Hanna. "Ever since I was led to the valley it has been my hope to get word back to the Masters about everything that goes on here — the good and the questionable. Not only am I am honoured that you will allow me to do this service for you, I will forever be in your debt. I vow to do whatever it takes to return you to your friends."

Nandin bit his tongue. He felt Jon was taking his role as messenger to the extreme, but at least he was on board with the plan. Hanna thanked him and resumed writing her letter in earnest. When she was done she slid the paper over to Jon along with the rock she had drawn on while in the pit.

She cracked a crooked smile and said with a confidence she didn't feel, "Alright Nandin, take me to your leader."

CHAPTER FOURTEEN

Meeting of Minds

THE BRIDGE LOOMED AHEAD.

As Nandin and Sarah walked towards it, they suddenly realized Hanna was no longer following them.

"What's wrong?" Nandin asked as he turned to face the frozen Hanna.

She motioned to the bridge and the castle floating above the pit.

"That's not natural."

"The castle has been there for over a century. It's perfectly safe," he reasoned.

"It's defying gravity," she responded stubbornly.

Nandin shrugged. "It uses a magnetic force or something like that. Come on, it's okay; you'll be fine."

"Maybe we should tell Mateo to come to the valley instead. In fact, now that I think of it, that's a better plan — I should have thought of it sooner. It'll be easier to escape after…"

Nandin closed his eyes, breathed deep and tried to hold onto his patience. "Mateo rarely leaves the castle, asking him to do so could make him overly suspicious. Of course he'll understand you not wanting to go to the castle, but how can I sneak you out to the woods or hide you in the valley if Mateo is in the valley with us?"

"But Nandin, the bridge…it's really…high."

Nandin glanced at Sarah and back to Hanna. It was not the

argument he had expected. "Yes, it is. It's also been here as long as the castle has."

"That doesn't mean we couldn't fall off of it! I can't float like Master Juro, I'd be dust by the time I landed at the bottom of the pit below it."

"Hanna, the bridge is wide. We don't have to walk on the edge. Come on, I promise, you'll be safe."

He offered his hand. Reluctantly, she took it.

"Kazi would be glad to hear that someone is still taking me on terrifying adventures," she grumbled.

He chuckled as Sarah bounded to her other side and linked arms with her and the three of them proceeded up the bridge. Hanna could feel the warmth of the Essence in Nandin's hand and it gave her strength; Sarah's infectious, carefree attitude helped calm the gut wrenching anxiety that took hold of her when she glanced down into the chasm. She wouldn't claim to have a fear of heights, just a deep-seated aversion to falling helplessly into nothingness.

Hanna focused her attention on the giant tower of the keep as they walked. Once they passed through the castle's outer wall, the anxiety of the bridge and depths below it were forgotten; replaced with unease for the upcoming meeting with Mateo. Walking towards them from the tower was a lone figure.

"Commander," Hatooin said with a bow as he reached them, "and Lady Sarah, always a pleasure." He grasped her hand and gently kissed it. Finally he acknowledged Hanna. "Honoured guest," he said silkily, "I am Hatooin, Master Mateo's assistant. Please…follow me."

There was nothing remarkable about Hatooin. He was rather plain looking; a face you would forget as soon as you saw it. He was immaculately dressed in his usual white robe and blue sash, and he was perfectly groomed; not a hair out of place. His soft, plump hands had neatly trimmed, clean nails. But something regarding this ordinary individual bothered Hanna. She didn't know why, she just knew she didn't trust him. She tightened her grip on Nandin's hand.

When they entered into the keep, Hatooin spoke to Sarah. "I believe you will find some of the staff in the great hall preparing for your wedding, I'm sure they would appreciate your input."

"I would love to but..." Sarah had offered to come to the castle in Jon's stead; she doubted he would leave Hanna to go decorate.

She eyed Hanna who motioned for her to go.

"Are you sure?" she asked hesitating a moment longer.

"I'm sure Nandin can find you if we need you."

"Oh, yay! Thank you!" she turned to leave calling over her shoulder, "Nandin, you'll come get me later?"

Nandin nodded as she disappeared down the side hall. Silently, Hatooin continued to lead the way up several flights of stairs and entered the library.

"Please make yourselves comfortable. Master Mateo will be along shortly."

When he left, Hanna let go of Nandin and grasped the nearest pillar.

"This place is amazing! Look at the details in this column." She spun around gawking at the enormous space, momentarily forgetting her concerns. The stained glass windows cast a rainbow of colours across the room. Sculptures, wooden desks with carvings and an ornate stone hearth large enough for her to stand in gave the place a feeling of opulence. Running to one of the spiral staircases she placed a hand on the rail to steady herself as she looked up to admire the chandeliers and the floor-to-ceiling bookcases. She was eager to climb the stairs to get a better look.

"I didn't know anyone on Galenia had so many books! Where did they all come from?" she asked as she took a tentative step up the stairs. "Who do you suppose wrote them all?"

"I did," Mateo said as he entered into the room. "A good portion of them in any case. I have a fair number of scribes adding to the collection."

Nandin stepped forward.

"Master Mateo, may I introduce you to Hanna?"

Hanna returned to Nandin's side, suddenly regretting that she let go of his hand, but too self-conscious to pick it up again. Mateo bowed slightly then extended his own hand. Automatically, Hanna reached out to shake it. It was electric. One hand grasped her, the other cupped over top — the Essence fizzled around and through her fingers.

"My pleasure," Mateo said. "Come, let us sit."

She was dumbstruck as he let go, feeling overwhelmed by his presence. As they made their way to a grouping of high-backed chairs, she couldn't look away even though the intensity of the Essence was almost painful to see. His whole body had an aura. She was dwarfed walking next to this impressive figure. Dressed in black satin, his long dark hair was loose down his back with the exception of a few tiny braids, he wore sandal-like shoes but kept his feet bare and his shirt was open enough to reveal his muscular chest. Hanna couldn't decide if he was handsome or not. His bronze skin was so smooth he could have been made of stone. And, although he smiled, it never reached his eyes. Her throat went dry. This was undoubtedly someone you did not mess with.

They took their seats in the deep-buttoned, leather chairs. Mateo reclined as he observed her.

"You can see my Essence?" he asked.

"Yes," she replied, barely above a whisper.

"And what do you make of it?"

"I can hardly stand to look at you...I mean, the Essence is so intense."

Mateo laughed. Hanna smiled weakly and glanced at Nandin who was sitting back with his arms crossed looking amused. Mateo continued to peer at Hanna. After an uncomfortably long silence he spoke again.

"And you have no Essence — aside from those few particles in that pouch your wearing."

Hanna refrained from grabbing her pouch that was hidden away under her shirt — since the castle was Essence-free she needed it while she was there, but it never dawned on her that Mateo would be able to see it. Quietly she berated herself for forgetting that little detail; what if he tried to take it? Unaware of Hanna's internal battle, Mateo continued.

"I understand you can also control the Essence. Would you mind a demonstration?"

Without waiting for a reply, he levitated a book off a shelf and floated it towards her. It was larger than most books she was accustomed to and she thought it was probably very heavy. When it hovered high above and directly over her lap Mateo dropped it. Instinctively, Hanna put her hands up. The book had barely fallen an inch before she had stopped it.

"Are you kidding me?!" she snapped finally finding her voice. She thought his test was a rude way to determine whether or not she could use the gift of manipulating the Essence, but she continued to float the book, twisting it into position and replaced it back on the shelf.

Mateo clapped his hands together. "Excellent! Well done! Now, let us talk. Nandin tells me you are not from Galenia. Will you share with me a little bit about the place you call home?"

"What would you like to know?" she said as she forced herself to relax. She had questions of her own, but she felt it was wiser to play it his way — for now.

He asked her the name of her world and how people lived without Essence. Instead of being confused by her answers, he seemed excited.

"At what point did you realize that you were not on your...*Earth*?" he asked unsure if he recalled the correct name Hanna had given him of her home world.

"I'm not sure the exact moment; there were a lot of little things that didn't add up. Seeing the map of Galenia for starters."

"So there was nothing that was extraordinary to you on Galenia? You have the same landscape, the same villages?"

"Well, not exactly. The land is similar, but the village was like something out of a history book. There is no electricity, no phones. I mean, it's not unheard of back home, some people chose to live like that I guess, but no one I've ever met. It's all very surreal."

The more they talked, the more at ease Hanna felt. He had such a calm manner and he was so interested in what she said. But she was not lulled into a false sense of security. She knew this man in front of her was dangerous.

Nandin finally interrupted the unceasing questions. "Do you believe me now that Hanna is not from Galenia?"

"Nandin, I believed it the moment I first laid eyes on her," Mateo confessed.

"So you'll stop the quarry?" Hanna asked.

"Of course," he said. "Now, tell me about these tears."

She didn't have much more to add to what Nandin had already told him, but it was the details of how it felt and what she saw that held his attention. Nandin smiled as any doubts that Mateo had disappeared as he spoke with Hanna. He seemed to accept every word.

"And you were not able to go back through these portals as you call them?"

"No. Master Juro said they're closed. He doesn't seem to think I'll ever be able to return home."

Mateo leaned forward. "I promise you, I will do everything I can to try and find a way back to your world."

"Thank you," she said lowering her gaze.

Home. That's what she wanted. Yet, coming from Mateo it didn't feel right. All these questions he asked, and yet, he didn't seem disturbed about the tears.

Nandin also wasn't comfortable with the idea of Hanna going home. She was proving to be instrumental in bringing Mateo and Master Juro together. Maybe not literally, but here they were, working on the same goal: the survival of Galenia. What would happen if she left? He was unwilling to confess, even to himself, he had a personal attachment to Hanna that he didn't want to lose.

Hatooin and a few other Kameil entered carrying platters of food and drinks. They placed them on the low table in front of them, then quickly left the three alone again.

"Ah, dinner. Shall we?"

CHAPTER FIFTEEN

Food for Thought

DINNER WAS CIVIL.

After a delicious meal of roasted fowl and vegetables, flat bread with oils for dipping and sweetened plum pudding, Hanna was more than full. She had the desire to question Mateo as to his goals, why he made the Yaru and what he planned to do with them, but for a change she aired on the side of caution. Currently they were getting along; what would happen if her questions upset him? She was pretty much at his mercy. She judged that it was a wiser approach to gather information on her own and keep Mateo in the dark as to her intentions.

Mateo sat back, legs out-stretched, his chin casually resting on his hand.

"I understand you've met Sarah," he said as Nandin refilled her glass with more fruit punch.

Hanna enjoyed the sweet drink. Juice of any kind was a special treat; she had to admit being at the castle had its perks. "Yes, she came with us up to the castle."

"Do you get along okay?"

"Yeah, she's cool."

She noticed his look of confusion as she stretched. "That means I like her; we get along great," she said with a yawn.

"I'm glad. Did she mention once married she will be moving with Jon into the castle?"

"Yes. She was very excited about it."

"That pleases me to hear. I think she will enjoy the suite I'm having done up for them. Did she explain she normally has to take Essence pills every time she comes here? And that I have offered to give her a permanent solution so she won't need to take them anymore?"

Hanna tucked her feet under herself getting comfortable as she wondered where Mateo was going with his new stream of questions. "Yes, she called it a cure."

"I'd like to think so. You know, I still have enough to offer it to you if you're interested," he said in an offhanded way. "It is much safer than that pouch your wearing. Beyond these walls that is a very dangerous thing to be carrying. There are all sorts who would happily slit your throat for it."

"Mateo — " Nandin started.

Mateo placed a reassuring hand on Nandin's shoulder. "I'm just saying, when she decides to leave us she will be vulnerable. I wish to give her the option of my help."

"Would it be safe to treat her?" Nandin asked. "She's not actually a Kameil."

"True, yet she carries Essence with her. If liquid Essence wasn't safe for her, neither would any other form of Essence be. I wouldn't offer if I thought it was likely to do more harm than good."

Hanna waited to see if Mateo would bring up the risk that she could die young or how it might affect her back on Earth. After a moment she realized her logic was fuzzy — why would he point out any possible flaws? And why was she so tired?

"Master Juro said Nandin was burning hot," she finally said. "That the extra Essence would shorten his life."

"Ha. So quick is he to come to that conclusion. I've been 'burning hot' for one hundred and twenty six years. Does that sound like a shortened life to you?"

"I guess not." She couldn't deny he looked great for his age. He obviously had extra Essence, even more so than Nandin. Was it possible Master Juro was wrong?

Mateo watched as Nandin contemplated the matter. He could tell Nandin was warming to the idea of giving Hanna Essence and that's what he wanted.

"It's getting late," Mateo warned as he stood and glanced out the window. When Hanna rose he reached out his hand to shake hers, again holding it uncomfortably long. "I can give you and Sarah each a room to spend the night so you don't have to cross the bridge in the dark, I've been told it can be rather daunting. I can tell you're tired; I wouldn't want you to put yourself at risk. "

Hanna was tired, extremely tired. In fact, she had the urge to close her eyes right then and there. And the image of travelling in the dark as the horrendous bridge collapsed filled her with dread. It was too risky. Aside from contradicting the laws of nature, the vast, stone pit beneath it was a death-trap; no sane person would attempt to cross it in the dark. Of course, lingering in a floating castle with Mateo seemed equally crazy, yet she couldn't will herself to object.

"Perhaps just the night," she yawned once again.

"Very good," he replied as he released her hand. "I must leave you for now as I have a few things that need to be attended to before the night is done. Hatooin will show you to your room when it's ready. I believe there are some on the floor below Nandin's that will do nicely."

CHAPTER SIXTEEN

Cure for All

SILENCE HUNG IN THE AIR.

Alone in the library, they both sat contemplating what Mateo had said. Finally Nandin spoke. "He has a point you know, a permanent form of Essence is worth considering."

She crossed her arms. "Really? I thought you were trying to convince him that giving me the 'cure' was a bad idea."

"If it was *dangerous* it would be a bad idea, but he said it was safe."

"Nandin, how naive are you?" she whined. "There's no possible way he can know that it's safe. Sure it sounds good, but I'm the only person from Earth on this planet. I would be an experiment. Plain and simple."

"His reasoning is sound, Hanna. And he's right. Carrying the pouch, or even worse, that gem you left back at the Citadel, is really dangerous. More so than taking liquid Essence."

"Only if people *know* I have it. It's not like I wave it around or anything."

"Okay, now who's being naive? Did you wear it in the baths at Kokoroe? Doesn't everyone you've met since you've been here know you don't have Essence and that you have to carry some with you? You even told me the whole village of Kayu voted to give you the crystal. It's just a matter of time before the Kameil beyond the valley discover your so-called secret. People who spend their every breath searching for Essence will find out about it; if they don't know now, they will soon enough. Finding out that sort of thing is what they do; it's how they survive."

"But, I...look, I don't plan on sticking around," she yawned once more. This conversation seemed exhausting; she felt he should already know what it was she was thinking. "I'm trying to get home. And now Mateo said he'd help me get there. Why do I need Essence if I'm going home?"

He shook his head. "You can't have it both ways. You can't trust that Mateo is helping you find your way home, but not trust him when he offers to help you with Essence. You either trust him or you don't."

"Oh please...nothing is that black and white. Are you saying I shouldn't trust that he'll help me get home?"

"No, that's not what I'm saying. But if Master Juro doesn't believe you can leave then that tells me, at the very least, it won't be easy. Mateo has accomplished many things that the Juro never could, still, none of it happened overnight — some things took years to achieve. Do you want to keep yourself at risk that long?"

"No," she groaned. Why was he still talking? "It's just, what if when I get home the Essence makes me sick or something? I can't take it off if he makes it permanent."

"There's no reason to assume it will make you sick...it doesn't make you sick now."

"You're exhausting me. Listen, I just don't want to be a lab rat. There are too many things I don't know. What I do know is that my crystal or these rocks work perfectly fine. I'll gladly hand them over if someone attacks me, I know how to survive for awhile without them. As long as there is Essence in the air I can pull enough out to keep myself alive."

The truth was though, the more they spoke the less valid her arguments seemed. There were the ethical reasons she had told herself: since Mateo had taken the Qual to make liquid Essence, parts of Galenia were dying. Of course, he had already done the damage. It's not like if she refused the treatment the world would heal itself. Through her growing fog, she also realized if she didn't take the treatment, he could use it to save another Kameil. On the other hand, maybe he'd use it to create one more Yaru. That raised another question.

"Why is the treatment different for the Kameil?"

"What do you mean?"

"Sarah said that she's getting an injection, but it's nothing like what the Yaru had to go through. Why? What did he do to you?"

"It wasn't pleasant. I wouldn't recommend it to anyone, but he's not making you Yaru. He's just providing you your own source of Essence."

"What's the difference?"

"When he treats the Kameil he's giving them what they should have had to begin with. The Yaru are a combination of the races. I have my Essence plus that of a Jagare's."

"Not the Juro?"

"No. He tried, but he hasn't managed to achieve that."

Hatooin came hustling in the room.

"My lady, I have your room ready. Shall we go find Sarah?"

"Finally. Lead on MacDuff," she said.

"It's Hatooin," he replied feeling insulted she had already forgotten who he was.

She groaned. "Nevermind"

* * *

Hatooin hastily entered Mateo's study eager to share what he had learned.

"Well? Did they continue the discussion after I left?" he asked impatiently.

"Indeed they did," Hatooin replied with a self-satisfied smile.

"I'm surprised she's still awake," he said, "with the amount of juice she consumed, I thought you'd have to carry her to the room. Are you sure you added enough of the koia mixture?"

"I did as instructed, perhaps she needs one more dose?"

"Good idea. Now, tell me every word; don't leave anything out."

Diligently, Hatooin complied. As Mateo listened, a sinister smile spread across his face.

"I particularly liked the part where he made a case that it was only a matter of time before the whole of Galenia knew about her pouch or a crystal that she wears around her neck," Hatooin noted.

"Ah, well done Nandin — just plant a notion in his head and he runs with it. Soon, she'll be begging for the treatment."

"There's more sir. She argued she didn't need Essence back on her world, which was where she wants to go. Also, she claimed that if she was attacked, she'd willingly hand over her supply. "

When Hatooin went on to explain that Hanna had then turned the conversation to inquiring about the difference between the Kameil and Yaru's treatment, Mateo shook his head.

"She's dangerously inquisitive. And rather resistant to my persuasion. Please tell me she didn't affect my influence over Nandin?"

Hatooin's grin widened. "It didn't. I chose that moment to arrive and explain that the rooms were ready. They didn't resume their chat in my presence and once Sarah joined us, the topic was as all but lost. They said their goodnights at the door to her room."

Mateo rubbed his hands together.

"Perfect. I will prepare to give her the treatment tomorrow."

Hatooin knew Mateo wanted the girl to stay at the castle, but it had to be her own choice; the sleeping draught was meant for extra persuasion. Beyond that, he didn't know what Mateo had in mind.

"You're not concerned the girl won't go through with it?" he asked.

"Of course not. I don't plan on giving her a choice. I just needed Nandin to go along with it. Do you have an issue with that?"

Hatooin smirked. "What would you have me do?"

"Start with giving her one more dose of the sleeping mixture. I don't want to risk her waking up before we've carried out the rest of the plan."

It was hardly the first time Mateo had asked Hatooin to do something others might have found questionable. His willingness to comply freed Mateo to spend his energy elsewhere; loyal servants with few scruples were hard to come by.

CHAPTER SEVENTEEN

Garden of Secrets

HER EYES SNAPPED OPEN.

Instinctively, Hanna reached for her pouch. She relaxed to find it still securely tucked under her shirt. She sat up too quickly and it made her dizzy. Stretching, she tried to bring life back into her limbs, they tingled and seemed slow to wake up. Swinging her legs over the bed she took a moment to steady herself. She didn't understand why it was taking so much effort to get up.

Waking up in unfamiliar locations had become routine. It struck her as odd that she hadn't taken the time to appreciate her room the previous night — she had been so tired, after her brief conversation with Hatooin she crawled in bed and went straight to sleep.

The room was simple, yet rather posh as far as Galenia was concerned. Although it didn't have the majestic four-poster bed, like her room at the Citadel, the marble fireplace, hand-woven area rugs, and table and chairs with carvings were all of the highest quality and exhibited incredible artistic detail.

When she discovered she even had her own washroom, including a bathtub with pipes running up the wall, she considered requesting an extended stay, but realized it wasn't worth the risk — she was far from trusting Mateo.

She took her time getting washed up and dressed; attempting to take full advantage of the space and allowing herself time to regain her stability. When she exited the bathroom she was pleasantly surprised, if not a little freaked out, to find juice on the table as well as clean clothes laid out on the bed. *Why is it that people like to drop off these niceties while I'm bathing?*

She lifted the delicate clothes and ran her hand over the burgundy designs that were embroidered over the soft, cream-coloured cloth. The undergarments were delicate and feminine, unlike the utilitarian ones supplied by the schools.

Since coming to Galenia, all her clothes had been supplied by other people; wearing ones provided by Mateo felt a bit too much like joining his cause. A note on top of the pile gave her pause.

It simply said, 'A gift. Thank you for saving Nandin's life.'

She wondered if it would be considered an insult to refuse the clothing. It was a safer bet to wear them and avoid such needless confrontation — she could always change back into her other clothes later.

As she changed, she was pleased to discover the pants were form-fitting and the draw string allowed them to fit snuggly around her hips. The shirt was tapered and gave her some shape. It had been a long time since she felt like she was wearing something other than pyjamas or hunting gear, let alone anything stylish.

She returned to the bathroom to do her hair and noticed ribbon sitting beside the comb. She used it to tie her hair in a high ponytail. It had been a while since she'd had a mirror to use while styling her hair so, on a whim, she pulled down a few strands to frame her face and curled them around her finger. She took an extra moment to admire herself in the mirror then headed back into the room.

Flinging the curtains wide she was taken aback by the view. She was surprised she could even see beyond the outer gate of the valley. Before she was able to step out onto the balcony and get a better look at the city and the castle grounds below, there was a knock at her door.

"Good morning," Nandin said as she opened it. "You look...nice. I feel underdressed."

Sarah pushed passed him and held out Hanna's arms. "Nice, are you kidding me? She looks amazing!"

Hanna did a curtsy. "Thank you."

"Well yes, that's what I meant," Nandin stammered as he gaped at her. "I came to invite you to eat."

"Great," Hanna replied, "I love to eat."

"Mateo asked if you would be willing to join him...I mean us. I mean we're going to go meet and eat with Mateo."

The girls chuckled at his awkwardness.

"Sure. Will we be dining in the library again?" she asked as she stepped into the hall, closing the door behind her. They made their way to the elevator — or the lift-lower platform as Nandin insisted on calling it. Hanna was pleased when Hatooin used it the previous night to take them up to their rooms. Especially after she learned their rooms were close to the top floor.

"No, he has a smaller dining room on the main floor that he uses when he's not eating with all the Yaru in the main hall."

When they arrived, Mateo was already sitting and the table was set.

"Please join me. Can I offer anyone some tea?"

"I'll have coffee with *white* sugar please," Hanna said recalling the time she had asked for brown sugar back in the clearing. After enjoying an instant of confusion from her host and the others, she laughed attempting to be at ease around Mateo to gain his trust.

"I've been wanting to say that for sometime, you guys sure

like your tea. I have to say, it's a nice change not having to worry about saying the wrong thing." She went on to explain, "Coffee is a hot drink we have back home. Of course, I didn't drink it — it was too bitter to me…hot chocolate! Now that's something I've missed." Mateo smiled patiently as her newfound friends continued looking perplexed. "Sorry, I'm babbling. Tea would be great, thanks."

"The clothes fit you well. You are stunning — a real jewel."

Sarah nudged Nandin and said, "Now that's how you give a compliment.

"Did you sleep well?" Mateo asked.

"Yes, thank you," Hanna answered feeling a bit uncomfortable with Mateo's flattering remark.

"And how was your sleep Sarah?"

"Great! The warm milk and cookies that Hatooin brought was just the thing. I finished them up, crawled into bed and went right to sleep."

Hanna nodded. "Yes, that was nice of him. I can't even think the last time I had warm milk."

"Milk and cookies?" Nandin said, "No one has ever brought me milk and cookies."

Mateo gave a wry grin. "You're not a guest Nandin."

"Does this mean when I move in I won't get bedtime treats?" Sarah said with a mock pout.

"Put your request in with Jon," Nandin replied, "I'm sure he'd do a kitchen run for you. Milk and cookies," Nandin said, shaking his head.

Some Kameil arrived balancing several plates of eggs and sausages, fruits and breads. When they finished placing them on the table, they quickly left the room.

"Did you give any further thought to whether or not you

would like to receive Essence treatment Hanna?"

"I have," she said. "Thank you for the offer, but I think I will pass."

She waited for him to begin another round of arguments as to why she should get it done.

"Hanna," Nandin began, but Mateo raised his hand to Hanna's surprise.

"Nandin, if this isn't something she wants, we shouldn't push her. So Hanna, what would you like to do today?" Mateo asked.

"I was hoping to go back to the valley now that the sun's up to light the way." She waited for Mateo to tell her she couldn't go. Again he surprised her.

"Certainly. I'm sure Nandin will see you safely to where you want to go." He tilted his head to Nandin who nodded his acceptance while sipping his tea. "Perhaps he will take you on a tour of the castle before you leave. It's rather unique on Galenia, and since you plan to be leaving the valley soon, this may be your only chance."

"Actually, that sounds fun," she replied. In addition to fulfilling her curiosity, she reasoned that it would double as a reconnaissance mission in case the Masters were interested in what she may find. "I'm up for it if Nandin is."

"Yes, sure. Of course."

"May I suggest starting with the gardens? They are quite exquisite — even better than Kokoroe if one were to compare," Mateo said.

Hanna had enjoyed her time in the gardens at Kokoroe, and even though she was excited to see the rest of the castle, her curiosity was piqued.

"Seems like a good plan to me," she replied.

"Sarah, did you want to continue to help with your wedding

decorations?" Mateo asked.

"Oh, yes please!"

"Nandin will know where to find you then when they are ready to leave."

"And what will you be doing?" Hanna asked Mateo. Nandin was startled. He couldn't think of a time anyone had asked Mateo what he was doing. Mateo just smiled, unfazed by the enquiry.

"After I order the work in the quarry to cease, I will be in my lab. In addition to making more Essence tablets, I need to devise a plan for studying the tears."

Nandin smiled at this bit of news; Mateo was keeping his promise as he had anticipated.

Mateo was the first to finish eating. He excused himself, wished them well and welcomed them to find him before they left the castle for the day to say goodbye.

* * *

The sweet fragrance of flowers and the mossy scent of greens greeted them as they exited out the back of the castle. Hanna followed the flat stones used as pavers through the rocky terrain to reach the gardens as she marveled at the display.

"That must have been a lot of work," she said pointing ahead.

"What do you mean?" Nandin asked.

She motioned to the sharp, red stones that made up the ground on either side of the path. "It seems to me this floating island is just a big rock which means they had to bring all the dirt and water up here, which would also explain why the garden is raised up." She quickened her pace as she went up the incline to the garden's entrance.

"Huh, I never really thought about it."

With her hands on her hips she scanned the area. The gardens at Kokoroe were tranquil, uncluttered and had a calming effect. They were beautiful in their simplicity. Mateo's gardens were busy with vibrant colours, had complex designs and fantastic variety. The fact that each of the same colours and varieties of flora were grouped together prevented the overall appearance from being overwhelming along with the water features and stonework that separated different areas. She couldn't say outright that Mateo's garden was better than Kokoroe's, but it was rather stunning. And it was full of life.

Not only were birds and bugs zipping to and fro, but also the plants themselves moved. When Nandin passed by, she noticed the tall grasses reaching out towards him. She watched a group of neon green flowers with rose coloured leaves open their petals as a small, fast moving bird hovered above them. Red flowers in the shape of upside down hearts appeared to be pulsing.

Two trees with long vine-like branches reached across the pathway making a canopy overhead, which they walked under. Nandin led her over a small arched bridge to a raised area with stone benches.

"You can see the whole place from here," he explained.

She spun in order to see all the fascinating features: white stone fountains with purple, trailing flowers, floating greens in a pond laid out to make spiralling designs and short, golden bushes that glimmered in the sunlight. When she paused to admire the greenery closest to the outer wall something odd caught her attention. Nandin followed her as she went to satisfy her curiosity. She hesitated as she scanned the area.

"What is it?" Nandin asked, noticing her intense gaze.

"All the plants in this spot are leaning or turning towards the wall, just like flowers turn to the sun."

"So?"

"So? Don't you want to know why?"

Nandin shrugged. The gardens were nice enough, but in truth he hadn't given them much thought. True there were a few rare specimens on display, but that was more Sim's passion — not his.

"Mateo always said the place had healing properties and I've noticed after spending extended amounts of time cooped up in the castle that when I come out here I feel better. I've wondered about that, but figured it was just the fresh air. I didn't pay much attention to the plants."

She let out an exasperated sigh. "This could *mean* something!"

Nandin stood back and watched as she left the stone pathway, carefully pushing aside the leaves following her own path.

"A-ha!" she shouted pulling back branches to reveal a grated opening in the stone wall.

He wasn't sure why she was so excited about a hole in the wall, but resisting the urge to shrug again he gave a weak smile and said, "Wow. That's really something."

"You have no idea why this is relevant do you?" she said.

"Nope, but I bet you'll explain"

"I suppose you couldn't know — after all, you can't see the Essence. This vent here lets in the air and dust, and therefore the Essence, from the quarry below us. Otherwise, the height of the walls would block it out completely." She inhaled deeply. "It's like a breath of fresh air, a ray of sunshine."

"But we don't need Essence," he reasoned. "Why would we need a vent?"

"Even though you don't need Essence to survive a bit of it in the environment is good for you...and the plants. It makes them grow taller and you feel better. That's why Mateo said the gardens had healing properties"

"Well…what do you know?"

She took one more deep breath. "Okay, let's go explore the castle a bit; I wonder what mysteries you've managed to overlook there."

"Hey!" he said in a mock hurt tone.

"Well?" she asked waiting for him to argue the point, but he knew better than to pursue the issue as he had been just as negligent in exploring the castle as he had been in the garden. His reasoning of being busy would hardly excuse his lack of interest.

CHAPTER EIGHTEEN

Out of Time

VOICES WERE MUFFLED.

Nandin thought the best place to start the castle tour was with a spot he knew well and it was one of his favourite floors. Leaving Hanna in the hall, he disappeared into a room and returned shortly after.

"What are we waiting for?" she asked trying to discern what the voices coming from the other side of the door were saying.

"I asked my friends if they would give us the room for a bit; I didn't think you'd care to walk in on a bunch of Yaru, particularly Blades."

"You've got that right. They didn't mind?"

"Nope, they were glad for the break actually."

"Break?"

"You'll see."

A moment later the door opened and a Yaru popped his head out.

"Okay, it's all clear," he said.

"Hanna, do you remember Nean?" Nandin asked.

"Of course, how could I forget? He's the one who brought me into the camp."

Nean grinned. "Not to mention, how could you ever forget my good looks and charming personality…Nandin, you sure I can't stick around? I'd hate to miss out on the fun."

Nandin shook his head. "Not this time, Nean."

"Fine. I'll accept that...only because it means there will be another time. I'd love to see what she can do."

On that mysterious note, he opened the door that led into the training room and left them alone. The strong smell of sweat accosted her and she tried to refrain from gagging. Having the open windows to vent the room was a slow way to purge it of odour. She stood in the doorway appearing to scan the space; she was really trying to acclimatize herself to the environment.

Aside from the pillars, it looked like a typical gym, although, much of the equipment was different than the ones back home. The ropes and punching bags were common enough, as was the running track, but most of those gyms didn't have a selection of swords on the walls or targets for archery. Although some of these elements were also in the training rooms at the Citadel, the bins of rice and pebbles were rather odd, as were the wooden stands with dowels sticking out of them.

When she felt ready, she followed Nandin into the room. Drawn to the swords mounted on the wall; she reached out to touch them.

"I've never seen swords like this on Galenia."

"That's because no one else makes them this way. There's a whole section of the market devoted to making these amazing weapons that we get to use. These curved swords take years to make. We have Kameil who dedicate their lives to creating them — it's truly an art form."

She had no doubt as to the quality and craftsmanship of the swords. *Why* they were made is what made her uneasy. Before she could voice her concerns Nandin beckoned her away.

"Check out these bins," he said. "Do you want to try them?"

"Okay, what do I have to do?" she asked leaving the

discussion of Mateo's weapons for another time.

"Just punch the rice," he paused as she complied. "Now the sand...great. Next are the pebbles."

"Yeah, I don't think so."

"Why not?"

"Cause it'll hurt! They're rocks."

Nandin chuckled. "You're so clever! Nean convinced me to punch each one and my hands were bleeding from little cuts and bruises. I was so mad at him! I can do it now though."

He proceeded to punch into each bin and then showed how he wasn't bleeding. Hanna just glared.

"What?"

"You were going to let me cut my hands? Thanks."

He had the good grace to look apologetic.

"Sorry, I didn't think that through. Did you want to try archery or climbing?"

She smiled. "I can climb."

He took her over to the wall and showed her where the hand and foot holds were. She patiently listened to his explanation.

"Want to race to the top?" she asked.

"Really?" he replied, "I'm pretty fast."

"Listen, if you don't want to be bested by an outsider I understand. You Yaru are sensitive about that sort of thing."

He laughed. "Alright, I'll race you."

"Good. Let's start back at that pillar there, so we have to run a bit too."

Nandin shook his head. "If you say so."

On the count of three they took off. When Hanna jumped onto the wall she was more than halfway up. She grabbed one of the handholds and swung herself the rest of the way and straddled the beam at the top.

"Need a hand?" she asked as Nandin, who was still two feet below her, continued to climb.

"How did you — "

"I told you I could climb."

"I guess so! Nean would be impressed. Any good at archery?"

"Want to find out?"

He grinned eagerly. They proceeded to compete. Nandin was better at archery and a faster runner, but Hanna was agile and was at least his equal at doing the flips. Awhile later though, she began to slow down; her limbs were getting heavy and the tasks felt harder to do than usual.

"Whoa," she said after she ran part-way up the wall and did a flip. She steadied herself using one of the pillars.

"Something wrong?" he said tauntingly. "Did a Yaru tucker you out?"

"Just have to...catch my breath," she stammered.

She took deeper breaths — it didn't help.

"Hanna, what is it?" he asked suddenly concerned.

"I don't...know."

She sank to her knees, wheezing. Grasping her pouch she spilt the contents on the floor. Any trace of Essence was gone; there were just clear specks in the rocks.

"My, my Essence..." she clumsily sat down, leaning against the post. She attempted to pull Essence from the air like Master Juro taught her, only there was no Essence in the air to pull. Too late she remembered what Sarah had told her, the castle's outer wall blocked the Essence from the quarry as did the thick bricks of the keep. This high up none would reach the open windows; if they had been closed, the Essence in the air from the Yaru's workout may have helped her, but now, there was no Essence. She was in trouble.

"Nandin," she wheezed barely audible, "help — "

She passed out. Nandin scooped her up and ran for the door. He didn't bother with the lift-lower platform; it would be much too slow. Down the stairwell he went, three stairs at once. When he reached Mateo's lab, he burst through the door.

"Mateo, help!" he hollered.

Mateo leapt up from his desk over to Nandin.

"What is it? What's happened?"

"She ran out of Essence! She needs Essence!"

"Place her on the table in that room while I get my supplies."

Nandin lay her down, unaware of the fact that he himself had laid on that very table.

"Please don't die," he pleaded, "please be okay."

A moment later Mateo arrived with a bag of liquid Essence and a needle.

"She didn't want that," Nandin began to protest, "can't you give her a capsule or something?"

"No time, it would take too long to get the Essence into her system. Besides she's unconscious, she can't swallow it."

"Right, of course…what about the gardens? They have healing properties."

"She would have to be awake to pull the Essence into herself. No son, this is the only way."

Nandin held her hand. He leaned down and whispered into her ear.

"Sorry Hanna, but I can't let you die."

CHAPTER NINETEEN

Force of Nature

NANDIN FIDGETED.

After retrieving Hanna's pouch and its contents, he had gone to the library to wait for word that Hanna was awake. He hated to leave her, but Mateo insisted that she required rest and with Nandin hovering over her, constantly checking if she was breathing, it wasn't likely she would get any. Mateo assured him she would be awake soon enough and he would alert Nandin right away when she was.

He attempted to get a book and sit in a comfortable chair to pass the time, but when he found himself rereading the same line over and over, he snapped the book shut and began to pace. So lost in his own thoughts he hadn't noticed the Yaru that entered the room.

"Well done, Commander."

He nodded, barely looking up. "Yeah...thanks."

When it suddenly registered who had spoken he stopped pacing and looked up. Thanlin and Blades faced him.

"What?" he asked.

Blades replied, "On bringing the Seer to Mateo. It's remarkable that you actually climbed up the walls of the Citadel to get into her room."

"Oh...that."

"And you even convinced her to come willingly. Like I said, well done."

Where is he going with this, Nandin wondered.

"It seems," Blades continued, "your girlfriend will make an excellent Yaru, what with having Juro abilities and all."

"She's just a friend. And she's not being made into a Yaru. "

"No? Where is she now? In the lab isn't she? Getting treatment I heard."

"Well yes, but that was an emergency. Mateo just gave her the Kameil cure so she wouldn't die."

Blades chuckled. "Oh come now, she's no Kameil. Why would Mateo treat her like one? She's much better than that. Think about it. Mateo has been striving to create people with the power of all three races. Isn't she the first one who contains those gifts? But still, she's limited. Even if he gave her Essence she wouldn't be our equal...that is unless she had the full treatment."

Nandin didn't bother to continue arguing with Blades. Of course, he didn't believe him, but Blades had raised enough doubt that Nandin needed to check it out for himself. He ran from the library and rushed to the lab, trying to get the picture of Hanna strapped to a table out of his mind. When he got there the door was locked.

He knocked.

He knocked again.

"Mateo?"

No answer.

"Hanna?"

Hanna's shrill voice cried out, "Nandin!"

He banged on the door louder.

"Hanna!"

"Nandin! Stop him, NANDIN!"

He slammed against the door. He kicked it and pounded it. It didn't budge.

"HANNA!" he hollered.

Mateo bent over her and whispered in her ear.

"I promise, it will only hurt for a moment. And then you will feel better than you ever have in your life."

The banging persisted. Mateo cursed.

"Where are Mayon and Thanlin? They were supposed to watch him."

Hatooin hurried to the door to listen. He heard raised voices outside.

"They've arrived."

"Good," Mateo said. "Now get over here and hold her still; I don't want to put this in the wrong spot."

"Come on Nandin," Thanlin said, "he's already started. He has to finish it now; it would be worse for her if he stopped."

Nandin glared. "You knew! Both of you...you knew he was going to do this!"

Blades shrugged. "Why didn't you? Besides, I don't see what you're so upset about. Now she's one of us and she'll have her own Essence. "

"Nandin, let's go back to the library," Thanlin urged.

"No. Back off, I'm going in there."

Hanna lay on her side strapped to the table wearing only the undergarments she had thought were so lovely. She wiggled and fought against the straps, but it only caused her more pain. Even her head was secured. Feeling utterly powerless, she had a small moment of triumph when Hatooin placed something in her mouth as she called out again, and she spit it out. Hatooin leaned on her to stop her moving as Mateo's large, warm, Essence-filled hand pressed on her bare back. And then she felt the cold pinch of a needle as he inserted it. As he forced it into her spine she let out a blood-curdling scream.

Nandin renewed his effort. Blades and Thanlin had grabbed his arms in an attempt to pull him back. He bent down and then quickly jolted up, slamming into Blades. He kicked out at Thanlin and when he released Nandin's arm, Nandin let fly a roundhouse that took Blades on the side of his jaw. With his arms free, he pounded on the door. He felt it give a little, but then pain erupted in his head and he fell to the floor.

A kick to his head and his eyes rolled back. The last thing he saw before he lost consciousness was the satisfied smile on Blades' face.

CHAPTER TWENTY

Wake-Up Call

THE ROOM SPUN.

Keenly aware of the throbbing in his head, Nandin reached up and felt a cool, wet cloth that had been wrapped around it. Moaning, he sat up slowly.

"Take it easy, there's no rush," Nean said.

"Hanna...Nean, he took Hanna!"

"I know. She's recovering in her room now. Hattie's caring for her."

Hattie had been the Kameil who attended Nandin when he was recovering from his Essence treatment. She was very kind and patient with him and he knew she would take good care of Hanna, but that was far from the point.

"I promised I'd protect her. Nean, *I promised*! She didn't even want a cure let alone to become Yaru. Why did he do it?"

"You don't know?" Nean asked.

"Mateo always gives people a choice; he doesn't force them!"

"That's not entirely true. He offers them a choice, persuades them to make the one he desires or chooses for them. There's a reason many of the Kameil don't trust him. I thought you'd have figured that out by now."

"You mean...you knew he'd do it? Just like Blades and Thanlin knew?"

"Not just like them, but I knew. I knew because I pay attention. I've learned to get past the words in order to find out the intention. Blades and Thanlin knew because they were sent to keep you away. They're thugs; they do his dirty work and thrive on it, as I'm sure you know."

Nandin was bewildered. "But this? Why didn't you tell me? And why do you follow Mateo? Surely, you're not okay with this kind of deceit."

"Of course I'm not okay with it. Like you, I came here believing in the ideals Mateo spoke of. I still believe in them, but I know now Mateo sometimes crosses the line. Overall though, he does more to help than to harm. He's saved a lot of Kameil."

"I can't believe you can still defend him."

"Why? What's he done that's so bad? Save your friend's life? Made her Yaru? Why is that so terrible?"

"Because she didn't want it! It was wrong."

Nean shook his head. "Life isn't just a choice of right or wrong. It's time you learned that."

Nandin eyed his friend suspiciously. "Did he send you here to appease me?"

"Yes. Just like he sent you to Jon."

"That was different," Nandin said, remembering how he had talked Jon out of his depression after his treatment.

"Why? Because you didn't know what you really signed up for?"

Nandin leaned back against the wall. He winced as the pain shot down his spine.

Noticing his pained expression Nean said, "If it makes you feel any better, you gave Thanlin a black eye and dislocated Blades' jaw; he looks pretty banged up."

Nandin grunted. "Yes, that helps a bit."

"Listen Nandin, you're Mateo's Commander. You still have a lot of say as to what goes on. Mateo may give the missions, but you are the one deploying the men and planning on how they are done. Why do you think I insisted he give you the job?"

"You did?"

"Yes, I did. There's no way I'd take orders from someone like Blades. His plans consist of 'kill now, think later.' He isn't interested in saving people or making Galenia a better place. He just likes having power over people. Mateo genuinely believes in everything he's told us, I think he just gets impatient. That's when the likes of Blades and Thanlin get too much freedom."

"Why didn't he make you Commander then?"

"Most likely because I know how to play his game. That and he has no idea of what I'm thinking."

"And he knows what I'm thinking?"

Nean chuckled. "Nandin, you're an open book. That's what Mateo likes about you: you tell it like it is. And that makes you trustworthy."

"Why didn't you tell me any of this before?"

Nean shrugged. "You weren't ready. But this is a longer conversation than I think you'd like to get into."

Nandin rose to his feet, pulling the wet towel off his head. "You're right."

"Where are you going?"

"I need to see her."

"I thought you'd say that."

"Don't try to stop me."

"I wouldn't dream of it. I like my jaw right where it is thank you."

Nean pushed back his chair and opened the door.

"I'll go there with you, if you don't mind. I'd like to make sure you don't pass out. It was a rather nasty whack to the head you took."

Nandin rubbed his head. "What did they hit me with anyhow?"

"You know those small chunks of iron they both carry in their boots? Usually they hold onto one when they hits things."

"Usually?" he asked as they made their way down the hall.

Nean winced, "Blades chucked his at you. Sorry about that, I should have been there. When Hatooin came and got those two, I should have known something was up. By the time it dawned on me what was going on, I ran to the lab, but you were already on the ground. I punched Blades in the gut for kicking you in the head. He didn't need to do that — he was just power tripping."

"He didn't need to throw a chunk of metal at me either. There were two of them after all."

Nean laughed. "Yes and you fought them both and managed to knock that heavy door halfway off its hinges."

"Good." He growled, satisfied he did some damage. "What would you have done if you showed up sooner?"

"Tripped you, sat on you and talked some sense into you. Probably tied you up while we had this talk."

"That doesn't make me feel any better."

"Knowing that Mateo is really furious with Blades and Thanlin might. You wouldn't want to be near him when he's angry.

"Why would he be angry? He sent them didn't he? What did he expect from his 'thugs' as you call them?"

"They were suppose to keep you in the library, restrain you if necessary, or get assistance if it came to it. Instead, as I understand it, they goaded you into going to the lab, let you get all riled up and then knocked you out. And no one get's away with attacking his Yaru, especially his Commander."

"Why?"

"You know how much work went into finding potential Yaru, collecting the liquid and making it into liquid Essence. And out of all the Yaru, you are the best one to lead and train the men. That's a man you treat with respect; you don't go kicking him in the head."

"What will he do to them?"

"I don't know, slap them around a bit, make them clean the chutes maybe."

"Ha! Fantastic, serves them right."

Cleaning the chutes was an awful job. Long poles wrapped in wool were used to scrap the sides of each chute. When that was done, the cleaners had to go outside where the waste let out and load the pile onto a wagon, take it to either be made into fertilizer or to be buried outside the valley. Nandin was gratified to think of those two up to their elbows in crap.

When they got to Hanna's room, Nean leaned against the wall. "You want me to wait out here?"

"Yes."

"Okay well, if you start feeling sleepy, call me." Nean knew head wounds were dangerous, even after the victim appeared to have recovered. He'd witnessed those who went to sleep with such an injury and never woke up again.

Nandin gently tapped on the door and then slowly opened it. Hanna was lying on the bed, neatly tucked in, eyes shut, mouth slack and he noticed traces of a bruise where a strap had held her head. She looked so frail and helpless. He knelt down and took her hand. Seeing her there like that was too much...his self-control finally broke.

"I'm sorry Hanna, I'm so sorry," he choked. "I didn't know, I should have, but I didn't."

"Yes, you should have," she whispered.

Nandin raised his head. "You're awake? How are you awake?"

"Am I not suppose to be?" she snapped pulling her hand away.

"After my treatment I was out of it for three days."

"Another mystery that is me," she mumbled. She was confused. The last twenty-four hours were a bit of a blur. Every time she gained consciousness she tried to puzzle out what had happened, but only bits and pieces made sense. She couldn't even understand how she'd been convinced to sleep at the castle; it seemed rather foolish in hindsight. Being tired was hardly a valid excuse to put herself in such a vulnerable position and yet she had stayed. Even her fear of crossing the bridge was something she could have normally conquered. They must have manipulated her somehow. The stroll in the garden, goofing off in the gym…why would Nandin bother? Once she was in the castle he could have just taken her straight to the lab. What was the point of all that?

"Why are you here?" she asked. "Is this another one of your diabolical schemes: to beg forgiveness while I'm unconscious?"

He lowered his eyes, unable to meet her gaze. "I didn't plan any of this."

She wanted to snap at him again and push him away from her. At the same time she was tempted to reach over and wipe the moisture from his cheek. She remained unmoved.

"You look terrible Nandin. What did you do, fall down the stairs?"

"I kicked Blades boot with my head and used it to stop a piece of metal from hitting the door."

"Lucky door."

"Not really, I ripped it half off its hinges."

"And how is it Blades got the better of you? I thought you were the best?" she said, bitterness still prevalent in her voice.

"He had Thanlin with him."

"Two against one? That's hardly fair. It seems there's a lot of that going around."

"Hanna, I — "

"Tell me how it happened...I remember seeing my rocks spill on the ground and the next thing I knew, I was strapped to a table being tortured."

Nandin cringed. The echo of her calling out haunted him; picturing her tied to the table caused him pain.

"When you collapsed I didn't know what else to do," he explained. "Mateo had to give you the cure."

"Why did he have to give me the injection?"

"Because you didn't have any Essence. I suggested taking you to the gardens, but Mateo said you had to be awake in order to pull the Essence into you...is that true?"

"Yes."

"He also said the pills wouldn't work fast enough, plus you couldn't swallow them when you were unconscious. I know you didn't want it, but I couldn't just let you die."

"Yes, but why couldn't Mateo have just given me the Essence gas? That's what Leader Chieo did when I was in Kayu."

Nandin's mouth dropped open. "I didn't think of that."

She sighed. "I'm sure Mateo did. He gave me the gas at some point and that damn needle in the back. Why did you let him do it?"

"I didn't! That's why Blades and Thanlin attacked me," he said. "They were trying to stop me from getting to you."

"But you brought me to him! Why did you leave me there?

You said you'd keep me safe."

"He was done. Mateo said he was done. You needed your rest and...and I was in the way. He said he'd let me know as soon as you woke up. He...he lied to me."

"You think?" She wanted to lecture him some more, but she was tired and she knew she had been just as foolish as Nandin. Her anger was not only at him and Mateo, but also of her own actions.

"All those things he did to me, all that Essence...is that what he did to you?" she asked less sharply.

Nandin's jaw tightened as he nodded.

"Does that mean I'm a Yaru now? Am I to follow your orders Commander?"

"I don't know what it means...I just want you to get better. Tell me what you need; I'll do whatever you want."

She leaned forward, gripped his shoulder, her nails digging in to keep her upright. "I need you to hold up your part of the bargain and get me out of here."

She collapsed back on the pillow, groaning from the pain that shot through her and the effort it had taken to move.

He leaned in close and grabbed her hand. "I will get you out. Once I know Jon has returned we'll leave. Until then, rest."

Hanna closed her eyes. Sleep came instantly.

CHAPTER TWENTY-ONE

Quest for Truth

NANDIN BROKE AWAY.

He pulled himself together as he closed the door gently; Nean was right where he had left him.

"Remember Nandin, you were out of it for three days. It was a full week before you were up and about; these things take time. Right now she's healing, she's resting — "

"She's awake," Nandin stated.

"She's awake? As in lucid?"

"Yes. Can we go somewhere to talk...somewhere we can't be overheard?"

Nean tilted his head. "You're finally catching on. Come on."

They didn't meet anyone as they went down the hall, took the lift-lower platform and walked out into the gardens. It was barely midday, but the sky was cloudy and caused a gloom over the valley.

"There are two places you can go here if you want to guarantee your privacy: the gardens and Mateo's study. Everywhere else is vulnerable. If you must talk there, do so quietly."

"How do you know those are safe places?"

"It's where Mateo holds his private discussions. The gardens are easy, you can see if there's anyone here." He said motioning to the gardens around them. "His study is well placed, there's no way to get to it to listen in — believe me, I've tried." He sat on a bench facing the castle. "So, what's up?"

For the last week he was constantly discovering he didn't know what he thought he knew. Darra was actually Hanna, Jon still chose the Masters over Mateo, Mateo used Yaru to do dirty-work and sometimes crossed the line. His trust had been betrayed too many times, but at the end of it all it was his own fault — Hanna was right, he had been naive.

"I want you to tell me everything you know or suspect. If I'm to be effective at leading the Yaru, I need to understand what's really going on and what's being done to achieve our goal. When I send someone on a mission I need to know what I'm actually sending them to do."

"Are you sure? You might get your hands dirty."

"They already are, but not intentionally. From now on I plan to make informed decisions."

Nean grinned. "It's about time."

When Nean was done speaking, Nandin stood up.

"Give me a minute," he said.

He walked around the gardens. The beauty of the flowers was lost on him. His newfound awareness altered his perception: the pulsing flowers were bleeding hearts, the greenery turned away in shame. Tears dripped from the fountains, and as a cloud extended across the sun the shadows seized him, pulling him into darkness.

He felt used. As Commander he had sent the Yaru on missions: Nean had told him what really went on during those missions, things he hadn't known or perhaps had chosen to turn away from. He wondered how many deaths he was responsible for. His face was set and grim when he returned to Nean.

"Why Nean? Why didn't you tell me this sooner?"

"I needed Mateo to trust you; he has a knack for knowing

when he's being deceived. If I told you any of this sooner, he may never have made you Commander. Besides, you hero-worship the guy; I doubt you would have believed me."

As Nandin resumed his seat on the cold, stone bench, Nean asked, "So what's your plan?"

Nandin hesitated. Nean had given him all sorts of information but, for the first time, he wasn't sure if he trusted him. He knew now that Nean helped Mateo manipulate him; Nean knew what was going to happen to Hanna and did nothing to stop it.

Nean nodded his head slowly. "That was the best answer."

"I didn't say anything."

"Exactly. For a change you stopped and thought about it. You're wondering if you can trust me, right?"

"Yes."

"Good. You should doubt me."

"I should? Why?"

"Trust has to be earned Nandin, not just given away."

Nandin scratched his head as he considered Nean's words.

"If I can't trust you, then everything you've told me is questionable."

"That's true. Time will tell, or you may find a chance to test me. That's when you can trust me; you'll know when you know."

Nandin grunted. "Helpful. And what do you propose I do until then?"

"Well, you can do what Mateo does, speak in half-truths, and only disclose the information you need to."

"What do you mean 'half-truths'?"

Nean tilted his head. "What did he say that convinced you it was okay to bring Hanna here?"

"He said he'd stop the quarry and he'd let her leave."

"Yes. But did he say when he'd stop it or for how long?"

"Well...no."

"And I'm sure he tried the same approach with Hanna. Did she start to trust him?"

"I guess...maybe"

"What did he tell her?"

"That he would help get her home."

"Did he? What were his exact words?"

"He said he would do everything in his power to...to find her home."

"Typical Mateo. He didn't actually say he'd let her go there, did he?"

"No."

"And now that she's had the treatment, do you think he will let her go?"

Nandin shrugged his shoulders. Even after everything he'd learned he hated the idea that Mateo would be so deceitful.

"That's his trick," Nean continued. "He tells you what you want to hear with enough truth that it's believable. Then he twists it. He may strive to find her home, but what you have to ask yourself is, *why?* You would help him because of what you assume his intentions are. It's not until the last moment you discover the truth."

"How do you know all this?"

"I've been a Yaru for six years. It's my job to know and it's what he taught me to do. It's what he asked me to teach you."

"What? When?" Nandin asked startled by this latest revelation.

"Last night, after he finished speaking with you and Hanna."

"Why would he want me to be devious; I thought he liked that I was an 'open book'."

"He did, but your role has changed. Just because Mateo can't read me doesn't mean I don't have value to him. Now that you've gone and gained the trust of Master Juro and Master Jagare he needs you to be more discreet. He wants you to be better prepared the next time you meet them."

"What?! I was scarcely allowed to leave the Citadel last time, why would he want me to meet with them again?"

"He needs you to tell them that he's stopped the quarry. That he believed your story and plans to visit the tears."

"And why would I do that?"

"Because he has stopped the quarry. This morning he ordered all the Kameil out of the dig site. And he plans to personally visit the tear sights."

Nandin crossed his arms. "Half-truths though?"

"Yep. Once you leave he's going to reopen the quarry and double the manpower."

"Why?"

"He wants that liquid, even more now that he knows Master Juro doesn't want him to have it. He hopes you'll buy him some time. This information you brought convinced him that he's onto something. Since the Masters know what he's mining, he's concerned they might try to prevent him from getting it. He needs to reach the Qual, as I understand they call it, before that happens."

"But I'm not suppose to know about that am I?"

"Correct...I'm not suppose to tell you his plans. I only know about them because I overheard Hatooin sending a messenger to have the lifers ready to work when you leave."

"And what makes him think I'd help him after what he did to Hanna?"

Nean grinned. "He doesn't. He thinks you'll help Hanna; take her back to the Citadel. What you tell the Masters is what you've learned and not been told. You would see that the quarry isn't being worked and learned about preparations for Mateo to go check out the tears. With a few suggestions from me, you'd make sure to tell them exactly what Mateo wants them to know.

Nandin was perplexed. He couldn't get his head around why Mateo would be so manipulative. Games within games. Still, he couldn't just walk away. He had come too far, too much had happened. He needed to see things through; he just wasn't sure to what end.

"How do you keep it all straight?" he asked, "Remembering what you said and to whom?"

"You need to know your goal — what it is you are trying to achieve. Not just for the moment, but overall. And you need to remember who you're talking to. Only give out the information that pertains to that person. Mateo gives me the details for my missions, but never for Blades'. Blades doesn't know what Mateo has told you and it's not always because he's hiding something. If you don't need to know it, Mateo doesn't say it. If you know a man's goal, you're that much closer to knowing what he *isn't* saying."

"Is that how you know so much? You know Mateo's goal?"

"That I have yet to learn, but I do listen in on conversations I'm not invited to," he said with a grin.

"Now that you've told me that he's going to continue digging you know I won't pass on the message that he's stopped. Don't you care if he can't cure the Kameil or won't able to make any more Yaru?"

"Nope. I'm not convinced he is trying to cure the Kameil. And I don't care about his dream of trying to create the perfect race either."

"What do you care about? What's your goal?"

"Ah, now you're testing if I trust you."

"And? Do you?"

"Yes, I always have. But that's not the issue. You need to become skillful at keeping secrets — conceal what you really think and feel. When I know you can do that, I'll gladly tell you my goal."

"What about everything you've just told me? If I can't keep secrets, haven't you said too much?"

Nean studied Nandin for a moment, a hint of a smile around his eyes.

"I don't think so. Mateo knew you'd come asking questions and he wanted me to reveal some things. He knows he's betrayed you and you're bound to be a more guarded. That's why I can finally reveal what's been going on — he won't suspect how much you know. Just focus on what's in front of you; it'll prevent you from slipping up."

Leaning over with his arms on his knees, Nandin stared at the ground. He started to understand what it was he had to do. What he wanted to do was run away from this mess, but he was more responsible than that.

Nean asked, "So, are you ready to tell me your plan yet?"

Nandin turned to look at him.

"I need to get Hanna out of the valley."

"That's it?" Nean pressed.

"That's all I'm going to tell you."

Nean patted him on the back. "Good man."

CHAPTER TWENTY-TWO

Held in Trust

TIME MOVED SLOWLY.

The cold stone floor of the hallway did not make for a comfortable resting place, but Nandin was being stubborn. Once he and Nean finished their discussion, he returned to the castle, and after a brief meeting with Sarah, sat across from Hanna's door and refused to leave. When Hattie came to check on the girl, he shooed her away claiming all responsibility for Hanna's care.

"All's fine and well when she's sleeping," he heard Hattie mutter as she walked away, "but when she wakes, I will be tending her. No man belongs in a lady's sick room."

He vowed he would not move from the spot until he was ready to take her from the valley. He held true to that vow until, after two hours at his post, Hanna poked her head out the door. He jumped up quickly, ushering her back inside, shushing her as they went. He followed her in, forcing her to sit down on the bed and closing the door behind them.

"What are you doing out of bed?" he said softly.

"I'm not," Hanna whispered back, "you pushed me back into it."

He looked at her sternly.

"What?" she asked. "And why are we whispering?"

"To start with, by all accounts you shouldn't be able to walk yet."

"Sorry to disappoint you."

He held up his hands to prevent her from talking.

"We're whispering so no one hears us; from our last conversation it might be known that you are awake. Nean seems to doubt they'd have anyone eavesdropping just yet as it usually takes three to five days for someone to recover from Mateo's treatment, not five hours, but I'm not taking any chances. I don't want anyone to know you're awake, let alone up and about. And that means no one will be expecting you to leave."

"What are you saying? I'm a prisoner here?"

"No, but I don't know what Mateo's plan are and I'm not taking any more chances."

"So when do we leave?"

"We'll go at night, as soon as Jon gets back. I sent Sarah home and told her to wait there until he arrives. At that point she'll come back here and let me know while Jon finds us a place to stay for the night."

Hanna laid back down and snuggled under the sheets.

"Well then, I may as well keep sleeping."

He watched her a moment and was glad when she dozed off. Now that he was in her room, he was hesitant to leave. Quietly he made his way over to the lounge chairs by the fireplace and sat down placing his feet up on a footstool.

With all that had been revealed to him that day, he had plenty to keep his mind busy. He started prioritizing his goals: first, get Hanna out of the valley and back to her friends. Then, he had to get back and stop the quarry somehow. He wasn't sure how to achieve that goal, but he hoped perhaps Jon and Nean would help him come up with a plan. What his future held beyond that was still unclear to him. He just knew, he wasn't going to let Mateo cross any more lines.

* * *

A soft knock on the door startled Nandin out of his doze. He had stayed in Hanna's room all night and kept drifting off to sleep as he watched her. The previous night, Hattie had stopped in and brought him dinner, but she hadn't returned since. Quickly he got to his feet and in two strides crossed the room to crack the door open hoping not to wake Hanna. When he saw Hatooin, Nandin entered the hall.

"Master Mateo wishes for you to join him for the morning meal."

"I'm not hungry."

"I see. Would you please come and speak with him?"

"No."

Hatooin went red in the face. It was probably the only time anyone had ever refused Mateo's invitation.

"Why not?" he asked indignantly.

"I'm not leaving her."

Hatooin softened. "I could get someone to stay with her. She will be in good hands."

"I'm sure she would be, but last time I left her in 'good hands' those hands stuck a needle in her back."

Clearing his throat Hatooin said, "Is there anyone you would trust to stay with her?"

On an impulse Nandin replied, "Sarah."

"We're in luck then! I saw Sarah approaching the castle as I was on my way here. I will bring her at once."

Before Nandin could argue, Hatooin was off. Pacing, Nandin realized he had painted himself into a corner. He had suggested Sarah, not just because he trusted her, but because he didn't think she would be in the building. Her return could only mean one thing: Jon was back. Now he was committed to meeting with Mateo, which was something he was not prepared to do. He knew too much now, yet lacked the skills required to play Mateo's game. With Jon's return, he needed to make preparations to get Hanna out of the castle and into the woods that night, but now he would be wasting time. He couldn't avoid the meal and he wanted to confront Mateo, but he was concerned he might not be successful at concealing his intentions. And his plan needed to work.

When Hatooin returned with Sarah, Nandin was still standing guard.

"Sarah, you're back so soon."

"Yes, I wanted to bring a little something to Hanna. A gift while she's recovering." Sarah indicated the large bundle she was carrying. "It's a quilt I made awhile ago; I thought it would add a personal touch to her space."

The gift was a prearranged excuse that Nandin and Sarah had devised before she had left the castle. Ordinarily she only came to the castle once a week so they needed a plausible reason for why she would return so soon.

"That's very thoughtful of you. She's sleeping of course. Would you mind staying with her while I meet with Mateo?"

"I wouldn't mind at all. I'm a bit tired from the walk anyhow; I'll go in and rest in one of the chairs."

Once Sarah had gone in the room, Nandin turned to Hatooin.

"Let's get this over with. Is he in the small dining room?"

"Some of the Yaru have chosen to dine in there this morning so he asked for you to meet him in his study."

"Fine." Pushing past Hatooin he said over his shoulder, "I know the way."

Hatooin was not pleased. It was his responsibility to lead people to Mateo or seat them where they would wait for Mateo to join them. It might seem an insignificant thing to a Yaru, but it was an valuable role. He knew the secrets, the plots and the schemes and he deserved the respect that Mateo gave him. Thanlin and Blades were always snubbing him, but they were uncouth brutes, incapable of manners. Nandin was different. He was the Commander, Mateo's right hand man, an example for the other Yaru. If he began treating Hatooin this way it was only a matter of time before the others did too. He hoped this was a momentary slip in manners due to his anger; it just better not become routine.

When Nandin walked into the study without knocking, Mateo was caught off guard. He snapped a black book closed and hastily closed it in a drawer. Nandin didn't recall seeing the book before, and wondered at its relevance. For the moment, catching Mateo unawares, which had obviously made him uncomfortable, gave Nandin a small sense of satisfaction.

"You wanted to see me?" Nandin said a little hotter than intended.

"Nandin…where's Hatooin?" he said lightly, although he was annoyed Nandin hadn't knocked.

"He fell behind."

Mateo chuckled. "Oh dear, that's likely to have offended him."

Nandin pulled out a chair facing Mateo's desk. He was taken aback though when Mateo walked around to sit next to him.

"You're angry with me."

"Yes." Nandin sat back and crossed his arms.

"I'm sorry I have upset you."

"Upset me? You experimented on my friend."

"I was saving her life."

"Initially. But giving her the full treatment was not necessary."

Mateo sighed. "I suppose your right. The opportunity was there and I took it. I hoped, when she recovered, she'd thank me. And so would you."

"Thank you? For betraying our trust?"

"No, for healing her and making her better. Don't you see? Not only does she have her own Essence, but her abilities will be amplified. Nothing can harm her now. "

"It was dangerous; you couldn't have known if the procedure would have worked."

"Didn't you notice the freckles on her arms? The small mole above her ear? She has another one on her shoulder. You know those are indications that the liquid Essence would properly bind. Besides, there was less risk with her than anyone who has undergone the treatment, she didn't have any Essence to begin with, there was no chance she would lose what she didn't already have."

Nandin glared. "She's not Jivan, Jagare or even Kameil, you had no idea what would happen to her. More to the point, she didn't want it."

"That is the point, isn't it? Again, I'm sorry. Sometimes, when I see what's best for people, I'm compelled to help them — even if they don't want to be helped. Right or wrong, for better or worse; if people don't want my help, I should leave them be."

There was a knock on the door.

"Come," Mateo said.

Hatooin entered and bowed.

"Thank you for knocking," Mateo said, unable to refrain from making the pointed remark.

Hatooin glared at Nandin as he entered pushing a cart. Sensing he had offended Hatooin, he reflected it was probably unwise of him. Hatooin was an integral part of the castle; if he spurned him it could only hurt any future endeavour he may have. Nandin stood up and approached him. Hatooin hesitated, unsure of the Yaru's motives and was surprised when Nandin bowed.

"I apologize for my rudeness earlier."

"I…I understand, sir. You were troubled. If it pleases you, I have brought food and drinks."

Nandin returned to his seat. "Thank you, that would appreciated."

Hatooin grabbed his cart and moved it further into the room. They allowed him to pour them tea and fill their plates before he left. Nandin found it odd that it gave the man pleasure.

"You handled that well," Mateo said approvingly.

Nandin acknowledged the compliment as he shovelled food into his mouth. He was in a hurry to get this meeting over with.

"I'm sure you are wondering why I asked you here?"

Nandin was tempted to say that it had to do with the fact that no one could hear their conversation in this room, but he restrained himself and said nothing.

"I know you spoke with Nean and you've learned a few things. I'm not the man you thought I was. I've made…mistakes."

"So have I," Nandin said.

"Like trusting me?"

"Yes."

"Again, I am sorry. You are important to me Nandin; I care about you. You're like a son."

Mateo swallowed. Nandin couldn't believe that Mateo was actually choking up. Was this another game?

"How can I earn your trust? What would you have me do?"

"Allow Hanna to leave."

"She's free to go. In a few days, when she recovers, take her back to the Citadel, if that's where she wants to go."

"Thank you." Nandin had no intention of waiting a few days.

Mateo sipped his tea as he watched him.

"Will you come back?" Mateo asked.

"I will," Nandin said without hesitation.

Mateo cocked his head to the side, "Why?"

He finished spreading jam on a biscuit and stuffed it into his mouth in order to delay answering. When he was done he said, "My place is here. This is where I belong. There's a lot of good we're doing and I plan see it through.

Mateo agreed, "So do I."

He offered Nandin more tea and then refilled his own cup.

"Did you know I stopped the quarry?"

"Yes."

"And I'm planning to personally go visit the tear sites on your return. I have to know if I caused them and if there's a way they can be to fixed."

Nandin nodded. "That would be good to know."

He sounded so sincere. If Nean hadn't told him Mateo's real intentions, he would have believed everything that was said.

"Of course, if someone else caused the tears it could all be for nothing."

"And if you can't find the cause, what will you do?"

"Then it makes sense for us to resume digging. We could heal the entire valley of Kameil with the Qual...I'm not about to walk away from that for no reason. But the Masters may not wish for us to heal them — they could be trying to stop the quarry for this reason alone. I just wish I knew how they'd try to fill it in if it continued. We must ensure the safety of our people."

Ah, there it is. The real intent behind those well-placed words — he wants me to find out their plan.

"Would you like me to find out?" Nandin asked

"You'd do that?"

"Yes. But I have a condition."

"Go on."

"Let Hanna go; keep her out of all this."

"I thought she wanted me to find her home?"

"Yes. But I don't want her involved in these politics. If you find a way to get her home, I will let her know."

"Hanna is free to come and go from the valley as she wishes. If she chooses to stay away, I will respect that."

Interesting, Nandin thought. He hoped Nean would be able to determine if those words had double meaning. He longed for plain speech.

"Do we have an agreement?" Mateo asked.

Nandin smiled. "We do," he said, although he doubted that either of them would uphold their part of the deal.

CHAPTER TWENTY-THREE

See the Light

THEY CREPT IN DARKNESS.

The few torches that were lit throughout the castle were spread out, making it difficult for Nandin and Sarah to see as they made their way down the stairs.

"Tell me…again," Sarah said panting, "why…the stairs?"

"No one works the platform at this hour," Nandin whispered, "I didn't know you were so out of shape."

"I'm not…I think I'm…low on Essence. I forgot my pill."

He shot her a worried look as he adjusted the large homemade quilt he cradled while trying to prevent the bag that was slung over his shoulder from slipping.

"Ah Sarah, I'm sorry…I think I have an Essence pill in my bag. I usually carry them — "

"No, no, I'll be okay," she said pausing a moment to lean against the wall and slow her breathing. "We're almost to the door. Once I'm outside I'll be fine."

They encountered no one as they made their way to the entrance and out into the grounds. Sarah breathed deeply; there wasn't enough Essence in the air to help much, but she knew on the other side of the gate there would be plenty. When they got to the gates the guard on duty called out.

"Ho there! Who's about at this hour?"

"It's Commander Nandin, I'm seeing to Lady Sarah's safe return home. Please open the gate."

"Yes sir, Commander!"

As the man ran to open up the gate, the quilt grumbled.

"Shh!" he said squeezing the quilt.

Once through the gate, they began the long walk down the arched bridge.

"That's better!" Sarah sighed as breathing came easier.

"Can I walk yet; I feel ridiculous," Hanna said from within the folds of the blanket.

"No you may not. Now keep quiet."

Sarah worked hard not to giggle as she thought the situation amusing; she'd never seen Nandin so serious. Smuggling Hanna out of the castle in a blanket also seemed rather comical.

* * *

Mateo and Nean stared out a window, watching Nandin and Sarah as they crossed the bridge.

"I don't understand why he can't let himself be happy," Mateo said,

"What do you mean?" Nean asked.

"He likes her, that much is clear, if the treatment was as successful as I think, she'll be a force to reckon with. But there he is, whisking her away. He's foolish not to wait," Mateo said.

"Maybe he doesn't trust you would really let them leave," Nean suggested.

Mateo sighed. "Yes, a thousand truths cannot mend one lie. I wonder how long it will take before he forgives me for giving Hanna the treatment without her consent?" he mused.

"Do you plan on stopping them?" Nean asked.

"No. I told them they could go; I just didn't expect them to leave so soon. I hope he knows what he's doing. Taking her out like this...he's putting her at risk."

"Why do you say that?"

"Would you want to be out there right after your treatment? And I assume he plans to take her out of the valley."

"What makes you so sure?"

"Now they'd both become overexposed from the Essence in the valley. My concern is if they encounter any beasts while crossing the rivers or in the forest. How can he ensure her safety in her current state? They'll be too vulnerable. I need to do something about that."

"What do you propose?"

Mateo studied Nean then looked back at the travellers.

"Take a team of Yaru and follow them, but keep your distance. I just want you there to make sure they're safe."

"Nothing more?"

Mateo sighed. "I don't trust those Vaktare; there's no telling whether or not they'd let Nandin leave a second time...or what they might do to Hanna, now that she's one of us. How many Vaktare are there? A dozen or so? Let's keep the odds in our favour, take ten Yaru," he said, a prideful smile on his lips at his unspoken claim that the Yaru outmatched any Jagare regardless of their training.

"I have to admit, I'm not sure why you're even allowing them to leave. Are you sure Nandin will return?"

"Of course he will," Mateo gave Nean a knowing look, "but you don't approve of their leaving."

"Every new Yaru you've made has been confined to the castle until you were confident they were one of us. Hanna still has doubts, even more so now. Plus she was extraordinary to begin with having Juro abilities. Letting her leave now seems counterproductive."

"True," he replied as he stared out into the darkness. "But like you said, she is extraordinary — winning her allegiance will require a unique approach. Each time she returns it will be harder to leave."

It fascinated Nean the things Mateo would tell him, but he'd been around long enough to know whatever insight he revealed had its purpose.

"What makes you so sure she *will* return?"

"Nandin. They have a connection; she will be drawn here like a moth to a flame."

"If Nandin is here that is," Nean replied as understanding dawned on him.

"Correct."

"And you want me to make sure that he is."

Mateo slapped Nean on the back. "As you have always done."

* * *

When they finally arrived at Sarah's, Nandin carefully put the Hanna bundle down on the couch.

"Well that was rather unnecessary. I really could have walked you know," she said as she untangled herself from the blanket.

"I don't know what you're complaining about," Nandin retorted. "You didn't want to cross the bridge in the dark, remember?"

Jon stepped into the room. "She's awake?"

"Yes she's awake," Hanna replied, "can't fool a Yaru."

"And back to herself apparently," Jon stated.

"I'm glad you noticed, Jon. Now can you convince Nandin here to stop mothering me already? He carried me like a child all the way here."

"I wasn't just carrying you for your own good; I was also trying to hide the fact you were with me."

"So what's the plan Nandin," Jon interjected, "did you really want to take her into the woods at this hour?"

Nandin rolled his shoulders to get the kinks out.

"We don't have much of a choice. I wouldn't have been able to take her out during the daylight."

"She could stay here until morning," Sarah offered.

Nandin shook his head. "She can't remove her Essence now, remember? And Jon's probably been here too long as it is; we should get going."

Jon nodded. "Everything is ready. I returned to the woods to set up camp after Sarah told me your plan. Will you be carrying her again?"

"Not a chance," Hanna piped up. "*Her* is going to walk using *her* own two legs."

Jon smiled and with a hint of irony he said, "Did you get up on the wrong side of the bed Hanna? You seem rather touchy."

"Really? Were you all cheery and chipper after your treatment?"

Jon's smile faded. "No, I wasn't. I apologize; that was rather insensitive of me. You just don't seem yourself — nor should you. I was just trying to lighten the mood a bit; usually that's Nandin's thing — "

"Yes," Sarah joined in. "But he's been so serious that I almost mistook him for you."

Nandin just raised his eyebrows. "Can we go?"

"Hold on," Hanna said as she stood up shaking the last of the blanket away. "I'd like to venture off into the woods with something a bit more appropriate on."

"More appropriate?" Nandin asked.

"Yes, something other than pyjamas? You're very fashionable in your black ninja suit, but I'd prefer something a bit more forest-friendly than this night gown."

Nandin had insisted she rest for most of the day and try to nap before he took her away that night; he didn't give her the chance to get dressed prior to wrapping her in the blanket.

Sarah took her by the hand. "Come with me," she said.

Returning to Sarah's room Hanna was relieved to change into the clothes she had worn to the valley. She felt much more comfortable in the cotton pants that she tucked into knee-high leather boots that were tied in place and the light, long-sleeved shirt which was covered by a leather jerkin and secured with her belt.

She retrieved her bag which she had left at Sarah's, not wanting to risk taking it to the castle, and returned to the room to find Nandin standing outside and Jon hovering in the doorway.

"What's he doing?" Hanna asked.

Jon replied, "Making sure no one followed you. So far it appears we're in the clear. Go ahead and join him; I'll be right there."

Hanna gave Sarah a hug. "Thanks for everything, Sarah. Can you tell the Kameil from Senda that I'm sorry? I know it doesn't change anything. I wish I had the chance to explain things to them. They were so nice to me when we stayed in the clearing. I felt bad for lying to them...and responsible for the deaths of their friends and family. I wish I...I wanted to do something to make it up to them...somehow."

"Stop that right now," Sarah lectured. "What those Vaktare did was not your fault. You've been a victim of this whole mess as much as anyone. And as far as keeping the truth from them? Well, we all have our secrets; it's how we survive."

Hanna knew the Kameils secret was the community of Kameil that lived under the city of Senda. Even the Yaru, having discovered their existence, still didn't know of the entrances and passageways of the sewer system. Hanna wondered what had happened to the copies of the map Master Jagare made and if he had ever figured out that they were for underneath the city. For the Kameil's sake, she hoped they hadn't.

"Thanks Sarah. I'll leave you two to your goodbyes." She winked as she went out the door. The night air was a bit cool; she considered if it was worth the fuss Nandin would make if she went back for the blanket.

When Nandin noticed her, he took her bag off her shoulder and threw it over his.

"Are you sure you're okay? You don't need to pretend to be strong."

"I'm not pretending, I feel really good; physically that is. Why is that so hard to believe?" she asked not bothering to object about him taking her bag; she was glad he wasn't still insisting on carrying her.

"It took Jon close to two weeks to recover. It was a week before I did much more than walk around my room."

"Maybe it's like the saying goes: the bigger they are, the harder they fall."

Nandin thought for a moment. Perhaps she had a point.

"You know," she said glancing around, "it's really dark out here. How are we going to see where we're going?"

Jon closed the door and joined them, "We're familiar enough with these roads. The woods will be a bit trickier; but we'll manage it." He placed a hand on Hanna's shoulder. "Now I realize you want to walk, but even I would feel better if you held onto one of us just in case."

"Fine, if it makes you feel better," she muttered.

"Good. I'll lead."

Hanna grabbed Nandin's arm and they began winding their way along the stone roads and through the village. She gazed into the darkness trying to make out the buildings and glanced down side roads as they passed.

"Why don't they have any of the street lamps on?"

"What for?" Nandin asked. "Everyone's sleeping."

As they walked, Hanna thought it odd that it was getting lighter out, either that or her eyes were just adjusting to the dark. There was the usual tinge of pink in the air, which was also strange because it was too dark to typically see it. When they passed the last of the brick buildings she peered into the woods until suddenly, they lit up.

"Wow...that's amazing!"

Nandin looked at her to see if she was being sarcastic again, but her expression was lost in the dark.

"What is it?"

She let go of his arm and ran ahead into the woods unable to look away.

"Wait, Hanna! Jon, where did she go?!"

"I'm right here," she called.

"How does that help? It's pitch black out here."

She backed out of the woods, still entranced by what she saw.

"That's so awesome!"

"What? What are you on about?"

"It's glowing! One minute it was dark and the next, the woods are glowing! The Essence is in everything and I can see it! It's like I have night vision goggles on, but everything is pink."

"You can see in the dark?" Jon asked.

"So it would seem."

"Is this...new?"

"Yeah, it's new! I wonder if Mateo or Master Juro can see like this."

She was practically bouncing up and down.

"Well, that's useful," Jon said, "I was going to go by memory. Now you can help."

"You weren't planning on lighting a torch or something?" she asked as she continued to stare at the glowing forest.

"No, it would be a beacon to anyone watching from the castle."

"I wonder why you didn't notice the Essence until we got here?" Nandin asked.

"I don't know...it didn't happen until I tried really hard to see into the woods...and then, I could."

She turned to look at them and jumped back.

"Whoa. Now that's freaky."

"What?" Nandin asked turning to glance over his shoulder.

"You...and Jon," she answered.

"What is it?" Nandin persisted.

"I can see the Essence moving through your veins. It gives off a kind of glow so I can just make out your faces and bodies, but you look...digital...electric...like a million tiny fireflies," she explained trying to put to words a reference they might understand.

They all stood there staring at each other, not moving. Finally, Hanna broke the silence. "Well, since I'm the only one who can see, I'll lead the way; you two can hold hands." She turned and continued into the woods.

CHAPTER TWENTY-FOUR

Take the Lead

THE WOODS WERE ELECTRIC.

As she walked, Hanna was compelled to reach out and touch the plants and trees as she went by. Seeing the Essence like this made everything seem like it was moving — even if it wasn't. It added another layer to the eeriness of the night. Being followed by two ghost-like versions of Nandin and Jon was also making her nervous.

"Do you really think anyone from the castle would notice if we had a torch?" she asked.

"The guard on the tower might if he looked this way," Jon said.

"And anyone else who was watching," Nandin added.

"Who would be watching this late?" she asked.

"Mateo and Nean," he replied.

"How would they even know we left the castle?"

"Because I told them," Nandin said.

Hanna turned around, not sure if she had heard him right.

"What do you mean?"

"I told Nean and then instructed him to tell Mateo."

"Why would you do that?!"

"Nean said Mateo always knows the comings and goings of the castle. I'd rather he found out from Nean than someone else."

"So what was the point of us sneaking out?"

"Mateo doesn't know that I know. I sent Nean to tell him and gain Mateo's trust. Mateo planned to let us go anyway, he wanted me to deliver a message to Master Juro, but he told me to wait a few days so you could heal. I wasn't about to stay, so I told Nean and now he can lead the pursuit."

"They're going to follow us?" She still wasn't sure his reasoning was making sense.

He nudged her forward as they talked.

"I'm sure they're going to try. Naturally they'll assume we went out the front gate. Even Nean doesn't know where we're actually going. They'll waste time going through the city and then discover we didn't leave that way. When he realizes where we must have gone, we'll be well on our way."

"I'm surprised you didn't tell Nean the whole plan," Jon said.

"I don't know how much I can trust him. He's been playing this game a lot longer than I have."

Jon nodded. "I'm glad you've finally clued in."

"I still don't get why you had to tell Nean anything," Hanna said.

"Because I trust him more than I do the other Yaru Captains. When I meet up with him, his men will all come back to the valley with me instead of continuing to follow you."

"Let me get this straight. Mateo knew you were going to take me out of the castle; in fact, he told you to go," Hanna paused.

"Right."

"But you chose to sneak out sooner because…?"

"Because I want to return you to your friends before the other Yaru catch up. Mateo doesn't know they are up in these mountains waiting for your return. I'm sure he thinks they're back at the Citadel so he's content to let us leave. Nean thought it was likely he'd have us followed so if we left during the day the Yaru would be our constant shadows. I don't know for what purpose, but I still have my doubts he'd really let you go."

"Why Nandin? What more can he do to me?"

"You're Yaru now. He said you were welcome to come and go as you please, but that doesn't make sense to me. Why make you Yaru and then let you leave? Anyway, that's not the point. The point is, I promised to get you back and I'm not going to risk breaking that promise."

Hanna reflected on the changes that were taking place in Nandin. He was far from the enthusiastic, committed person she had met in the clearing. After he spoke with Mateo when they first came to the valley, she saw a glimpse of that Nandin. Now he had a significantly different view of things. She wondered if this change was for the better. Obviously being more guarded and suspicious of the company he keeps was smart, but what happened to his spark? His passion was being replaced with a cold determination.

Jon brushed past her. "This is it; the camp should be through the trees on the right. I left this marker here."

He reached out to remove a branch that stuck out across the path at knee height.

"How did you know it was there? Did you see it?"

"No, I felt it when I walked into it, but I knew it was coming up soon. I remembered it being just beyond that little incline we took. Watch your step, lots of stuff to trip on."

Hanna grabbed Nandin's hand to lead him through the dark. Jon seemed to know the way well enough as to not be hindered by the lack of light. The warmth of his hand reminded her of the bridge crossing, but something was different; it was as if she could actually feel the Essence moving through it.

When they cleared the brush, she looked around the empty space of the camp. There was not many Essence-rich plants or anything to allow her to see well. Jon lit a small fire that he had previously prepared since they were now far enough away from the valley and the trees surrounding them kept them hidden. Hanna made her way over to the stones and fallen logs that had been arranged for seating. She observed the pico wraps that hung in the trees and found it odd that two of them hung between the same two trees. Noticing Hanna looking up at them, Jon explained.

"Nandin mentioned you'd slept in the wraps before so I thought that would be the easiest and safest way for us to camp. There are bags hanging over here that contain food, water and a few other items that may come in handy. There's a knife on the outside pocket of one of them in case you need it."

"Thanks. Why is there one wrap on top of another?"

"I don't know if you can tell with the Essence, but if we had more light you'd see these woods are mostly evergreens. It's hard to attach the wraps to those so my options were limited. This is the best I could come up with.

"Which one's mine? I'm ready to crash for the night."

"Yours is slightly smaller and since your lighter it's the one higher up, but don't worry, the trees are plenty thick enough not to bend and break."

Jon pointed hers out and handed her the rope that was already in position for her to climb. Nandin came to stand beside her.

"Need any help?" he asked.

"Help climbing? From you? I seem to recall I won that contest. Maybe you need my help?"

"Hanna, I hate to keep reminding you, you just had treatment — "

She placed a hand on his arm. "Please stop reminding me. I'd like to forget. I'm fine, I promise. If I need help, you'll be the first to know."

She started to pull herself up into the tree, paused and called back.

"Thanks for your concern though. Goodnight."

Without much effort she hoisted herself the rest of the way and was quickly nestled into her hammock-type bed.

CHAPTER TWENTY-FIVE

Foes for Friends

THE BIRDS SANG.

By the time Hanna woke the next morning, there was a crackling fire and the smell of sausage filled the air. She peeked out of her wrap to see Jon diligently cooking breakfast. Carefully she undid her ties, pulled herself out of the covers and used the rope to descend.

"Good morning Jon."

"Morning Hanna. Sleep well?"

"I did thanks. That smells good," she said as her mouth watered.

"It'll be ready shortly."

Nandin entered the clearing carrying more wood for the fire.

"Morning," Hanna said waving as she headed into the trees.

"Hey, where do you think you're going?" Nandin asked.

"Nature calls," she replied.

"What?"

Hanna moaned at having to explain. "I have to pee."

Jon laughed. "Ha! Nature calls. Bring that wood over here, Nandin." Seeing Nandin hesitate he added, "She'll be fine."

Once she was alone, Hanna reflected on Jon's mood. He was so serious when she first met him. Now he was quick to laugh. She figured it might have something to do with his upcoming nuptials, but it was odd that when he was with Sarah he hadn't been in as good a mood.

When she returned to the campsite, she joined them by the fire. Jon passed her a small wooden board that held fried eggs, sausage and bannock. Hanna recalled when her family went camping and her dad had taught her how to cook the bread on a stick over the fire. She smiled at the memory, but knew it was unwise to linger there.

"These are nice plates," she said running her hand along the smooth underside of the treated wood. Both ends were angled allowing it to be held easily.

"They are, aren't they? Sarah's father has a wood shop in the market; he made these for me. You can keep that one as memento if you'd like."

"Great, thanks!" Using her bread, she scooped her egg into her mouth. "You seem to be in a fine mood today, Jon," she said around a mouthful of food; feeling in lighter spirits herself.

"He's in the woods, it's his happy place." Nandin said.

"And why not? We've got clear blue skies, birds are chirping, I'm spending time with friends — "

"And you're in love," she teased.

"That too," Jon said with a grin.

"Speaking of friends, I haven't asked you yet if you found Karn," she said.

"Indeed I did...Nandin, why didn't you tell me it was Karn?"

"You know Karn?" Hanna asked.

"We both do," Jon said.

Nandin looked up from his plate. "I don't know him...I mean I didn't know him before all this."

"Karn, Matthews-son of Senda?"

"Oh. That Karn. Well I never really met him."

Hanna grabbed the cleaning cloth hanging on a pot of water and wiped off her plate.

"How do you know him, Jon?"

"We went to school together, Tasha too. She an I were a couple years ahead of Karn and Nandin. He was in your year though, wasn't he?" he asked Nandin.

"He was a semester ahead of me; we never had any classes together. I was a Jivan then, remember?"

"Right...I actually forgot."

"Why does that matter?" Hanna asked.

"At the Citadel, all the Jagare are in the same classes regardless of age so I was with him for a bit," Jon explained.

"That's like the Juro at Kokoroe. There were classes I had with students who had been there for years."

"I was already at the Citadel when Karn went to Kokoroe," Jon continued, "but most Jagare had heard of him by the time he met up with us there. He was top of his class, a truly gifted Jagare. And not the type to brag. I'm not surprised he's received special assignments."

"Yes, I bet he'd make a great Yaru," Nandin grumbled.

They both gaped at him, disbelief on their faces. The thought of Karn being strapped to a table and injected sent shivers down Hanna's spine — the experience was far too fresh in her mind.

Noticing the sudden distress of his companions, Nandin held up his hands. "Kidding, I was just kidding," under his breath he mumbled, "he doesn't have the markings to be a potential."

Turning away Hanna said, "What did he say when you met him, Jon? Did he recognize you?"

Jon nodded, "Once I introduced myself he did. It's been a few years since I'd seen him."

"Not to mention your Yaru transformation. What did the great Karn have to say about that?" Nandin said brusquely. He didn't understand why, but something about Karn rubbed him the wrong way.

"As a matter of fact, he was really good about it. I told him why I came to the valley to begin with and then why I stayed. It was my hope that bringing all the Kameil here and teaching them how to hunt and protect their farms would stop the raids on the towns and save lives." Jon stared at the remaining embers still burning in the fire. "Karn said he was proud of me...and the sacrifice I made," he confessed.

Nandin knew that being Yaru weighed heavily on Jon's mind. He had been a proud Jagare and was devoted to protecting the people. His intention when joining Mateo was to find out what he could and report back to the Sanctuary in order to put a stop to the madness the Kameil brought to society. What he discovered though, were a gentle people, struggling for survival. Most attacks were out of desperation, not greed, and by helping in the valley he was protecting all races. In doing so; however, he'd severed all ties with those he'd left behind.

Watching his friend, he realized that for the first time since they had meet, Jon was untroubled — happy even. Sarah had done much to lift Jon's spirits, yet even his relationship with her had left him unsettled. It was an unwritten law that Jagare marry Jagare. His bride to be was Kameil, and even though Jon came to accept the Kameil, it was hard to erase generations of rules and prejudices.

Feeling ashamed of the glib remarks he had made towards Karn, Nandin was aware he was not acting like himself — ever since the attack at the Yaru's camp, his usual good humour and optimistic persona had been slipping away; he wasn't sure he liked the man he was becoming. As he stood up he announced that he would retrieve the pico wraps and bags while the others finished their tea.

"I can help," Hanna said.

"No thanks, but if I need your help, you'll be the first to know." He gave her a wink and went over to the trees.

CHAPTER TWENTY-SIX

Take a Hike

THE PATH WAS OVERGROWN.

It didn't take them long to pack and begin their hike in earnest. When the path diverged, Jon chose the one on an incline; the breaking of branches and the crushed leaves showed others had been here recently.

"I thought Karn and his team would be waiting for Hanna towards the base of the mountain...doesn't this path take us further up?" Nandin asked.

Jon explained. "When he said he really wished he could see the valley and everything that Hanna had described, I told him about the look-out at the top of the mountain. He was eager to check it out so I showed him how to get there."

"You what?!" Nandin cried taken aback by Jon's statement. "The whole reason they came here was to get Hanna back to the safety of the Citadel — this is putting her at risk."

"It's safer than being in the castle," Hanna argued.

Ignoring her comment, Nandin continued to scold Jon. "Don't you realize what you've done? They could use this information to come up with a way to attack the valley!"

"Think about it, Nandin," Jon said, "when they see the Kameil families peacefully living out their lives they'll come to the same conclusion I did — the Kameil aren't dangerous people. Maybe they'll even help us bring the other Kameil here where they are safe and well cared for."

Nandin ran his hand through his hair. Perhaps if he hadn't had such a bad reception when he was at the Citadel, he too would believe some good could come out of showing others the workings of the valley. His recent experience made him doubt it.

"And how do you suppose they'll react when they see the quarry? I'm assuming Hanna told them in the message that the Qual is the liquid Mateo is mining…Master Juro already threatened to fill in the pit if that was the case and when they see that it's still operational — "

"Wait, didn't Mateo stop the quarry?" Hanna asked.

"He did, and I'm to pass on that message to Master Juro. But Nean informed me that after we left, the quarry would start up again. Mateo thinks Master Juro is exaggerating the seriousness of the situation or trying to stop him from curing the Kameil. He's hoping I can stall for time and gather intelligence so we'll know how to counter the attack." Nandin adjusted the packs on his shoulders. He didn't care how good Hanna felt, he still wouldn't let her take her own bag.

"Nandin," Hanna said becoming exasperated, "I thought you agreed the pit needs to be filled!"

"Yes, but only if it's causing the tears, which we still don't know for sure. Besides, this is the Yaru's responsibility — not the Juro's."

"What do you plan to do?" Jon asked.

"Once Hanna's safe, I'm going to go back and see if I can stop the mining somehow."

"Let Jon take me the rest of the way; then you can stop it sooner," Hanna suggested.

"No. I made a promise to you…and Karn. I said I would get you back to them and I mean to do it. No offence to Jon, but I have to do this. I assumed he'd be taking you away from here...heading further up the mountain is putting you and your friends in danger. If the other Yaru find them here I don't know what they'd do."

Jon nodded. "As long as they're with us there shouldn't be a problem, but it's better not to push the issue. Let's convince Karn not to linger. Shall we pick up the pace?"

They hiked for most of the day, stopping briefly for lunch. Instead of getting tired, Hanna kept passing Jon, she felt he was going rather slowly.

"We're making camp now," Jon said calling Hanna back.

"Why?" she asked. "I was thinking maybe we should run for a bit, I still have energy."

Jon and Nandin exchanged startled looks.

"That's good to know Hanna, you can help set up, but this is the best place to camp for tonight. We should meet up with Karn and the others by midday tomorrow."

Hanna felt restless sitting in the camp. She had set up all of the wraps while the men gathered the wood and got the fire going. She was completely bored by the time Nandin started cooking.

"It'll be worth the wait," Jon assured her. "Nandin is a great cook."

"I know. He did all the cooking when we travelled from the Citadel to the valley. But I don't feel like just sitting here."

"Karn felt the same way when I told him I was going back to get you."

"You weren't gone that long, shouldn't we have meet up with them by now?"

"They didn't follow Nandin's instructions to stay put as they had a talented tracker with them — "

"That would be Dylan," Hanna said with a smile.

"Well, he successfully managed to find his way without

174

getting too turned around so they were closer to the valley than I expected. But it's a good thing I found them when I did because if they continued on the track they were on they'd have been stuck on the wrong side of a chasm. Once I put them on the path to take to the top of the mountain I came back to get you as I figured they didn't need me to escort them at that point." Hanna nodded keeping her thoughts to herself; she didn't know how she felt about Karn's decision to press on. She wasn't sure if his desire was something he had said in the moment or if it was his plan all along — she certainly didn't know about it, but like Nandin she felt it was unwise for them to be here.

"You seem to be feeling well," Jon said pulling her out of her musings. "Does the Essence look different in the day time too?"

Nandin looked over, curious as to Hanna's response.

"It looks the same, but there is something that's changed. I use to need to concentrate and shift my perspective in order to see the Essence. Now I can turn it on and off with ease. If I want to see it, it's there. If I don't, it's gone."

"Interesting. Anything else?"

Hanna stood up unable to sit still any longer.

"Just that I want to be moving. Even when we were hiking it felt like we weren't going fast enough. I don't know if you two were slowing down or if I'm going through some sort of massive caffeine rush, but I just want to run."

"Well then, tomorrow we run. Why don't you find a tree to climb? Take a look around and see what you can see. Stay close though."

She nodded and began scrutinizing the trees searching for the best one. When she made her choice she carefully started to climb.

Jon turned to Nandin. "What do you make of that? Another side effect of the treatment?"

"I guess. Makes me glad we left when we did. I think Mateo would want to study her, give her some tests, you know?"

"I think you're right."

By the time Hanna returned, the night had rolled in and the light from the fire made it appear darker outside its glow. As she sat down Nandin turned to greet her, but was startled.

"Jon! Jon, take a look at this!"

"What?" Hanna asked as Nandin leaned closer to peer at her.

"Your eyes! You've got cat eyes!"

"I do?"

"He's right," Jon said kneeling down to get a closer look. "They're bright green except the centre part which is black of course, but that part is now a narrow slit instead of circular."

"Were they like that earlier?" she asked as she touched her eyes. They shook their heads. She leaned to the side to gaze into the fire then looked back at them. "What about now?"

"Wow...they look normal again! That's fantastic!" Nandin exclaimed.

"Hmm, cat eyes. I guess that's why I can see at night, but why do you suppose they weren't like this last night?"

"They probably were," Nandin said, "but I wasn't sitting this close to you last night." She leaned back.

"Can you see my eyes now?"

"From the light of the fire I can, but now that you're not staring into the dark they're your typical eyes."

They continued testing the odd transformation of her eyes, confirming that they only changed when she was in complete darkness and Nandin had to be no more than a hand span away to see them.

"If you two are quite done, I believe the food needs tending."

Hanna resumed her seat on the log and attempted to sit still, but her leg bounced up and down and her fingers were incessantly tapping. She smiled to herself as she mumbled, "Cat eyes…cool." Hanna watched as Nandin flipped the meat on the hot rock in the fire. "Hey," she said as something dawned on her, "I didn't know you had cats here. I mean, I've never seen any."

"Count yourself lucky," Jon replied.

"Why, Jon? Don't you like soft, playful little kittens?"

Jon chuckled. "We have very different opinion of soft and playful — unless getting your throat ripped out is your idea of fun."

"Noooo…that's not really typical behaviour of house cats. What kind of cats are you talking about?"

"In these mountains? Cougars mostly. They're big, auburn-coloured beasts; with razor sharp talons. And fast, they're wicked fast. Do you have cougars back home?"

"Yes, I don't think they're auburn though…and I have this feeling Galenia cougars are larger — seems to be a trend, everything seems bigger here. Except the Juro, but I guess they have big brains."

Jon looked up from sharpening his knife. "Hanna, let me know if you need to go into the woods at all," he said motioning into the black.

"I can see just fine, remember?" she said mistaking his concern.

"It's not that," he said as he put his knife aside and poured her some tea. "There are traps laid all around the camp. I don't want you inadvertently stepping in one."

"When did you do that?"

"A long time ago. I often stay here when I'm hunting. That's why I knew this was were we needed to stop."

Hanna nodded then realization dawned on her.

"Traps? For cougars?"

"Sure, and wolcotts, bears, wolves...pretty much the type of beast you don't want sneaking up on you and catching you unawares."

"Great, welcome to Oz: 'lions and tigers and bears, oh my'," she grumbled, glancing up at her bed swinging slightly in the tree.

"We'll be safe up there though...right?"

"Yes...and no," Nandin answered.

Jon explained, "The wraps will keep us safe from most of the beasts, but to the Mystic Flyers, they make us a meal wrapped to go. They are drawn to the Essence and well, we have a lot."

"Great, we're take out. And how likely are we to encounter any Mystic Flyers?"

Jon shrugged. "We're a small group and aren't making much noise, so the odds are in our favour. Although..." he left the thought unspoken.

"What?" she snapped.

"The fire will also draw attention to us."

Hanna stood up, hands on her hips. "Well put it out then!"

Jon shook his head. "Can't. It keeps away the other beasts — they don't like to get burned."

"And the Mystic Flyers do?"

"The draka are immune to it. They breathe fire themselves and their hide is protected from it."

Hanna sat back down. "So how do you kill one?"

Jon reached into a bundle behind the log they sat on and pulled out a spear. The handle was longer than Hanna was tall and was made from a thick, hard wood. The spearhead was triangular and barbed and nearly the length of her arm.

"Where did you get that?"

"I keep a few weapons stashed here. When you went climbing

I got out my supply. I keep a wooden box sunk into the ground and then cover it with some deadfall. It's easier than having to drag all my weapons up here every time I come."

Hanna was hardly listening. "So where do I stick it? Anywhere?"

Jon knelt down and smoothed out the dirt in front of them. Using a stick, he made a rough sketch of the Draka. Hanna particularly loved the emphasis he put on the fangs, claws and spiked tail.

"Like the wolcott, it only has a few vulnerable spots. The eyes, this spot here behind its ear just above its jaw and the areas where the legs join its body. When I'm hunting them, I try to put an arrow in its eye or by its ear. That'll cause it to drop to the ground. Then I use my spear to finish it off."

"He's gets them every time," Nandin said as he handed them their plates.

"True, but that's during the daylight. If one attacks at night I'd be content to stick with scaring it off. Poke it a few times to convince it to let us alone. I can't shoot what I can't see."

He studied Hanna; she didn't look overly reassured.

"Listen, one of us will be keeping watch. If we spot one, we'll call out. You'll need to cut open the ties on your pico wrap and get down here as fast as you can — I'll take it from there. You sleep with your shoes on and your knife close by, don't you?"

"I do now," Hanna said, the sound of doubt all too present in her voice.

"Maybe after dinner we can do some sparring?" Jon suggested. "I could teach you a trick or two that might help you if we're attacked."

"That would be great!"

Nandin nodded. "I'd be up for that."

"Really?" Hanna said. "I was totally expecting you to say no or try to talk me out of it."

"Hey, you've been hiking all day and have energy to burn. Obviously you don't need to rest. In fact, tomorrow you can even carry your own bag."

"Gee thanks, my own bag! I feel so privileged."

CHAPTER TWENTY-SEVEN

Be on Guard

Hanna waited eagerly.

She rushed through her dinner barely tasting it. Being the first one done, she got up and began doing some stretches.

Nandin leaned over to Jon. "You know, the odds are in her favour. We'll scarcely be able to see."

Jon slapped him on the back. "It'll be great practice for us."

"Alright," Nandin uttered, "let's get this over with."

Jon jumped up and over the log.

"Shall we start without weapons? Just see if we can knock each other down to warm up?"

He couldn't see the smile on Hanna's face; this was something she was good at.

"Hanna, do you want to watch while Nandin and I have a go? Sort of give you some idea of what it's all about?"

"Oh yes, by all means, give me a demonstration," she said, betting that observing their tactics would give her an advantage. Like Nandin, the challenge Jon had proposed had lightened her mood; the concerns of Karn lost for the moment.

She backed up towards the fire to give them room. They slowly began circling each other. Jon feigned a step forward then quickly pulled back before Nandin could grab him. Hanna thought it was funny seeing Nandin being goaded into reacting, that was until the next time Jon leaned forward when Nandin snatched hold of his arm, tugged him forward off balance, then pushed him to the ground. It happened so fast; even Jon was perplexed how he was on the ground looking up at the sky.

"Well done Commander," he offered out his hand and Nandin helped him to his feet. Brushing himself off he backed up. "I'd like another try, if that's okay with you Hanna."

"Go right ahead," she replied.

This time Jon didn't wait and he went directly towards Nandin. Nandin was caught unawares at the sudden attack as Jon grabbed his shoulders trying to push him to the ground. Nandin seized Jon's arms, which prevented him from falling over. Twisting, Nandin was able to get himself in a more stable position, but as he did so Jon stuck out his leg and swiped Nandin's feet from under him. Nandin landed on his backside, cursing as he fell. Jon bowed to him then offered his hand to help his friend to his feet.

"Again?" Jon asked, but Hanna jumped in.

"No, no. It's my turn."

"Okay, who do you want to face?"

"Go ahead Jon," Nandin said. He had been bested by Hanna before and thought he'd like to see what she was capable of before going against her.

Jon went to circle her like he had with Nandin, but Hanna didn't move. She stood upright and just watched him approach. As he got closer he said warningly, "You know, you're should be on guard."

Suddenly, she bent down and ran under his outstretched arms, seizing his foot as she passed by and kept running. He did a face plant.

Nandin laughed. "That was great!"

Hanna offered a hand to help Jon stand. The moment he lent his weight, she let go and he fell back down.

"What?" he cried; Nandin laughed harder.

"Didn't Biatach tell you not to trust your opponent? It was the first thing he taught me."

"Tahtay Biatach taught you to fight?"

"Well *yeah*...and Karn. You didn't expect them to send a helpless girl into a camp full of Yaru did you?"

Nandin added, "You heard what she did to Blades, right?"

Jon groaned as he got up, dusting himself off again. He turned to Nandin, "This hardly seems fair then. She can see in the dark and has had specialty training. How shall we even the odds?"

Nandin grinned. "Two against one?"

Hanna laughed, "Bring it!"

Jon, who had his back to Hanna, gave Nandin the slightest nod. He spun around and together they advance on her. They both grabbed her shoulders to push her down, but instead of resisting she bent down and did a backwards summersault causing both of her opponents to stumble forward, then she took hold of their feet and flipped them all in one fluid motion. WHOMP! They landed flat onto their backs. She chuckled as they groaned.

"You know boys, I could keep this up all night, but I doubt this will help me face a draka. Can we proceed onto something a bit more...educational?"

Jon just shook his head as he got up. "Well, that was certainly educational for me."

"Considered yourself schooled. Now...spears?" she asked.

They spent the next hour practicing how to handle the spears. They were heavy and Hanna wasn't sure if she would be able to pull it out of the draka if she did managed to stab it. At this point, the best she could hope for was to stop one from coming closer.

"I'm sure glad I didn't have to face a draka when I was on my own. I'd be lucky to heave the spear up high enough to hit it."

"No, if you're alone it's best if you don't even try — just run," Jon said. "Run into the trees and keep going. They can't manoeuvre in them too well and they just give up. There's easier and bigger prey to be found."

"Good to know. As long as I don't accidentally land in one of your traps."

"Or one of the Jagare's. You won't find their traps in these woods, but they have them in the forests outside any of the towns or schools."

Hanna remembered a pit with sharpened stakes that a wolcott was coaxed into the time she was attacked out by Kokoroe. She cringed at the thought.

"Well, I think I'm ready to relax for a bit."

"Finally," Nandin said collapsing next to the fire.

"All tuckered out?" she teased.

"A bit. Mostly though, it's that I'm not a fan of the spears. I'd rather a bow and arrow…or a sword."

Jon sat by the fire, placing the spears within reach.

"Nandin, I'll take the first and last shift if you'd like."

Nandin nodded. "Okay, thanks. I'll go get some sleep then."

"Wait," Hanna said, "I can take a shift. I'm not sleepy yet. Why don't I start and then wake one of you?"

Nandin stalled, trying to come up with a valid reason why she should head to her pico wrap and have a solid night's sleep. He could think of many, but he knew Hanna wouldn't agree with any of them. Sensing Nandin's hesitation she pressed her case.

"Listen, when you first met me I was Darra, the orphaned Kameil who was surviving on her own, following after a wagon of people who pretended I wasn't there. I realize it was a set up and they were my friends, but I *was* alone. I had to hang my own bed, steal my food and be by myself. All I'm proposing is to stay awake by a nice warm campfire, which I didn't even get back then. I can see well enough — I'd be able to see if there was danger before either of you could."

Nandin shrugged. "Have it your way; more sleep for me. Jon you want the late shift or the morning one?"

"Between the two of us, I'm more of a morning person so I'll take the last shift."

"One thing though," Hanna said, "how will I know when to wake Nandin?"

Jon reached into his bag and pulled out two candles and a wooden stand. He set up the first candle as Nandin made his way up the tree to bed.

"Each candle burns for three hours, which is the typical length of each shift. When it burns out, wake up Nandin."

"Okay, will do. Um…Jon? I've never done this sort of thing before, what will I do for three hours? I imagine it would be pretty easy to just…fall asleep."

"I put some note paper in your bag if you want to write, you'll need to keep the fire going, get up and walk around the camp, stretch and help yourself to the dry rations that are also in the bag. I'd avoid drinking too much or you'll need to relieve yourself."

The idea of going into the woods when everyone was sleeping made her nervous — even if she could see; it didn't mean she could react in time if a beast came and she was preoccupied, not to mention the traps Jon warned her of. "I don't want to be caught with my pants down — literally," she said visualizing a bad scenario.

"Exactly," Jon agreed. "Keep your back to the fire so your eyes aren't constantly trying to adjust to staring in the dark. If you're finding it hard to stay awake and three hours is too much, just wake Nandin sooner. We've had a lot of practice with guard duty so we can handle the longer shifts."

"Okay, thanks. Hey Jon, why didn't we do this last night?"

"We were still relatively close to the valley. The beasts have learned to avoid the area; I cleared out any of the predator dens and set lots of traps to keep it clear." He rose and made his way to the tree with his bed. "Have fun," he called over his shoulder.

"Thanks. Goodnight," she replied thinking that guard duty probably was Jon's warped version of fun.

Hanna watched him as he made the climb up the tree. She lit the candle by holding it close to the flames in the fire, then placed it on a flat surface nearby. Picking up a stick, she attempted to pull off the bark. When it proved too difficult, she got out her knife and started whittling it to a point.

She made a plan to change activities prior to becoming bored of it, so when she removed half of the bark from the stick, she got to her feet and walked around the camp. Watching the Essence move in the night was mesmerizing, but again she stopped before too long. She continued through all of Jon's suggestions including stoking the fire and doing the stretches. It surprised her when she saw the candle had burn two-thirds of the way.

The last third seemed to burn slower. She found she could only sit for short periods of time as her head became heavy. She was able to amuse herself for a time drawing in the dirt and was curious if the others would notice and appreciate her masterpiece. It was times like this that she really missed having electronics to pass the time. She wished she could listen to the music she loved or watch one of her favourite movies. Time alone was rare and was also the hardest for her to handle; it was when she was the most homesick.

When the time came to wake Nandin, midnight felt much more like the middle of the night than it ever had before. She didn't even complain when Nandin helped her up the tree into her hammock. She had just settled in, relieved she could sleep, when she remembered her knife was still on the ground. Fortunately, Nandin had noticed and was already on his way back up the tree to give it to her. He showed her a special pouch in her pico wrap where she could safely store it before he left. She closed the wrap, snuggled in and was instantly fast asleep.

CHAPTER TWENTY-EIGHT

Get Caught Up

BOREDOM SUNK IN.

The number of Juro that joined their party had been increasing steadily over the week since they left the Sanctuary. By the time they left Thickwood Forest and entered into the Valley of a Thousand Rivers, Kazi estimated their number was in the seventies. Their arrival proved to be less and less exciting with each passing day. He was no longer sitting in Master Juro's inner circle, which typically included other Juro leaders and if they weren't in some deep discussion, they were meditating.

The Vaktare, whose numbers had also increased, stopped spending time training Kazi as they concentrated their efforts on scouting and guarding the area or hunting. Kazi still wasn't allowed to hunt, he had no interest in Juro meditation, he was not included in the Master's discussions and was, therefore, left with nothing to do but march and think about his battle song. The idea of coming up with a plan was completely useless as he had no idea what the Juro had in mind, how they proposed to attempt to rescue Hanna or fill in the quarry if that's what it came to.

Finally, they arrived in the mountains. A Vaktare from Karn's team had met them on the edge of the river valley and led them to the mountain pass. Kazi was disappointed that the trek didn't allow them the chance to see the fabled fortress; he'd only heard rumours of the wall that was stretched between two mountains. Hearing his grumbling, Zane was quick to point out they were not on a sightseeing expedition.

The camp where Karn had initially stayed just inside the mountain pass would not accommodate the number of people they had with them so many of the Juro stayed at the base of the mountain until the Vaktare could secure the area. Since Kazi was included in the smaller group that went to the camp, he was able to listen in on the plan which consisted on staying put until another one of Karn's team members arrived with information. Staying put with nothing to do was much worse than hiking forward with nothing to do.

As the Juro sat around, once again in meditation, and the Vaktare stood guard and scouted the area, Kazi felt more than a little restless. He took up his parchment and pencil and wondered into the woods; he planned to stay close to the camp, he just wanted to get away from the mumblings of the Juro.

Looking at his notes, he puzzled out what he would say next. So far, marching through the woods, into the valley and sitting in the mountains was hardly much of a tale to tell. He paused a moment to add a word or two and then resumed walking; he found it easier to think when he moved.

He yelped as a net jumped from beneath him and wrapped itself around him as it pulled him up into the air, the tight ropes digging into him and squeezing him in half. He cursed his luck as he dangled in the air. The branch that held him was thick and strong; there was no way he could break it if he were to bounce, also the net was high enough above the ground that if he should fall he was likely to break something. As he observed the ground below, he figured he hung well over a Jagare's head, but still within their spear reach, or more to the point, a Yaru's. The trap was obviously to catch prey and then skewer it as it hung helplessly in the net. Kazi had no weapons to defend himself and in the awkward angle that he was crumpled, had no hope of avoiding attack.

As he recalled his offer to be bait, he realized he was currently an easy meal to any draka that happened by. Being in the mountains where the draka frequented he knew he was in serious danger. He sighed as he came to terms with what it was he had to do; he could already hear the lecture he would receive.

He took a deep breath and shouted, "ZAAAANE!"

* * *

Nean held up his hand to silently signal for the Yaru to halt. He thought he heard something unusual...there it was again! Someone was yelling in the distance. He signalled the men to hide up in the trees while he scouted ahead. Even in their own mountains, the Yaru didn't make such noise. Unless Nandin was in trouble, he would be moving silently through these woods, which meant it was likely there was someone else here.

Nean left the path that they had been following and made his way stealthily further down the mountain to investigate — he was glad he did. He thought he had been tracking his friend, but for some time, something seemed off. There were signs of more than two or three travellers and the tracks were heading in the wrong direction. Even so, for all this, he didn't think that he would find what it was he discovered.

He quietly watched as a Jagare cut apart a net, freeing a young Jivan who had been caught in one of Jon's traps. It was this Jivan who had alerted Nean — thankfully. If it hadn't been for the boy calling out for help, the hidden Jagare sentries would have seen Nean and the Yaru coming down the trail without them knowing. He wasn't sure what would have happened then, but he thought it doubtful it would have resulted in anything good.

He ghosted his way through the woods, careful not to become a victim of another one of Jon's devices or to be detected by the Vaktare. The armour, weapons and whole demeanour of the Jagare warriors, made them easily distinguishable as the special forces known as the Vaktare. Unlike most Jagare, they were not mere hunters or defenders of the people — they were trained to kill, and the Yaru were their targets.

Silently he cursed his luck for already sending one of his men back to the valley; he had done so to alert Mateo that Nandin had not gone out the front gate, but had left through the woods. Nean acknowledged that it had been a wise choice on Nandin's part as it had slowed Nean down considerably. Now he wished he had held off sending the message, as he would have requested back up; the nine Yaru could hardly take on the number of Vaktare and Juro that Nean had discovered. As it was, he counted fifteen Vaktare and twenty-some Juro. He hadn't gone around the entire camp, but he was confident there would be more of the warriors hidden in the woods. Their presence was worrisome, even more so, as there had been no sign of Hanna or Nandin.

When he arrived back to his men, he apprised them of the situation and devised a plan: they would remain hidden in the trees and wait to see what transpired before they acted.

It was only a few hours later when a runner came from the opposite direction heading towards the Vaktare and Juro's camp. Shortly after the runner's arrival, the intruders broke camp and headed further up the mountain. Careful not to be detected, the Yaru followed.

CHAPTER TWENTY-NINE

Looking for Trouble

HANNA FLEW.

After a restful night — no draka in sight — she was anxious to meet her friends. She raced along the path, right on Jon's heels. It sent a thrill through her to be able keep up with a Yaru. The memory of being caught in the clearing by Blades was motivation to excel.

Her increased stamina left her with mixed feelings: on one hand she was still angry that Mateo had experimented on her, yet she felt better than she had ever felt in her life; plus she had more abilities than before. Still, there had to be a downside; the realist in her knew there was always a downside.

After running for over an hour, Jon raised his arm to indicate he was stopping. As tempted as she was to jump over him, Hanna decided precaution was the smarter choice. They waited a moment for Nandin to join them. He smiled as he approached.

"That was quite the sprint! Are we needing a break?" he asked.

"Not from me," Hanna said. "I could keep going."

"It's nice to know you two can keep up," Jon said. "But it might be wiser if we didn't run up on Karn, I'd hate to have an arrow accidentally shot at us because we startled them."

"We don't startle so easily."

A figure materialized in front of them covered head-to-toe in leaves.

"Dylan!" Hanna shouted bounding forward to greet him. She went to give him a hug, but he held up his dirt-covered hands to stop her. He didn't want her to risk poking an eye out with one of the many twigs he'd attached to himself.

"Rockin' the camo I see."

Jon and Nandin exchanged puzzled looks, but Dylan just laughed. He'd spent enough time with her during their training at the Citadel to appreciate, if not fully understand, her eclectic speech.

"Are the others near by?" Jon asked.

"Yes. It won't take long to catch up. I stayed close enough that I could get a warning to them quickly if needed."

The path became more of a goat trail forcing them to walk in single file as trees gave way to the rocky terrain. Dylan took the lead and Nandin brought up the rear. A short time later they came upon Karn and Tasha who were poised on large boulders on the side of the path, with weapons at the ready.

Karn leapt down, greeted Jon and Dylan before grabbing Hanna in a hug lifting her off the ground. Nandin cleared his throat, feeling a little uneasy at the display. Karn placed Hanna back on her feet and approached Nandin. To his surprise, Karn embraced him as well.

"I'm sorry I doubted you Nandin; I didn't know if you would bring her back. But here you are and Hanna is safe. I should have known that her trust was well-founded."

Nandin sighed as his guilt surfaced. "I fear your doubts were appropriate. I never should have taken her to the valley."

Karn looked at him questioningly, but Hanna interjected. "At least, not to the castle," she said brusquely, but eased off a bit as she added, "You got me out though, Nandin."

"What's this?" Karn said picking up some friction between

them.

Jon spoke up, "May I suggest we continue on around this bend? There's a better place where we can make camp."

Karn motioned for Jon to lead the way. Once they reached the suggested area, they laid down their packs. Clumps of trees stood like islands amidst the flat, rocky ground. The area looked as if it had been scooped out of the rock face leaving high rock walls on three sides. The open cliff side had thick trees that grew at an angle and the view one could make out between them was of more trees. The valley remained hidden; they could only see the other mountains that surrounded it. As Jon and Tasha went about preparing lunch, Dylan built a fire while Hanna, Karn and Nandin resumed their conversation.

"Where's the rest of your team, Karn?" Hanna asked. "Aren't you a few Vaktare short?"

"After Jon left us to get you I sent them back to our first camp…now tell me about your trip to the castle."

Taking turns, they filled Karn in on everything that had occurred once they were in the valley. He cringed at the explanation of the injections; Nandin held his head in his hands, unwilling to make eye contact. Jon added his amazement at her recovery and her increased skills. When Hanna complained about Nandin's treatment of her afterwards, insisting on carrying her and his constant coddling, Jon explained how most recoveries took days — if not weeks.

"So she probably still shouldn't be walking," Karn said in all seriousness.

Hanna punched him in the arm. "Not you too."

Nandin looked up, a worried expression on his face.

"Do you think I should have insisted on her taking it easy?"

"Like you could!" Hanna scowled.

Karn sighed, "I somehow think you would have ended up flat on your back if you tried."

Nandin nodded his agreement. "She had fun proving that point last night. Jon and I have had our egos checked."

"She does that," Karn said remembering any number of times she had bested him both at Kokoroe and at the Citadel.

"You're taking this rather well," Nandin said. "I thought you'd want to kill me when you found out what happened."

"It was touch-and-go there for a bit, taking her to the castle was a big mistake, but then again, if she had run out of Essence out here, she would have been dead by the time you reached us. So I guess you saved her life, and by the sounds of things, you did everything you could to keep her safe. Besides, Hanna said she chose to go with you. We may not like that she has a mind of her own, but we have to accept it."

Hanna wanted to argue Karn's point about her dying in the woods as she had learned how to keep herself alive, as long as there was Essence around, but as Nandin bowed and shook Karn's hand she felt keeping the peace between them was better than arguing the point.

"Thank you," Nandin said. He now understood exactly how Jon felt. Karn's words had a way of lightening their emotional burdens.

Unable to completely let the issue drop Hanna said, "I might have a mind of my own, but Mateo forced the treatment on me — he didn't have to do the whole thing in order to save my life."

"I'm not saying what Mateo did was right, or that you deserved the consequence," Karn said, "but as consequences go, you seem to be doing alright. According to Jon, better than alright."

Hanna rolled her eyes. "Yes. Fine. Fantastic. And when I get back home, my head might explode."

"What?" they all said as they looked at her.

"Well I don't know! We didn't have Essence there — it could be...toxic or have the opposite effect. Maybe instead of Yaru, I'd be sick like the Kameil," she stomped away feeling everyone's eyes on her as she went.

"Jon," Karn said, "how far do we have to go before we can see this valley of yours?"

"It's just a bit further. I suggest we leave our gear here — the path is narrow and we'll have to do a bit of climbing to get around the rocks."

They tossed their bags into a pile, but kept their weapons as they followed Jon, with the exception of Dylan who chose to set up camp.

When they finally crested the ridge, they walked among a field of boulders and at the edge of the cliff the view of the valley spread out below them. Karn and Tasha stood in awe. He didn't disbelieve Jon's account of the size of the city, the details shared about the floating castle, or the depth of the quarry, yet seeing it made a much bigger impression on him. Even at this height the quarry was impressive. The details were hard to make out, but one thing was clear, there was a great deal of activity.

"It's like looking at an inverted ant hill," Hanna stated watching the Kameil at work.

"It looks like trouble," Karn replied.

Nandin had to agree. "I'll stay the night with you here and see you part way down the mountain. Jon can take you safely back to the start of the northern pass, but I need to get back to the valley and convince Mateo to stop the mining."

"There's no need for either of you to stay," Karn said, "I'm sure Dylan can find the way back."

"At this point, I'm more concerned with who you might run into out here than I am of you getting lost. If Jon and I are with you no one will attack." Jon flashed Nandin a concerned look; he had neglected to think through what would happen if the Yaru tracking them encountered Hanna's friends. If it were Nean's team there wouldn't be an issue, but if Blades or Thanlin had tagged along, it could get messy.

Karn's face creased with concern. "Do you expect more Yaru out here?"

"Potentially," Nandin replied. "I'm betting Mateo is having us followed, but we should still be a day or so ahead of them since they don't know where we went."

Tasha sidled up to Karn. "Perhaps we should go back and warn Master Juro."

"I doubt we could offer any more protection than the Vaktare who are escorting him."

"Escorting him where?" Nandin asked, concern evident in his voice.

"Here," Karn said waving his hand around him. "He wants to see the valley for himself."

Nandin threw his hands in the air. "Great...this just keeps getting better and better," he grumbled. He hadn't liked the idea of showing Karn up the mountains. Master Juro's presence could complicate things — especially with a Vaktare escort. He wondered what Nean would do when they came across them.

CHAPTER THIRTY

Mighty Have Fallen

Darkness fell.

By the time Hanna and the others returned to camp, the pico wraps had been set up. The few tall clumps of trees dictated that the wraps had to share space and were, therefore, grouped in threes. They put Hanna in mind of bunk beds as they were hanging one above the next.

They gathered around the cook fire and as they talked, the tension that she had felt over the last week started to subside. Her tantrum earlier had actually helped as she had been holding onto that fear and resentment. Going home was not something bound to happen any time soon; there was no point feeding the fear of 'what if.' At least with Master Juro arriving, she could get his thoughts on the matter.

As they spoke, it dawned on her that she had completed all the stealth tasks she'd been given. She was done. No more pretending to be Kameil, no more intelligence gathering. Even if she wanted to, Mateo and the Yaru knew who and what she was, her days of being a spy were over.

"You can see in the dark?" Karn asked, snapping her out of her reverie.

"Oh, uh yes, sort of. I can see the Essence in the dark. I can't make out lots of details or non-Essence things like dead trees or clothes, but I can see everywhere the Essence is."

"That would be handy," Dylan said. "What else can you do?"

"I have more energy and I can run faster."

Dylan nodded his head. "Nice, but is there more?"

"Why…what do you mean?"

"Well if the Sight is different isn't it possible manipulating the Essence could be too?" he reasoned.

"I haven't really tried anything. Let's see…"

She looked around observing all the Essence-rich things in the area. The trouble was, no one would be able to see what she was doing or, if they could, it wouldn't prove to be anything new. That gave her an idea. She crouched down by the fire and cleared a space on the ground to sit. Legs crossed, eyes closed, she gave herself a moment to feel the Essence. As with seeing it, the instant she willed it, she could sense it. A smile spread across her face; this was going to be fun.

She raised her hands and began pulling the Essence from around the fire. Faster and faster she moved it causing the flames to spiral. She moved the Essence to make the fire fork, or dance. Once before, she had manipulated flames, but had no real control. Another idea came to her. Using a combination of the Essence in the air and what was left in the embers, she was able to toss the embers up so they hovered above the fire. Then she rearranged them. At first she made a circle, then a heart, followed by a star — it was too easy. She tried a happy face, a snowman and a dog. As quickly as the thoughts occurred to her the picture appeared. Searching for something more complicated, she recalled her reflection in the mirror at Mateo's. When her own face was staring back at her, complete with the loose strand of hair, she turned towards her friends. They were speechless.

"Well?" she coaxed.

Finally Dylan responded. "I guess that answers that question."

"That is truly amazing," Nandin said.

Karn asked, "Were you able to do that before?"

"Not with that kind of accuracy. I could move the flames or embers, but I couldn't shape them."

"Do you mean to move them now?" Jon asked pointing to the fire.

Glancing back at her art, she realized it was moving dangerously close to her. She gave it a mental push and it dispersed, falling back into the fire.

"That was close; thanks for the warning."

Tasha leaned forward, offering Hanna a hand up. Hanna accepted and resumed her previous seat.

"That was rather trusting of you Hanna," Jon said.

"I'm not her adversary," Tasha replied, "If we were sparing, she wouldn't have been foolish enough to accept my help."

Hanna and Nandin laughed as they recalled Jon splayed out on the ground.

"Yeah Jon," Nandin chided, "you should be able to tell the difference between friend and foe."

The words hung in the air.

"Not always an easy task," Karn said. "It's getting late. Perhaps we should get some sleep?"

Hanna was relieved when they turned down her offer to help with guard duty. Last night she felt the need to prove herself; now she just wanted a full night's sleep. It was agreed that Tasha, Jon and Karn would take turns guarding and then the next night the other three would.

Hanna shinnied up her rope to her pico wrap. She was grateful that two tents had been assembled for some of their supplies; it had the extra bonus of allowing them to change in privacy on the ground instead of attempting to do it up in the trees. She no longer had to bring a change of clothes up with her. The only thing

Hanna needed in her wrap was her blade, which she tucked away in the pocket Nandin had showed her. Tasha had even provided Hanna with lighter leather shoes to sleep in to replace the thicker, dirty ones she wore all day. Taking a minute to gaze at the stars before tying herself in for the night, she thought, at the moment, there was nowhere she'd rather be.

* * *

It was not the safest place to stay for the night and Karn knew it. High up on the mountain, they were open on many sides to predators capable of navigating the rocky terrain. Although the six travellers were only able to enter the area from a narrow, broken path, there were animals that could gain access from the higher ridge that surrounded the place. What was worse were the trees that lined the ridge, making the approach of predators practically undetectable.

The sound of howling wolves sent shivers down his spine, but they were far enough in away as not to concern him. He paused in his patrol of the perimeter of the camp, stared into the gloom and met a pair of yellow eyes that reflected the fires glow. Karn raised his spear and braced himself as the large cat lowered its head, ready to pounce, but before Karn could raise the alarm the beast changed directions and disappeared back into the trees. Puzzled, he cast about to see what had caused the creature to retreat. That's when he saw the enormous shadow blocking the stars in the sky.

One word shattered the peaceful night air.

"Draaakaaaa!" Karn yelled, terror stricken as it dove towards the pico wraps.

Hanna fumbled with her knife as she willed herself to consciousness. She cut the ties and pulled back the covers.

"Hanna, look out!" Karn screamed at her.

Instantly she rolled out of her wrap, grabbing the branch her bed was attached to. She felt the Draka brush by as she hung down, holding on tightly as the tree shook when the creature's wings knocked against it. She swung herself up so she was perched on top of the branch. Her heart pounded as she took in the sight of the flying beast. Essence coursed through its massive body, and it spewed flames as it shrieked, angry at missing its prey and at the arrow that had hit it and now dangled from its side. It flew around the trees, revealing its spiked tail, then looped back to hover in front of her. Knife in hand, Hanna did what seemed to be the safest thing to do as its powerful, reptilian-like jaws snapped at her. She jumped.

Flipping over its head, she landed on its scaly back, facing its tail. It twisted and turned trying to snatch at her, but she was high on its neck and it couldn't reach her.

"Shoot it!" she heard someone holler.

"Throw something!"

"I can barely see; I might hit Hanna!"

Hanna knew she needed to get a better grip; she was starting to slip as the creature thrashed. Holding her blade in her mouth, she managed to reach behind and grab hold of one of its many spikes as the Draka beat its wings and flew straight up, causing her legs to dangle in the air. The only thing preventing her from falling was her grip on the spike. Up and up it flew. When it changed direction and dove towards Nandin, who now stood on a branch in the tree, Hanna was able to pivot so she was facing forward and then clamped her legs around its neck. Withstanding the wind that pushed against her as it dove, she pulled herself up its neck, scraping her hands on the barbed scales as she went. She inched her way up using the many spikes as leverage for her feet.

When she was next to the great horn on top of its head, she grabbed her blade and plunged it behind the draka's ear. Its cry was deafening. Resisting the urge to cover her ears, she drew the knife up in a slicing manner until it caught on bone. The beast's wings went limp and the creature's dive became a fall taking Hanna with it.

"HANNA!" Nandin called out, as he grabbed the branch above him, lean forward and thrust out his other arm.

As she hurtled towards him, she reached out and seized his offered arm. He caught her as she fell past and swung her up on top of the branch. The beast continued to plummet, shaking the ground as it crashed. As Nandin steadied her, she was hardly aware of the others who, using spears, put the wounded beast out of its misery.

"Okay," she said still clinging to Nandin for support, "that's twice you've saved my life; I think I can forgive you now."

He smiled as he held her, "I'll say this for you Hanna: you're not boring."

* * *

They stood around the fallen creature. Crumpled as it was, Hanna thought it seemed smaller. She supposed a plane without its wings would also appear diminished in size.

"Careful," Hanna said as Karn reached out to touch it, "the scales have spikes."

"I'm aware of that," he replied turning towards her, casting his torch light upon her, "I have fought one or two before. I'm just trying to figure out how you stayed on and apparently unscathed."

She held up her bloodied hands to show the damage she'd endured. Taking in the tattered and blood-soaked state of her clothing, he realized more than just her hands were cut.

Karn shook his head, "Why the heck did you jump on it?"

Hanna shrugged. "It seemed the quickest way to get away from its teeth."

"Jumping down would have worked too," Nandin said. "I did catch you after all."

"But how was I to know you would? And it's not like I had a lot of time to think it through. I just reacted."

Dylan patted her on the back. "I thought it was utterly amazing. And the way you flipped yourself around as it flew straight up!"

Karn managed to chuckle. "Yes, again with being backwards. It appears to be a thing with you."

Hanna recalled how embarrassed she was at the crossing by Kokoroe when she swung up onto a log and was facing the wrong way. At the moment, the thrill of riding the draka still fresh in her bones, she was simply elated that she didn't die.

"It was also pretty reckless when you stabbed it; how did you hope to survive that fall?" Nandin asked.

"I was thinking more along the lines of how you weren't flame proof." She threw her hands up in the air. "You and Karn are a bunch of worrywarts. We all lived through it, didn't we? In fact, I think a thank you would be more appropriate than this lecture."

Jon put an arm around her. "She's got a point. I think we should be applauding her efforts; it was a little unconventional, but she did marvellously."

Tasha took her by the elbow. "And I think we should see to those cuts. Dylan would you boil some water and bring it to us in our tent?"

"I'll get her some food too; I always feel the need to eat after death defying experiences." Jon gave her a wink as Tasha led her away.

Karn and Nandin continued to grumble about the way Hanna dealt with the situation.

Dylan laughed. "You two are so biased. If Jon, Tasha or I did what Hanna just did, you would be jumping up and down, congratulating us on how impressive and brave we were. Hanna deserves no less."

"But she's — " Nandin began to protest.

"No. He's right, although I don't know if I'd be jumping," Karn said with a sigh, "I know I'm protective of her. She's young and her training is limited, but she's not a typical fifteen-year-old; we have to stop seeing her that way."

Nandin nodded, but he knew that's not how he saw Hanna. It didn't matter if she was twice her age and had years of training, if he saw her on another draka he'd feel the same gut-wrenching fear he had just felt.

"Well, aside from having enough meat to last a lifetime, there's an additional benefit to having this beast among us," Karn said.

Dylan and Nandin looked at him, waiting for an explanation.

"We shouldn't have to worry about any more predators. Even another draka won't attack us if they see one of its kind here."

"Even though it's dead?" Dylan asked.

Karn gave him a tired smile. "That's the kicker, we're going to have to pose it. Make it look like it's attacking, not just laying here."

Nandin raised his eyebrows, as he looked the beast up and down.

"And how do you propose we do that?"

"We have to gut it first. Its skin is more of a shell, so it will hold its shape even after we take the meat."

Nandin groaned. Gutting animals was the task he dreaded most.

"Look at the bright side," Dylan chirped, "we get fresh meat to eat."

Walking towards them with his dagger in hand Jon said, "Let's get to work, shall we?"

"Can't we just leave it for now and do it in the morning? I'm sure we'll be fine for another few hours."

"You know the meat won't be any good if we leave it and I'm not about to let that much food go to waste. You know how many people I could feed with this beast?" Jon said rolling up his sleeves.

Karn nodded his agreement. "Not to mention the other animals that will be attracted by the smell and if it looks dead — "

Nandin relented. "Yes, fine, let's get on with it."

Once Jon sliced the soft areas under the legs, Karn took his spear to pry the shell open. Grudgingly, Nandin grabbed a dagger and resigned himself to the bloody task before him.

CHAPTER THIRTY-ONE

Over the Top

CAMP WAS SILENT.

Since the draka had been successfully gutted and hung across several trees, Karn and Jon felt it was safe for everyone to sleep in the tents. After the attack, Hanna for one didn't think she'd be able to sleep in a pico wrap any time soon and as comfortable as the swinging hammocks may be, she wouldn't miss the hassle of climbing up and down the tree; that novelty had long worn off.

When morning arrived, Jon and Dylan went to seek out the Vaktare from Karn's team and discover if there had been any sign or word from Master Juro. As they waited for their return, Hanna observed Nandin sitting by himself looking deep in thought. He sat on the ground, leaning against a log and staring at the remains of the previous night's fire.

"What's on your mind Nandin?" she asked sliding beside him.

"I'm trying to figure out our next move," he paused as he looked at her, "Nean has most likely found our trail; he won't be more than a day behind. There's no way to get you and Karn and Master Juro down the mountain before we meet up with them."

"Do you think they'll attack?"

"There's no reason to think they would; my mission is to gather intelligence. I don't know Nean's, but it's probably to make sure I get away and return to the valley."

Hanna placed a hand on his leg and gave it a squeeze. "You don't have to you know...go back to Mateo that is. You don't belong to him, even if he did make you Yaru."

"I know. I doubt I'd be welcome back into society; I might not be Kameil, but aside from being different, the Yaru are not well liked. I could manage on my own somewhere if I wanted to. But I have responsibilities and I'm not walking away from them...not this time," he said as he took her hand observing the cuts that were almost healed.

"I know the quarry has to be stopped, but after that— "

"The Kameil still need my help." He wanted to share his burdens with her and let down his guard, but it wasn't the time or the place. He also didn't want Master Juro to know the things he had learned and Hanna was under no obligation to keep his secrets. "I don't belong to Mateo, but I am responsible for him. Someone has to keep him in line — no more forced experiments."

"Good, he needs to be held accountable," she said leaning against him. "I'm proud of you." She meant it, although the thought of Nandin going back made her a little sad.

"Mateo said he'd still try to find a way back to your home — even though you won't be in the valley."

"Do you think that's true?"

"He'll search for it. If he even gets remotely close, I'll come find you. I don't know if his plans include letting you go back home, but I'll get you there."

"Promise?"

"I promise. But can you still trust me?"

"What have I got to lose?"

Nandin took her hypothetical question seriously and tried to puzzle out what it was that could go wrong. His thoughts wavered between nothing and everything — he just didn't have enough information to go on yet to really think it through.

"What?" Hanna asked watching his face as he slipped back into deep-thought mode.

"Huh? Oh nothing. So what about you? What are your plans now? Are you going back to the Citadel to finish your schooling? That is if they let you."

"Ug, what a depressing thought," she replied. "I probably will, but I think I'll start with a party before hitting the books."

"A party?" Nandin laughed. "You can throw a party for returning to school?"

"Kazi gave me one when I first showed up, sounds like a good tradition to start. Besides, my birthday is in a month — I could have an early party."

"Sounds like a good time. This is fifteen?"

"Sweet sixteen actually. Darra was younger, remember?"

"Sorry, it's hard to keep track of the truth verses the lies."

"Hey!" she said shoving him

Karn stuck his head between them.

"I'd hate to interrupt what I'm sure was a deep and meaningful conversation, but we have company."

They jumped to their feet and turned towards where he motioned to watch as Jon and Dylan entered the clearing followed by Master Juro. Nandin noticed Jon's face was drained of all colour; when he saw Juro after Juro enter the camp with the occasional Vaktare in the line, he understood why.

Nandin leaned towards Hanna, "Looks like the party is coming to you...this can't be good."

They rose and went over to greet the new arrivals.

"Good morning Master Juro," Karn said with a bow.

Master Juro returned the greeting then motioned to the beast in the trees.

"It appears you have managed to find a way to feed all of us."

Karn smiled. "You can thank Hanna for that," he said as he led Master Juro further into the camp.

"Whoa!" cried Kazi as he entered the area. "Is that a real draka?"

"Of course not," Dylan answered, "we decided we had nothing better to do, so we created one out of clay and painted it."

"Kazi!" Hanna yelled running towards him. "What are you doing here?"

He ran to meet her and they embraced. "Hanna, I'm so glad you're okay! Hey," he said pulling her back, "you've grown!"

"I have?"

"Yeah, your above my chin now."

"Really? I grew a whole inch?"

"That's pretty impressive; you've been gone less than two weeks."

"I was taller after my treatment too," Nandin whispered in her ear as he joined them.

"How did you convince Master Juro to let you come?" she asked Kazi, choosing to ignore Nandin's statement; the idea she was a Yaru still didn't sit right with her.

Kazi smiled. "Karn informed him I was going to chase after you even though I was told not to, so Master Juro suggested I stay with him."

"And? Were you going to follow us?"

He shrugged. "I don't know. I was just starting to come up with a plan when he approached me. He didn't give me a chance to figure something out."

"Kazi," Hanna whispered, "what's with the Juro army?"

"Army?"

"You know, the mob that is still pouring into the area? How

210

many are there?"

"I didn't count, but I'd say roughly seventy, maybe eighty. Plus the Vaktare — there's twenty five of them."

Nandin shot Jon a nervous look; the situation was rapidly getting worse and they weren't in a position to do anything about it.

"What's going on?" Nandin asked. "Are they planning to attack?"

"I have no idea. No one tells me anything — anything of importance anyway. I've just been tagging along…it's been a real drag actually. The Sanctuary was neat at first, but after a bit, it was rather boring. I bet you've had a much more exciting time than me."

"Of course, time of my life," she replied sarcastically. "Let's see, I overdosed on Essence and passed out, had to cross this very questionable bridge over a rocky pit of death to get to the castle, came face-to-face with Mateo, passed out *again* from lack of Essence and nearly died, was experimented on and last night, to keep it really interesting, I was attacked by a draka."

"See? You get all the fun!"

"Fun? Were you even listening?" she said exasperated. "I just told you I almost died, twice actually, and I was experimented on!"

Kazi shrugged, a grin lighting up his face. "Yes, but you seem okay now. Your trip was definitely more exciting than mine."

"Kazi, I worry about you."

"Surely riding the draka consisted of some excitement," Jon pointed out.

Kazi's mouth dropped and he stopped walking as he gaped from Hanna to the beast.

"You rode it?! No way!"

211

"Kazi," Master Juro called, "I would also like to be part of this conversation. If you would be so kind as to join us?"

Nandin nudged him forward and then he and Hanna took the remaining seats on a log in front of the cold fire pit. Kazi was content to sit on the ground; Karn and Jon stood unobtrusively behind them while Dylan and Tasha took charge of organizing the incoming Juro and Vaktare.

Hanna glanced around the circle of Juro that had assembled there, and considering the limited space, she figured these must be the most senior Juro present. Aside from Master Juro, she recognized Tahtay Etai from Kokoroe and Tahtay Puto from the Citadel. They both acknowledged her, but the seriousness of the moment left little chance for happy reunions.

Noticing Nandin's jaw clench, she knew he was tense. She wished she could reassure him, but had her own doubts about the situation.

When everyone was settled, Master Juro spoke. "I received your note a few days ago. I am most anxious to see this quarry; however, first I would hear the whole tale. Hanna, if you would start from when you arrived in the valley?"

She explained her walk through the city and her stay with Sarah and of Jon's immediate trust and assistance to both of her trips to the quarry. She watched Master Juro closely as she confessed her acceptance of Mateo's offer for a meeting. Silently they listened until she reached the part of Nandin and Jon helping her escape into the woods.

"In the castle, you collapsed from lack of Essence?" Master Juro asked. "You say your stones were empty. I wonder…do you still have them?"

"No."

"I do," Nandin said. He excused himself and went into his

tent. When he came back he carried the pouch of stones Hanna had worn around her neck.

"I went back and got them when I thought you were recovering. They've been in my pack since I carried you out of the castle. I forgot all about them."

He handed the pouch to Hanna who then gave it to Master Juro. He emptied the contents on the ground. All the surrounding Juro and Hanna stared at the stones. Master Juro turned them, but all the crystal flecks were clear; no Essence could be seen.

"There was plenty of Essence in these when you left the Citadel. There is no way they would be so depleted. The Essence has been...drained from them."

"I wondered about that, but I've been a bit preoccupied to give it much thought," Hanna said. "I checked the stones before I went to the castle and I wore them the whole time I was there. No one took them from me. How could they be drained?"

"You stayed the night. Could someone have taken them while you slept?"

"I doubt it. I wore my pouch around my neck the whole time. I would have woken up if someone tried to take it, just ask Nandin, I'm a light sleeper."

Her experience when the draka attacked was the most recent example, but their nights in the forest and even when he came through her window all lent weight to her reasoning. "You were pretty exhausted that night though," Nandin said recalling how she could barely stay awake. Then something else occurred to him. He smacked his palm to his head.

"Milk and cookies!"

The statement confused the others; only Hanna seemed to understand where he was going with this. All eyes turned to Nandin. He wished he hadn't spoken out loud as he had no desire to share his thoughts, but he couldn't think of a way to get out of explaining now. "Hatooin doesn't give people warm milk and cookies before bed," he said, "but he gave some to Hanna and Sarah...the milk could have been drugged."

Master Juro stroked his pencil-like beard. "That is a possibility. The koia bean can be crushed and would then dissolve in liquid. It would put you in a deep sleep for most of the night, yet one glass of milk would hardly contain enough."

"Can it dissolve in juice?" Hanna asked with a sinking feeling.

"Yes. Did you have some of that too?"

"Practically a whole jugs worth...it was so good."

Master Juro raised his eyebrows. "If it was drugged you would have most definitely been in a very deep sleep. Tell me, when you woke, how did you feel?"

Hanna tried to recall how she felt the morning before her ordeal. "I remember feeling a bit woozy and my limbs felt kind of numb, like I had been sitting on them for too long."

"Those are the side effects the koia bean has," Master Juro said and the Juro supported his claim. "I believe we can say, with some certainty, that you were indeed drugged. Once you were asleep, someone removed your pouch, gave it to Mateo, who was obviously able to remove the Essence, then returned the stones to you before you woke."

"If they drugged me, why didn't they just take me to the lab and give me the Essence then?"

"Because he didn't want to lose me," Nandin said softly. "If you had been taken to the lab like that, I never would have forgiven him. With you collapsing, it was me who brought you to him to save your life. He may have broken my trust, but he didn't completely alienate me...games within games."

She was all for throwing stones at Mateo, yet it didn't all add up. "How did I last so long? It was at least two hours after I woke up that I collapsed. If there was no Essence in my stones I should have passed out much sooner."

Master Juro said, "That is true. Were you exposed to any Essence?"

So much had happened since that morning she was at the castle. It started with a gift of clothing, followed by breakfast with Mateo before going on a tour of the castle — stopping first at the gardens. "The gardens!" she exclaimed. "I found a vent in the outer wall that let Essence filled air into the gardens and I sat there and breathed it all in. That's why I lasted so long."

"A bit of a coincidence you went there then," Master Juro said.

"Not really," Nandin mumbled. "Mateo suggested we go there. Although, if he wanted her to pass out so I would bring her to him why would he send us there? Surely he would have known it would've helped Hanna."

"If she went unconscious shortly after your morning meal together you may have expected foul play. Perhaps his intention was to postpone the moment in order to prevent suspicion. Tell me, did you ever suspect that Mateo was the cause of Hanna's collapse?"

"If I did," Nandin said, "I wouldn't have run straight to him...or at least I wouldn't have left her alone with him. I really thought he just wanted to help her."

Master Juro stroked his beard. "It appears he has."

"What?" Nandin and Hanna said together.

Master Juro tilted his head as he observed Hanna.

"He has provided you with your own source of Essence. It appears to be stable; it has bound to you as if you were born to it. You shall never need to fear dying due to a lack of Essence again."

"What about too much Essence?" she asked. "I never had Essence on Earth…what affect will it have on me there?"

"That I can't say for sure…you mentioned there was no Essence in Mateo's castle?"

"That's right."

"That is unique on Galenia. It is also like your home — Essence-free. Unless there is something else in your environment that would react to Essence, it is possible the effect would be the same as your time at the castle." He paused as he studied her. "How do you feel?"

"Great actually. I have a lot more energy and it's much easier to see and control the Essence."

"Is she burning hot?" Nandin asked recalling Master Juro saying that Nandin was dying because of what Mateo had done to him.

Master Juro shook his head. "Not like you. Your Essence has been layered, Essence on top of Essence. Hanna had no Essence to begin with. Now it is evenly spread throughout her body. It seems, Mateo has achieved Kenzo's dream."

"Who?" Kazi asked

"Mateo's father," Nandin said to the surprise of the Juro around him.

"What was his dream?" Hanna asked.

Master Juro seemed distraught as he answered. "To create a perfect blend of all three races in one person. You had all the gifts prior to meeting Mateo, but with the Essence you are now truly the complete combination."

The Juro muttered and shifted uncomfortably.

"Now may be an appropriate time to show us this quarry," Master Juro suggested.

"No," Kazi said loudly, then shrunk back as everyone stared at him, "I want to hear about the Mystic Flyer. They said Hanna rode the draka — we haven't heard that part of the story yet."

All eyes flashed to the beast in the trees as more mumbling rippled around the circle.

Master Juro stood. "We have more pressing matters to attend to." Seeing the dejected look on Kazi's face he added, "It does sound like another tale worth hearing; Hanna can tell it as we walk."

Hanna suddenly felt overwhelmed. She was just informed that she was officially a Juro, a Jagare and a Jivan, but she didn't want to be. She just wanted to be human and go home. Her head was buzzing, *what was it that Master Juro had just asked?*

Nandin grabbed her by the elbow and helped her stand as he started telling the tale. It helped focus her and she contributed details to Nandin's recounting of the previous night's adventures as she walked in a daze. Even with their less than enthusiastic explanation, it did make for a great story.

CHAPTER THIRTY-TWO

The Devil's Advocate

THEY WERE AWED.

A handful of Juro joined Master Juro on the edge of the field of boulders, to survey the valley. There was a lot to take in. They had all seen the massive wall that spanned across the valley barring the entrance, but what lay past that wall was beyond their imagination. The market, the people and all the houses that filled the majority of the area were more than any of them had anticipated, as was the castle and quarry. Even though Hanna had mentioned their existence, Master Juro expected a smaller, more rustic community.

As Hanna, Nandin, Kazi, and Karn approached, it was Kazi who uttered the first words.

"Look at the castle!" he exclaimed, "Is it really floating?"

"There is much more here than I imagined," said Tahtay Etai, "the city, the people — "

"There are so many," said another Juro leader, "how could we not know?"

Master Juro nodded. "Leader Michi you make a valid point. We should have climbed this mountain some time ago. It was foolish of us to have left Mateo alone to his own devices."

Leader Michi replied, "Yes, with this many Kameil, he could over take any number of the nesting grounds."

Nandin cleared his throat. "No, that wouldn't be possible.

Once the Kameil leave the valley they are without Essence. They would never even make it to a nesting ground let alone be in any condition to seize it."

"Is it not true that Mateo has made Essence capsules so that they can survive outside the valley?" Master Juro countered.

"Wait a second," Hanna interjected. "You are all missing the point." The Juro exchanged startled glances, they were not used to anyone rebuking their opinions — to speak to Master Juro in such a fashion was unheard of. Even at the Sanctuary there were certain formalities when presenting an opposing view. But Hanna was unconcerned with protocol.

"The Kameil don't attack just for the sake of it — it's an act of desperation and those who live in the valley are not desperate. If Mateo wanted the crystals from the nesting grounds he'd just send the Yaru. They could take out the guards easily enough."

The Juro nervously look about, as if just mentioning the possibility of an attack would cause one to occur. Nandin wondered where she was going with the dangerous line of thinking.

"The point," she continued, "is that they can survive *here*. The point, is that Mateo is not interested in causing harm to people; he's trying to help them."

"That's right," Nandin said standing taller, surprised that Hanna came to Mateo's defence. "Even what he did to Hanna was for her benefit, even though it was against her will. This whole quarry, the Essence tablets, making liquid Essence, is all to cure the Kameil. Even the Yaru were created to help them. We protect their farms, teach them to hunt and seek the Kameil outside the valley to bring them here."

Master Juro studied Hanna for a moment. "I would not have believed you would be such an advocate of someone who has drugged and experimented on you."

Hanna crossed her arms as she gazed towards the castle. She hardly wanted to defend Mateo, she didn't trust his motives or his methods, but the issue was about the Kameil.

"I'm not his advocate; his methods border on the psychotic. He's been in charge here so long he just does whatever he wants…but that doesn't make the Kameil your enemies. You can't judge an entire race of people on the actions of one man."

Leader Michi added, "You can if that one man is in charge. They do his bidding and they've brought this disaster down upon us. He'll destroy the world with this foolishness and the Kameil will help him do it." He waved towards the quarry. "We should have sought out Mateo sooner, contained him before he did this damage."

Hanna gaped at them, astonished by the Juro as they muttered their agreement, all of them except Master Juro, who kept his opinions to himself.

"And then who would help the Kameil?" she asked the leaders. "Would you?" When no reply was forthcoming she proceeded with her case. "The people I've met since coming to Galenia are not the type to leave whole families alone to die. During the Time of Endurance, each race was fending for itself, struggling and often dying. What the Kameil are going through isn't any different. Just because their ancestors made bad choices, doesn't mean they should be abandoned."

Master Juro raised his hands. "These are issues we will need to bring back to the Sanctuary to discuss. The quarry is what we need to deal with now, or there will not be a home left for any of us."

"What do you propose to do?" Nandin asked raising his eyebrows; this was what he had been waiting and fearing to hear.

"From what we now know, I believe the safest thing to do is fill in that pit before the Qual is released," Master Juro said as he studied the landscape.

"I agree," Tahtay Etai said solemnly. "Do you think we can we do that from here?"

Master Juro walked along the edge, deep in thought. "If all the Juro coordinate their efforts we could. We can toss these boulders down into it. It won't be enough to fill it completely, but it will be a sufficient start."

"There are men down there, working in the quarry," Nandin protested. "They'd be crushed!"

"Then I suggest you get them out of the way. How quickly can you get down there?"

Nandin hesitated. There was no way he and Jon could stop all the Juro from lobbing the boulders down into the valley. The quarry and the people would be completely vulnerable. The best course of action was to go back. "If I travelled through the night, I could reach the valley around this time tomorrow. Then I could start the evacuation."

Master Juro nodded. "I will give you until then; however, if Mateo uncovers the Qual any sooner, we will have to act. I fear what kind of damage will be caused by the release of that much Qual."

"Give us a chance to fill the quarry in. Mateo was unaware of your immediate threat, but given the circumstances, he will act. It would be much safer if we filled it in down there than if you just started throwing stones at us."

"Mateo has already made a mess of things. We can not sit here and wait for him to do what needs to be done. Hanna explained that she already told him about the tears and the damage they caused. Obviously it had little effect since the mining is still

221

in progress. Nandin, I am giving you a chance to save your people, but do not mistake my generosity for patience. We are almost out of time."

Nandin ground his teeth in frustration as he turned and hurried back to the camp to find Jon. He hoped together they could empty the quarry before the Juro acted.

CHAPTER THIRTY-THREE

Together We Stand

TIME WAS OF THE ESSENCE.

It didn't take long for Jon and Nandin to gather their things while Hanna ran to her tent. She returned to them with her bag, dug around in it and pulled out a piece of parchment. "I should have given this to you earlier."

"What is it?"

She leaned in closer feeling the need to be discreet. "It's a map of Senda...Nandin, you've got to get the Kameil out of the sewers. Master Jagare has a copy of this and it's only a matter of time before he figures out it's for under the city. I don't know what they'll do if they find the Kameil there...you will save them won't you?"

"Of course, that's what I do."

"I'll try to stall Master Juro...maybe I can convince him to go and talk to Mateo. If they worked together — "

"I don't think Mateo would do that if they fill in the quarry, but you're right — if they worked together it could solve a lot of problems."

She grabbed his arm. "Nandin, whatever happens, don't let him change you. Remember who you are. And be careful down there." Rising up on her tiptoes, she gave him a quick kiss on the cheek before turning to Jon.

"Good-bye Jon, thanks again for everything. I hope you have

beautiful wedding, sorry I'm going to miss it."

"We'll be thinking of you. Come on Nandin, let's get going."

Nandin hesitated. He wanted to go save the Kameil, but hadn't expected that leaving Hanna behind would be so hard. Jon tugged at his arm; reluctantly he turned, glancing over his shoulder as he jogged out of sight.

Hanna hugged herself. After everything that had happened and the effort it had taken to get her out of the valley, it seemed ironic to her how tempted she was to join them.

* * *

They passed a couple Vaktare who kept watch of the trail. It seemed wrong to be leaving them there to spy on his home and plan an attack, as that was how he thought of Master Juro's plan to fill in the quarry.

He fretted as he raced through the trees and down the mountain following Jon. They hadn't gone far when Nean jumped out of a tree right behind them, catching them off guard.

"You know Commander, you're suppose to set an example," Nean said as he tossed a small stone at Nandin, "that could have been an arrow in your back."

Nandin and Jon stopped to greet Nean as more Yaru descended from the trees.

"So you are here...been hanging out long?" Nandin said unable to resist the wit.

Nean raised an eyebrow as he replied. "We were heading up the path when we heard a bunch of wolcotts crashing through the woods, so we thought it safer to let them pass by being up and out of the way," Nandin and Jon cast about for signs of the wolcott. Nean casually continued, "Turns out, it was just you two."

Nandin crossed his arms. "Very funny. So you managed to pick up our trail."

"You certainly didn't make it easy to track you. You set me back by going into the mountains and not out the front gate. I was delayed again when you didn't actually head out of the mountains. When we came upon a pack of Juro and Vaktare, I frankly wondered if I'd ever see you again. How did you manage to escape?"

"They let us go."

"Putting those great diplomatic skills to use again?" Nean asked.

Jon said with some urgency, "We need to get warning down into the valley. They plan to fill in the quarry. We have to go back and get everyone out."

"Why not stop them?" Blades said as he emerged from behind a tree further along the path.

Nandin resisted the urge to swear; Blades presence was bound to make things more complicated.

As more of Blade's and Thanlin's teams emerged, Nean explained, "When we learned you didn't leave through the main gate, I sent Sim back to let Mateo know. Apparently it made him more than a little concerned so he sent the rest of the Yaru to help find your trail. They joined up with us a couple hours ago."

Blades grunted. "It's a good thing we came too, so we can remove the invaders from our woods."

"Blades, there are twenty-five Vaktare and seventy-some Juro. You're not going to be able to just throw them out," Nandin reasoned.

"And why not? We can stop their attack instead of fleeing from it. There are twenty-six of us; seems to me the odds are in our favour." The men around him laughed.

"No," Jon said sternly. "Nandin and I are going back to the valley."

"Afraid?" Thanlin taunted.

Nean waved the comment aside. "No, he's right; they should go. It would take us awhile to deal with the Vaktare in order to stop the Juro. A lot of people in the valley could be dead by then."

"Right," Nandin agreed. "Which means you need to hold off on attacking them until Jon and I get down to the valley, otherwise the Juro might not wait for the quarry to be cleared before they start tossing rocks. We were given until this time tomorrow, but Nean, if they begin before then, get the Yaru in there."

Nean nodded. "We'll be in position."

Leaving the Yaru to attack the Vaktare and stop the Juro was a dangerous plan; he hated abandoning his men at a time like this.

He hesitated. "Maybe I should stay — "

"No Nandin," Jon said with some urgency, "You're the only one who has a chance to reason with Mateo. Once he sees what we're doing, I'm sure he'll come down to the quarry. You'll have to convince him to let us evacuate."

Nandin knew there was no time for a debate so he turned to go calling back over his shoulder. "Nean, if you have to engage, disarm them, but try not to kill anyone."

Nean sighed. "I'll do what I can. Good luck."

Nandin raced after Jon who was already running back down the trail. Blades smirked at Nean as he flipped his dagger in his hand. "He really is naive, isn't he?"

Nean sighed, shaking his head. "I'm afraid so." Nean knew he could order his men to stop at incapacitating the Vaktare, but Blades and Thanlin lived for the moments they could kill indiscriminately. The Vaktare camped out in their territory provided just such an opportunity. Nean figured once he had told

Nandin about some of the missions they went on he would understand Blades would not hold back. "Alright, let's figure out how we're going to take their camp."

The only way to prevent Blades and Thanlin from killing anyone was to take them out of the equation. Surrounded by their own team of Yaru it wasn't something Nean could do beforehand without causing trouble. The best plan he could come up with was to coach the Yaru he trusted to incapacitate instead of kill until he could deal with the situation. He knew though, things were about to get very messy.

* * *

Kazi was fit to burst by the time he finally got a chance to talk to Hanna alone. For her part, Hanna was lost in thought and hadn't noticed her friend's mounting restlessness. They wove their way through the Vaktare and Juro who were starting up the cook fires. Hanna proceeded to a quiet and empty area by the rock wall farthest away from the cliff edge and had just sat down when Kazi could contain his curiosity no longer.

"So tell me, what was he like?"

Hanna took a second to think it through. "He was too trusting and a little naive when I first met him, but a lot has happened since then — I think he'll be more cautious now. I believe he means what he says: he's really just trying to help people. I thought I'd hate him forever for letting Mateo hurt me...but he was so torn up about it, I even felt bad that my pain caused him pain. Geez, that sounds really cheesy. It's just...I can't help but like him."

Kazi chuckled. "Yes, I figured as much, but I wasn't asking about Nandin."

Her eyebrows knit together as she tried to figure out who it

227

was that Kazi was referring to. He shook his head and rolled his eyes. "Mateo! Tell me about Mateo!"

"Oh...him."

"Well yeah! Come on Hanna, the guy's a legend. You remember back in Kayu that most the people didn't think he even existed? No one's ever seen him before; you're the first! So...what's he like?"

"To start with he's massive. He's even bigger than Master Jagare. His Essence is so intense it is hard to look at him for very long," she paused as she tried to formulate the words to describe who he was as a person. "He is eager to learn things. He tries to be charming, but frankly I don't think he pulls it off very well; I found his attempts at flattery sort of creepy actually. He was pretty convincing about his cause and desire to help people, yet something makes me a bit uneasy about him."

Kazi nodded. "I'd say being strapped to a table and stabbed in the back had something to do with it."

She cringed at the memory. "That definitely confirmed that he's a controlling, inconsiderate, manipulative jerk...still, he was so convinced he was doing the right thing — like he really was trying to help me. It just made me so mad. I'm still mad. I'd love nothing more than to clock him one, but..."

Kazi waited. When she didn't resume her sentence he felt the need to ask. "What?"

She sigh as she leaned back against the rock wall. "He was right. Since he gave me the Essence treatments I've felt better than ever. I'm stronger, faster...I can even manipulate the Essence more easily."

"I guess that's a good thing then."

"No, it's not. Right now it's great, but I still don't know what happens when I get back home. And I didn't like being forced into it. He does whatever he wants and even though he says he cares about the Kameil, I don't think he really does. The day he decides he doesn't want to deal with them, he'll end up walking away and they'll be left to fend for themselves."

Ever since Kazi told Hanna about the Kameil, she had shown her concern for them. Now that she had met them and learned first-hand how they live and struggle to survive, she was even more compassionate towards their plight. Kazi realized he had accepted the twisted stories of who the Kameil were. Thinking back on it, he recalled when his village was attacked the Kameil had stolen simple supplies and food — hardly the act of raving, hardened criminals.

"What about the Yaru? Won't they stay and help them? Nandin seems like someone who would."

"I agree, but why should the Kameil be afraid for their lives? Why must they be tucked away in the valley in order to survive? If the people of Galenia accepted the Kameil and helped them they could...they could all live happily-ever-after. Sorry, I don't mean to rant on and on about this. Let's change the subject. Tell me about your trip with Master Juro. Isn't he just a barrel of laughs?"

Kazi was delighted to tell his tale. After spending his time with the Vaktare and the Juro he was so relieved that he finally had someone whom he could really talk to. The others had barely tolerated his presence; Hanna was actually glad he was there.

CHAPTER THIRTY-FOUR

Plans of Attack

THEY MOVED STEALTHILY.

The Yaru ventured deep into the woods and off the trail to prevent anyone from stumbling onto them. The five leaders stepped aside to discuss their strategy before they gave out orders to their men. They quickly agreed that they needed to use an alternate route into the Vaktare's camp as the narrow path could easily be defended preventing their advancement.

At one point in each of the Yaru's training, they had been taken to the mountaintop and instructed to climb the rock face to reach the clearing so they knew that it was a viable option. The downside to that plan was that the climb was difficult, slow-going and required a lot of their energy and concentration. Fortunately, Nandin said they had a twenty-four hour window, which was plenty of time to make the climb and rest before they needed to be in position — if the Juro didn't attack before then.

They still had half a day before they lost the light so the leaders were confident they could be above the camp before dark. The rest of the plan was much more difficult to get agreement on. Blades' strategy was to wait until dark and storm the camp. It would be difficult to see, but easier to take out the Vaktare and many of the Juro in the process; he revelled at the idea of the mass slaughter. Thanlin agreed whole-heartedly that the plan was a good one.

Plyral and Sim were in agreement with Nean's proposal. Under cover of darkness they would attach ropes to the trees along the cliff's edge and keep them out of sight until they needed them to make the descent into the camp. Once they determine the best position, Plyral would instruct a team of bowmen to set up their weapons where they could see, but not be seen.

Everyone would sleep throughout the night keeping at least two sentries on duty and switch them often so all the men would get enough sleep to be well rested for the coming confrontation. In the morning, Nean would be able to get a better look at the Vaktare's position before finalizing the plan, but the overall idea was to have Plyral and his archers cover the Yaru who first entered the camp, among them would be the other four Captains. Blades' and Thanlin's job would be to keep any attacking Vaktare engaged as the rest of the Yaru descended. Meanwhile, Nean and Sim would make a beeline for the far side of the camp where the goat trail led to the lookout; it was the only feasible way to reach the Juro as climbing to the lookout made them easy targets if the Vaktare also had archers. Once Nean and Sim reached the trail, they would hold the position until the rest of the Yaru joined them.

Nean patiently reminded Blades that the Vaktare wore full body armour and going for the kill would be time consuming; it was faster and easier to disarm and incapacitate them.

"If I cut off their legs, that should incapacitate them alright," he snickered.

"Nean what will we do once we get all the Yaru to the lookout?" Sim asked.

"That's easy," Thanlin replied, "without their Vaktare protectors we can just slice and dice."

Nean scoffed, "Not so easy; they can use the Essence you

231

simpleton. If you go in there swinging, what's to stop them from lifting you up and tossing your sorry butt over the cliff?"

Thanlin crossed his arms and held his tongue to wait for either Blades or Nean to make the call as to what they would do.

"Not to mention," Nean continued to scold, "if you commit mass murder of the Juro, the valley would be under a full scale attack within the month. The Jagare will come in and wipe us out. As amazing as we may be, twenty-six Yaru and one Mateo will not be able to withstand any long term siege — if we could, I'm sure Mateo would have been less reserved in our operations over the years." Seeing that his point had been made he continued explaining his plan. "Once we get to the look out we'll just hold our ground and keep them distracted. We won't be able to hold them off indefinitely, but we can give Nandin the time he needs to get people to safety. We need to contain the situation as best as we can, not make it worse."

Thanlin grumbled, but Blades smiled grimly and said, "Don't worry my friend, the Vaktare's armour isn't invulnerable. I'm sure we'll have plenty of time to get our point across."

Nean hadn't expected any less from either of them. At least they were willing to follow the logistics of his plan. When the time was right, he would deal with them accordingly.

* * *

Jon and Nandin continued to run through the night, stopping for short breaks; the torch that Jon carried provided just enough light to make out the path in front of them. When they rested along the way, they were content to eat their dried rations instead of spending the time to cook. Also during their stops, they saved time by napping on the ground. Jon was confident that his ability to sleep lightly was sufficient to warn them in case of danger. Nandin was skeptical, but figured for the short while they would be resting the risk was minimal.

Entering the valley at midday, they paused for a minute to catch their breath and to devise a plan. Jon would make for the quarry and sound the alarm, which was typically used for cave-ins, machinery collapses or as an avalanche warning system; it had never been used for the latter. Nandin was to warn Sarah and together they would initiate the avalanche evacuation procedure; they would alert the residents closest to the quarry who would then notify the next house and it would repeat down the line until all houses were clear. It had never been done before and was likely to be chaotic.

"Jon, are you sure you don't want to go with Sarah?" Nandin asked knowing the quarry was the riskier location to be.

"No, you need to deal with Mateo and getting to the bridge will be quicker from the streets. It won't be long before Mateo discovers what's happening; I guarantee he'll come down in person to find out why. Hopefully you can stop him from interfering with the evacuation...try to convince him to start filling in the quarry — "

"If he's willing to fill it in, we can help him and then the Juro won't need to act. I'll keep an eye out for him; he'll be easy enough to spot coming down the bridge. Are you sure you want me to get Sarah's help? I could send her to the wall to begin with."

Jon shook his head. "She won't go. She'll know you need help getting the evacuation started...after that, send her to the wall."

"Alright...let's get on with this," Nandin said as he wiped his brow and started running once more.

CHAPTER THIRTY-FIVE

In too Deep

INDUSTRY WAS BOOMING.

When Jon reached the quarry, he was surprised how busy it was. Twice the number of people were hauling stones and the tumbling machines were not able to keep up so the rocks were piling up in rather random places: in-between the towers and grinders as well as on some of the pathways. He recognized one of the rock cutters busy chiselling inside the sheltered work space.

"Hello Jon! What brings you to the quarry today?" the man shouted above the din as Jon approached.

"Afternoon Marcus. We have a situation."

"Oh?"

"I need to get the Kameil out of the quarry and as far away as possible…to the market would be best. Can you sound the alarm? There are signs of a rockslide from the mountain — we have to clear the area." The agitation in his voice was clear.

All the colour drained from Marcus's face. He could imagine the damage a rockslide could do; it was not a warning one took lightly. Seeing his explanation had the desired effect Jon added, "I'll go down into the pit and get the men out, you sound the alarm and spread the word up here. Once you get people running, no one will bother sticking around to see why the alarm is going off."

"Bless you Jon. May luck be on our side."

Jon nodded his thanks and ran towards the road down into the pit. Marcus's words made his throat go dry; in the event of a real rockslide, being caught in the pit was a death sentence. Having giant boulders thrown in it would be no less hazardous — he hoped the Juro would wait.

Nandin took a moment to drain the glass of water Sarah offered him before he told her what they needed to do.

"Okay, follow me," she said as she exited the house.

Nandin knew the layout of the city, but typically only travelled from the main gate to the bridge leading to the castle. He didn't know the quickest routes or his way through the back alleys. Not only was Sarah efficient at navigating through the maze of houses, she also knew which houses were most likely to have people currently in them.

Although Nandin had told her what the Juro planned to do, she agreed the excuse of a rockslide was the best way to get people moving without question. It was a threat that the residents in the valley feared most; being surrounded on three sides by rocky mountains, one would often wonder what would happen if those rocks came loose.

* * *

As Jon sprinted towards the quarry, he swore as he saw the undeniable figure of Mateo standing at the edge of the pit. Mateo's presence in the quarry was rare and it complicated matters. He could stop the evacuation before it even got started. Jon made straight for him.

"Jon, there you are!" Mateo shouted above the noise of the mining around them. "I was wondering where you got to."

"I went with Nandin," Jon said.

Mateo nodded. "Of course you did. That's why he went into the woods instead of out the front gate…was that your idea?"

"No. Mateo, we have…we have a situation. We need to evacuate. I sent Marcus to sound the alarm — we've got to get these people out of here."

"You what?" he barked. "How dare you! Have you any idea how close am I? They could reach the Qual any time now!"

"I had to," Jon replied, raising his own voice, "they'll be crushed otherwise."

Mateo paused mid rant. "Crushed? What do you mean?"

"The Juro. They plan on filling in the quarry. They gave us a day to get the people out and time is almost up!"

"How is this possible?" he asked glancing around for any Juro in the area.

"There," Jon said pointing to the cliff on top of one of the mountains. Mateo squinted, attempting to see the Juro and then literally staggered back when he saw them. "Once we get everyone out, we could start filling it in ourselves…maybe then the Juro won't — "

"I need to get the Qual while there's still a chance." Mateo said as he stepped closer to the quarry.

"No, you can't! The moment you do they will begin to throw the boulders. The Kameil could be killed!"

"I have to do this! It has taken me too long to get this far!"

"If we fill it in ourselves they won't have to. Don't you see? It's the only way to stop them."

Jon grabbed at Mateo who flung him to the ground.

"Let me do this," Mateo roared, "Save the Kameil if you can."

Seeing the determination in Mateo's eyes, Jon knew there would be no reasoning with him. He leapt to his feet and bolted towards the pit just as the alarm sounded.

"Get out!" he hollered as he ran. "Rockslide! Run!"

Panic ensued. Tools and buckets of stones crashed to the ground as people abandoned their posts, yelling as they frantically tried to flee.

Jon leapt over equipment and debris to aide whoever needed help. One man was desperately trying to free the mules that were attached to a wooden plank that sat on top of a stone basin.

"Go, I've got this," Jon yelled, but the man refused to leave the animals whom he cared for.

Jon released the leather belts that attached one of the mules to the plank and then removed it from its neck so it to wouldn't become entangled. He whacked it on its hindquarters and yelled "heeya" at it to get it moving. As the man finished untangling the other mule they heard a rumbling sound. They both looked over to where Mateo stood on the edge of the quarry and saw a boulder flying over his head and crashing to the ground.

"It started!" Jon shouted.

Without further hesitation the man fled. Jon loosed the final mule and glanced up to the mountaintop, cursing the Juro for not waiting when he caught sight of another boulder out of the corner of his eye. Turning to watch it, he realized it came out of the pit, not from the mountain. Mateo was using the Essence to rip the boulders free and was hurtling them out of the quarry.

"Not good," Jon said and rushed through the quarry to help any others who had yet to make their way clear.

As he ran, he heard Mateo cry out. Glancing over his shoulder he saw a fountain of Qual, bursting forth from the quarry. Time was up.

* * *

Not one person hesitated at their warning; few even bothered to gather any belongings as they fled. Most people remembered it was their job to alert their neighbour before retreating to the wall, but some panicked and fled without helping. Sarah hoped she would be able to alert enough people that no one would be missed.

When the alarm sounded, doors randomly opened as people stuck their heads out. Seeing the throng of people running from the quarry or in the streets heading to the market, the curious onlookers joined in not waiting for an explanation.

"Still no sign of Mateo?" Sarah called as she ran across the street to Nandin.

"No. I'm going to the quarry to help Jon. I'll double back and meet Mateo when he comes. You head to the market and knock on doors as you go."

"I think people know to leave now…I need to get Jon."

"He'll be on his way — I'll make sure of it. You should go."

"Yes, you're right…I'm going to get Jon," she yelled as she veered off to take a short cut to the quarry. Nandin sighed as he took off after her; he realized there was no way she would go without Jon.

CHAPTER THIRTY-SIX

Divided We Fall

THE JURO PREPARED.

"He's done it!" Master Juro cried as the Qual was released. "We cannot wait a moment longer. Send the rocks."

Seventy-five Juro faced the field of boulders; using Essence, seventy-five boulders lifted into the air. As one, they turned towards the valley and hurled them.

"Wait!" Hanna cried lifting her hands in the air. They all looked towards her, shocked as she had used the Essence to stop the boulders and was holding them all in midair; not even Master Juro had that kind of power.

"Hanna, what are you doing?" Master Juro shouted, overcoming his awe at her newfound strength.

"The quarry's not empty yet! We have to wait," she managed to plead, barely able to maintain the effort of holding the stones.

"Karn," Master Juro said sharply.

Karn grabbed Hanna's arms and spun her to face him breaking her hold on the boulders. Out of reflex she ducked her head, but the Juro had once again resumed their control of them and tossed them down to the valley below.

"No!" Hanna cried pulling away from Karn as she helplessly watched the boulders fly out of her reach. Nervously she waited to see what kind of damage they'd cause.

The rumbling, booming sound of the boulders crashing to the ground echoed around the valley. Dust billowed, covering the scene. They all scrutinized the valley below, trying to get a glimpse of what had happened. A high-pitched cackle reached their ears and as the dust cleared they saw Mateo surrounded by the stones, but the Qual still came forth.

"He must have deflected it," Leader Michi said. As he spoke another spout of Qual burst out of the ground.

"Again!" shouted Master Juro. "Karn hold her."

"No wait!" Hanna said.

"We can't — "

"I…I can feel it…oh no!"

"What?" Karn asked as she collapsed to the ground.

"The world…it's being ripped apart. Master Juro, you…you have to stop this!"

Again they cast down their resolution to the quarry, this time unhindered by Hanna. When the dust cleared they were able see an additional geyser break through.

"It's not enough!" Leader Akira yelled, panic thick in her voice.

"The mountain!" Master Juro exclaimed. "We will have to bring down the mountain. Everyone, cast another boulder, this time aim it at the rock face behind the quarry."

The cries of the people below echoed up to them, but Hanna knew she could not save them. Tears came to her eyes; she knew what she had to do. Gaining her feet she lifted her hands again.

"Hanna, this has to be done," Karn said.

"I know Karn," she said steadying her resolve, "and I have to help."

As the boulders hit the mountain, she reached out and pulled the rock face to shift the balance; once again astonishing those around her. The mountain started to slide.

"Master Juro!" Hanna yelled, "Master Juro, I can feel it! A

portal…he's opened a portal…it's pulling me!"

Master Juro whipped his head around to look at her, "Go child, go now!"

Hanna didn't wait to see if the rockslide would successfully fill in the pit — this could be her only chance. Instead, she dashed to the path leading back to the campsite.

"Hanna, wait!" Kazi called.

"Karn, stop him!" Master Juro commanded.

"Hanna!" he yelled again.

Karn grabbed Kazi by the wrist.

Master Juro said firmly, "Kazi, you can't go where she's going."

Knowing there was no way he'd be able to break from Karn's grasp, Kazi hung his head. "I know," he said as he stopped resisting.

Karn let go of him and started to turn back to the valley when Kazi bolted after Hanna. Karn cussed under his breath and went after him.

* * *

The Yaru were in position, watching the camp below. Nean figured that Nandin should have reached the valley and the evacuation would be well underway. He didn't want to wait any longer; if the quarry wasn't empty by now and the Juro began trying to fill it in, a lot of people would be dead before the Yaru could intervene. Nean gave the signal and the first group quickly dropped the ropes and rappelled down them.

They landed before the Vaktare were aware of their presence, but as Nean and Sim began their sprint around the clearing, keeping close to the rock walls, the alarm went out and the

Vaktare took up arms. They made it three quarters of the way around before they were intercepted. Blades attacked careful not to venture too far from the wall leaving the Yaru descending the ropes as easy targets and to keep out of the way of the archers who provide Nean and Sim as much cover as they could until they were out of range.

Over the shouts of the men, off in the distance they heard a rumbling sound that echoed up the mountain. Nean sighed; it had begun.

As Hanna entered into the campsite she slowed down, trying to make sense of the chaos in front of her. Black clad figures danced between the Vaktare, some with swords in their hands, others held daggers or staffs. The ground was littered with arrows and several Vaktare.

"What's going on?!" she screamed. Between the clashing of weapons and the rumbling of the mountain her words were all but lost — no one stopped what they were doing to answer.

The Yaru closest to her pulled off his mask after he disarmed his opponent and knocked him to the ground.

"Hanna, are you crazy? Get out of here!"

"Nean, what's going on? Why is everyone fighting?"

Nean parried a blow from a sword with his staff from a new adversary.

"I'm a bit busy…just get out of here!"

When Karn and Kazi arrived behind her, she was barely able to perceive the distinctive *'shing'* of a sword as it pulled free from its scabbard. She turned to see Karn, his face a mask, a blade in his hand.

"Oh my god, oh my god! What are you doing?"

"He's right Hanna, go! Kazi, get back to Master Juro, let him know what's happening."

"Hanna wait!" Kazi shouted and jumped in front of her blocking her path.

"What is it Kazi?!" she hollered.

"I just wanted to say goodbye. I — "

Suddenly, Kazi eye's widened and Hanna saw a sword protruding from his gut.

"Kazi!" she shrieked.

He gazed at her with a pained and confused expression and gasped, "Hanna?"

He groaned as the sword was pulled out. Grabbing at his gut, he looked down, noticing his hands were covered in blood before he collapsed to the ground leaving Hanna face to face with a Yaru. Blades.

He slashed out in an attempt to strike her down, but she jumped back and without thinking blasted him with Essence causing him to fly across the clearing. The Essence flowed through her veins and she began to shake with anger and the desire to attack him again. He sprung back to his feet, but before she could react, he moaned and fell to the ground, cradling his neck where a dart protruded from it. With Blades dealt with, her attention went back to her friend.

"Kazi," she cried as she fell to the ground beside him.

"Hanna, there's nothing you can do for him, please, go!" Karn pleaded as he pulled her to her feet. "We'll take care of him, I promise."

Her grief and anger bubbled inside her, fuelled her. She wove in and out of the fighting men, dodging the ones that attempted to lunge at her and leapt over the fallen before finally disappearing down the goat path, tears streaming down her face.

CHAPTER THIRTY-SEVEN

Out of Order

THE KAMEIL FLED.

Jon had gone to the pit to ensure all the workers made it out. The Kameil were oblivious of the Juro threat as they evacuated the pit and assumed Mateo's desperate attempts to reach the Qual stemmed from the impeding doom of the rockslide Jon had warned them about.

The ground rumbled as the first boulders hit; the dust rolled towards them making it hard to see. The Kameil didn't bother to watch as they ran for their lives. Mateo's laughter echoed around them.

"Why does he persist?" one Kameil shouted, being careful not to trip as he fled.

"If that liquid is buried; he can't cure us," another man grunted as he climbed over a large rock.

"But he could be crushed!"

"Just run!" Jon barked. "Save your breath."

They were out of the pit and in less danger, but he felt anywhere near the quarry was not safe. One of the Kameil tumbled over as he tripped on a pile of stones that had been dumped when those working the machines fled. Jon leapt to the man's aide and helped him over the rest of the rocks as the second volley hit.

"Are you okay," Jon asked supporting the man's weight.

"I think I sprained my ankle," he coughed as dust filled his lungs, "but I'll manage."

He released his hold on Jon and continued to run; a painful limp slowing him down. If the mountain was truly coming down, Jon knew the man would never make it.

And that's when he heard the rockslide. The ground shook as a thundering sound reverberated around the valley. It was not the sound of boulders landing in the pit, but he did not take the time to see what the Juro had done; every fibre in his bones told him to flee. His heart almost broke in two when he saw Sarah push passed the last of the escaping Kameil. She headed towards him with Nandin close behind.

"Jon!" she wailed.

He waved at her, "Go! Run, Sarah, run!"

She didn't hesitate; seeing Jon sprinting towards her was enough for her to know he would come. She spun around and ran.

"Run Nandin," Jon yelled as he had just about caught up with Sarah. Nandin ran backwards until he saw Jon swing Sarah over his shoulder. Nandin turned and took off towards the city. He had seen the rocks sliding down the mountain and cursed the Juro for such a reckless solution and their disregard for the Kameil's lives; they could have at least waited for them to clear the area. He hoped that the pit would swallow most of the rock so they could all make it to safety; little did he know, Mateo had refused to take cover. So intent on his escape he didn't see the rock that crashed into Jon, crushing his legs.

Mateo watched in horror as the boulders crashed into the side of the mountain. There was no way he would be able to outrun the avalanche they had caused. He had never been able to float like Master Juro did and he realized there was nothing to offer him protection. He did the only thing he could: he created a dome of

Essence. The first few boulders bounced off of it, but the quantity and speed of rocks proved even too much for the great Mateo and ultimately, he was buried.

* * *

With the death of Blades, Nean called out.

"Enough! Yaru, stand down!"

The Yaru knew it was Nean who gave the order. Without Blades to rally them on, even Thanlin would turn to Nean for direction. The Yaru backed away from their opponents. Seeing the black-clad warriors lower their weapons gave the Vaktare pause.

The force of the rockslide shook the ground and as it reached the valley, the last mighty thundering crash drew everyone's attention towards the cliff. The Vaktare were startled when the Yaru suddenly sprinted past them and headed to the goat trail. Cursing at being tricked into lowering their guard, the Vaktare took after them concerned what would happen to the unprotected Juro. When the Yaru burst into the lookout, they paid no attention to the Juro, but headed straight to the edge of the cliff to gaze down into valley. What they saw brought them to their knees.

The Yaru removed their masks, completely disregarding the Juro as they helplessly gaped at the valley below where the quarry had disappeared from site; the pit was filled and the first few rows of houses were demolished by the torrent. As the Vaktare finally caught up Master Juro signalled for them to lower their weapons. They complied, but strategically placed themselves between the Yaru and the Juro.

"What have you done?" Nean whispered.

Master Juro sighed. "What we had to. Did Hanna get away?" he asked, concern in his voice.

"Yes," Karn replied, "She may not have if it wasn't for this Yaru." He indicated Nean who cast him a concerned look and shook his head ever so slightly — he didn't want the Yaru to know it was he who fired the dart that killed Blades. Karn acknowledged the man's silent communication.

"He called an end to the fighting," Karn said instead of divulging the fact that he had killed one of his own men in order to do so. "And the odds were in their favour, they could have defeated us instead of telling his men to stand down."

Master Juro nodded. "Go," he said to the Yaru. "Your people will be in need of you. From what we could tell, most of the workers made it out of the quarry before the avalanche — casualties should be minimal." The Yaru stood, uncertain how to take the news. "I can't say the same for Mateo though, he was standing by the quarry when the rockslide hit."

The Yaru exchanged concerned looks.

"We will go," Nean said firmly, "but you will leave first."

The Yaru all stood and faced the Juro, their determined faces revealing their intent should the Juro and Vaktare wish to remain. Master Juro nodded his head; they had done what it was they came to do; there was no point in staying. He glanced back at Karn, and was suddenly aware of Kazi's absence.

"Where is the boy?" he asked.

Karn replied dejectedly, "At the camp. Dylan is with him, he was stabbed...I don't think he's going to make it."

Master Juro hastily rushed back to the camp; followed first by Karn and Nean and then the Juro. When he arrived, he rushed to Kazi's side where Dylan had been keeping pressure on the wound. He moved aside as Master Juro ripped open Kazi's blood-drenched shirt revealing the wound and set to treating it. "This does not look good." He called over his shoulder, "Tahtay Etai I

247

will need your assistance! Karn, see to the dismantling of the campsite and send our people on their way as soon as they are fit. This may take me some time."

Nean and Karn wove their way through what had become the battlefield and sought out survivors amongst their fallen comrades. The rest of the Yaru and Vaktare had yet to arrive as they followed behind the Juro who still made their way down the path from the lookout. Of the Yaru casualties only one survived; his injuries were serious, but not life threatening. Nean moved the bodies of his men so they lay side by side. There were five in all.

Karn was surprised to discover some of the Vaktare were simply knocked out.

"I don't understand," he said as he approached Nean. "Why are they still alive? The Yaru could have killed them all."

"Those weren't Nandin's orders. He wanted us to stop the Juro's attack or at least postpone it, but no one was to be killed."

Karn scanned the area. Of the sixteen Vaktare that lay on the ground at least half were dead. Understanding the confusion on Karn's face Nean explained, "Not everyone chose to follow those orders."

"Before we leave, I would see to our dead," Karn said resigning himself to the grim task ahead.

"As will I."

As the rest of the Vaktare and Yaru entered the campsite, they joined them in burying their dead while the Juro rested.

"Why do they just sit there? Why aren't they preparing to leave?" one of the Yaru ranted. Nean detected the man's resentment as well as the urgency in his voice.

An exhausted Master Juro approached, wiping the blood from his hands on a rag. Nean asked, "Will he live?"

"It's too soon to tell."

Nean nodded. He had no desire to be indelicate, but he wished to get to the valley sooner rather than later. "Aren't your men leaving? The Yaru are all here; no one will attack them."

"Soon, they need to recover first. Using the Essence like that is draining."

"Hanna didn't seem drained, but then…maybe she didn't take part?"

"She did more than her share. It appears she has strength that most Juro do not have."

"Why did she run through here? Where was she going?" Nean questioned, knowing that both Nandin and Mateo would want to know — that is, if either of them had survived.

A hint of a smile pulled at Master Juro's usual stoic face. "She was going home."

CHAPTER THIRTY-EIGHT

At a Loss

TEARS STREAKED HER FACE.

Hanna dashed from the path and headed into the trees. She felt the rumbling as the mountain came crashing down and the guilt pressed against her. As she continued to run, the evergreens gave way to the more familiar deciduous trees of her woods back home. Trees grew further apart and when she looked back, there was no sign of the forest she had been in moments ago.

She became aware of a dog barking, and the noise of cars as they whizzed down some unseen road. *I'm back!* The realization was bittersweet; she now understood the cost of her return. Releasing the Qual had opened the portal, but in doing so it ripped the life source from the planet; the damage it would cause would be catastrophic. She could only hope that by burying the geyser Mateo had caused, the damage was minimal.

As she passed her tree with its mossy cushion, she noted it was unchanged after all this time. Racing towards her house she saw the car in the driveway. She took the stairs two at a time and burst through the unlocked front door.

"Mom, I'm home! I'm home!" she bellowed, short of breath as she staggered into the house.

Her mom poked her head out of the kitchen.

"What? You're speaking gibberish."

Hanna was baffled, not only at her mother's calm demeanour or by the odd statement she had made, but how strange the words sounded. That's when it dawned on her; she hadn't heard anyone speak her own language for over a year. Feeling a little dizzy, she made her way through the house pushing the thought aside — she would reflect on that later.

When she entered the kitchen her mother was standing by the sink drying her hands on a tea towel.

"It's me mom; I've come back," she said hoping for a bit more of a reaction.

Her mother nodded. "I can see that dear. Are you feeling all right? You look rather flushed. You must have been in the sun too long; you probably have heat stroke."

Hanna couldn't understand her mother's cavalier attitude, but it didn't stop her from wrapping her arms around her and hugging her tight. The tears streamed down her cheeks.

"Ouch, Hanna! Too tight. What is it? What's wrong?"

Hanna loosened her grip, but continued to hold her mom. "I haven't seen you for so long; I missed you."

"Rough day was it?" she said patting her on the back.

Hanna pulled back. "Year mom, it was rough year!"

Her mother sighed. "I know sweetheart. School has been hard on you this year, what with those headaches and all. Maybe we can figure out something to help you make it through the rest of the school year; you've only got a month."

She stumbled back to look her mom in the eyes.

"Mom, when was the last time you saw me?"

Her mother gave her a smile. "This morning of course. Hanna, did you grow? You seem taller to me."

She vaguely recalled Master Juro saying it was possible time moved differently between Earth and Galenia, but a year? She faltered as her legs grew weak. Her mother led her to the table to sit down.

"It's the heat stroke," she heard her mother say, "I'll get you some water and an ice pack; just rest here."

She shook her head trying to clear it — it didn't make any sense. Had she imagined it? Had she dreamed the whole thing? She looked down at her arms and saw the Essence coursing through her. As she slid back her sleeve she noticed the mark left by one of Mateo's injections and became aware of the clothes she wore. Her beige cotton pants were covered in dirt and were still tucked into her leather boots tied around her calves. The leather jerkin was still done up tight and she felt for the knife still attached to her belt.

When her mother returned she too observed Hanna's attire. "Interesting getup you have on. Are you in a school play?"

"What? No. I just...a friend gave these to me, I thought they looked cool," she answered trying to sound calm, but feeling anything but.

"Very medieval, are you planning on hunting in the woods?" she said sarcastically.

Hanna sunk back in her chair. The image of Kazi laying on the ground and the Vaktare and Yaru killing each other was imprinted on her brain. It was because of her they were there. She laid her head on the table as she was still dizzy and feeling rather weak.

"No mom," she sighed, "I think it's time I stayed clear of the woods."

* * *

Nandin bent over, hands on his knees panting as the sound of the rockslide abated. He wiped his brow, as he turned around and realized he couldn't see his friends. Quickly scanning the area and seeing no sign of Jon and Sarah, panic set in. Fighting off his fatigue, he ran back towards the debris. Wounded Kameil lay battered and beaten from various sized stones they hadn't out run. Several times he stopped to uncover one victim or another. The amount of debris that had pushed its way into the streets could have buried many people. His anxiety grew.

He came upon a small, frail hand that stuck out between the rocks and clumps of dirt. As he got nearer, he discovered the clump of dirt was actually the dust-covered form of Sarah. Small rocks littered part of her upper body and one stone, just smaller than her head rested nearby and was spattered in blood. The gash across her skull was indication enough — she had been killed instantly.

Carefully he brushed her off and discovered that the majority of her body was underneath Jon. Without hesitation he set to removing the rubble in earnest.

"Nandin," he barely heard Jon utter.

Nandin knelt down to the prone figure. Jon was on his stomach; his battered and bruised head cocked to the side.

"I'm here Jon; I'm right here."

He grabbed his friend's hand and squeezed; Jon's fingers just twitched in return.

"Look....after them...the Kameil. You've got to —" he rasped.

"I will Jon, I promise."

"And Sarah...take care...of her?"

Buried as he was, there was no way for Jon to know Sarah's fate. Nandin's eyes began to water. Taking in the giant boulder that lay across Jon's legs and lower back and the way is friend was struggling for air, he knew — Jon didn't have long.

"You know I will," Nandin said.

Jon closed his eyes a second and lay still before he spoke again.

"They were…right," he gasped. Nandin waited, not wanting to miss his friends last few words.

"The Juro…they did it…they saved — " he started coughing and barely managed to finish his words, "the world."

Nandin regarded the chaos around him. It sure didn't feel like the Juro had done them any favours.

He leaned closer to Jon. "You did it," he said, "you saved the Kameil."

"And a mule." Jon attempted to laugh, but broke out in another coughing fit.

Nandin put a hand on Jon's forehead.

"Rest," he said. Nandin stood, discontent to simple sit by as his closest companion faded away in front of him. He placed his hands on the boulder and tried to lift it, but it didn't budge. Digging his shoulder into it, he screamed as he tried to push it aside. It rocked ever so slightly then settled once more on Jon's crushed body. Nandin collapsed; anguish and tears overtaking him.

* * *

For a time, the quarry lay silent and still as the dust settled. Then a few pebbles started to roll. Suddenly, boulders and debris exploded as Mateo burst forth with a roar. He had been unable to keep the torrent of stones from coming, but he was able to surround himself in a protective Essence bubble.

Filled with anger and despair as he took in the wreckage, he howled again as he shook; partially from his rage, but mostly from the effect of having the Essence course through him. The quarry was completely buried; the pit was now a mound. Some of the houses nearest to the quarry were also covered and half of the bridge to the castle was missing, leaving the rest dangling from above. Mateo glared at the mountaintop and cursed the Juro, but no Juro remained to hear him.

He stumbled among the rubble towards the city caught between two emotions. Anger boiled inside him as he thought of their attack, but coming so close to an endless supply of Qual, pained him. His life's work, in ruins! And then he saw a figure crouched low on the ground at the edge of the rockslide and despair won out.

"Nandin! Nandin are you hurt?" he screamed finding the last reserves of energy to run towards him.

Nandin looked up, unashamed of his tear-drenched face. As Mateo reached him, he repeated his question.

"Are you hurt, son?" he asked in a raspy voice.

Nandin shook his head.

"Oh, thank goodness!" Mateo reached down and lifted Nandin off the ground as he embraced him.

"Jon," Nandin muttered.

Mateo set Nandin on the ground and glanced over to where he had motioned. He knelt down and lay a trembling hand on Jon's back.

"His breathing is shallow," Mateo said also struggling to breath.

Nandin nodded. "I couldn't move the rock."

Hearing the helplessness in Nandin's voice, Mateo put his hands on either side of the giant boulder, paused a moment to steady himself and with greater effort than usual, moved the boulder. He knew it would make no difference to Jon's fate, but it would be a small consolation to Nandin.

Nandin wondered why Mateo didn't just use the Essence to remove it as he watched Mateo lift and toss it aside. Mateo stumbled to the ground to join Nandin who hovered over Jon. A spasm shook the dying man's body and he let out his last breath.

"I'm sorry. There is nothing else I can do, I — " Mateo's breath stuck in his throat and suddenly he began to shake uncontrollably.

"Mateo! What's wrong?" Nandin said. When Mateo's eyes rolled back and the convulsions took over the whole of his body, Nandin knew he had to get him to the castle as soon as possible. He glanced about hoping to find someone close by who could assist him, but those he could see were injured or dead — he was on his own.

CHAPTER THIRTY-NINE

Sick and Tired

THE CONVULSIONS STOPPED.

Nandin picked up the unconscious form of his leader and carried him over his shoulder. By the time he reached the partially collapsed bridge, guards from the castle had arrived to help. Having the advantage of being stationed high up on the walls on the floating island they had helplessly watched everything that had transpired. Seeing the Commander climbing over the rubble carrying Mateo prompted them to leap into action.

They lowered a rope and Nandin tied it under Mateo's arms. It took several men to haul up the massive figure; they had no idea how the Commander had managed to carry the man on his own. By the time Nandin had climbed the rope, Hatooin had appeared with a stretcher and ordered the guards to carry Mateo to the lab.

He enquired as to what Mateo's symptoms were before he had lost consciousness; with a bit of prompting, Nandin was able to give a fairly accurate account. He had witnessed people succumb to an overdose of Essence before, but the shaking was new and it had him worried.

"It's not from him breathing in the fumes," Hatooin explained, "when he sent the Essence streaming through his body to repel those boulders, he caused a different type of Essence sickness."

"Will he recover?" Nandin asked, surprised to hear of Mateo's heroic effort to counter the Juro's attack, unaware that Mateo's actions triggered the Juro's actions.

"Most likely…I'll need to flush out his system."

"How do you know?"

"It's happened before," he said hurrying back to the castle without explaining further. "I could use your help."

"Of course, what can I do?"

"Go get cleaned up and then meet me in the lab. Make sure you change your clothes and get all that dust off your hands and face; I don't want you to contaminate the room or the procedure."

As soon as Nandin entered the lab, they set straight to work. He cringed when Hatooin inserted a tube into Mateo's arm. Even though he was unconscious, Mateo flinched. Nandin held onto Mateo to ensure he didn't move: either from flinching or the return of the convulsions as Hatooin hung the animal bladder on the wall. It was filled with the fluid that dripped down the tube into Mateo's arm.

The next part of the procedure involved bringing up Mateo's temperature. Nandin felt inducing a fever was counter-productive, but Hatooin insisted it was required to fully flush out Mateo's system. Hatooin set to filling a tub with hot water and once the bladder was empty and the temperature of the water was right, they lifted Mateo into the tub. When the fever had sufficiently taken hold, Nandin and a few Kameil used the stretcher to take Mateo back to his own room.

Nandin wanted to stay with him, but there was likely to be other casualties in the valley. He was doubtful that any of the buried Kameil had survived, but he was not going to chance leaving them there to die if they had. He left Mateo in Hattie's care with instructions that he be notified at once when Mateo gained consciousness or if his conditioned worsened.

He laboured in the streets clearing debris and searching for survivors alongside the Kameil who came to help. Some were there only out of the desire to lend aid, others were desperately searching for loved ones. Every few hours Nandin would return to the castle to prevent himself from becoming overwhelmed by the Essence. He would return to the valley with renewed strength and a greater skepticism of finding survivors. As darkness fell, they lit torches to help them see and worked in shifts so no one would collapse from exhaustion.

In the castle, Nandin dozed in a chair beside Mateo's bed, his arms crossed and legs stretched out in front of him. Mateo called out in his fever, chattering away about some madness, but Nandin listened intently in case any lucid thoughts came through. At one point, Nandin assisted Hattie in replacing the bed sheets, as they had been soaked from sweat. Between moving the rocks, recovering broken bodies, and the restless naps at Mateo's bedside, it was a very long night.

By morning, Mateo's fever broke and he settled into a deep, undisturbed sleep. As exhausted as he was, Nandin continued alternating between removing debris in the valley and sitting by Mateo's bedside. Graciously he ate the food that Hattie or Hatooin brought, but refused to follow their advice of going to his own room and getting a more restful sleep. It was mid-afternoon when Mateo finally came around.

"Thirsty," he muttered through parched lips.

Nandin's eyes popped open and his head snapped up making him keenly aware of the kink in his neck. He looked over, not sure if he had imagined the noise. When he saw Mateo's eyes open and his tongue desperately trying to bring moisture to his lips, Nandin got up and poured some water, eager to do something useful.

He placed his arm around Mateo's shoulders to help him sit up. Slowly Mateo sipped the water, enjoying the coolness as it trickled down his throat. When he had his fill he adjusted himself so he could sit up and lean against the wall; Nandin fluffed the pillows for him then pulled a chair closer to the bedside.

"When did the fever break?" Mateo asked.

"Early this morning...about six hours ago. You were aware you had a fever?"

"No, but I have experienced this previously so it was expected."

"That's what Hatooin said."

Mateo nodded. "He would know; he was there."

"When did it — "

"Years ago. I use to be careless when I used the Essence. After my last...episode, I vowed to be more reserved in my manipulation of it."

"Until now."

"Yes."

"So you knew this would happen," Nandin said, admiring the risk Mateo took.

"Yes," Mateo sighed.

"Thank you for trying to protect them; your efforts were not in vane...many of the Kameil escaped the quarry."

Mateo studied Nandin for a moment. He realized that Nandin had not witnessed him releasing the Qual and it made Mateo look like a hero instead of the instigator of the attack. It was likely those that had been at the quarry who knew what actually had happened were dead, including Jon. People from the castle may have observed the whole thing; he would get Hatooin to find out so he could keep the truth from spreading.

"I felt it would be worth the risk," Mateo said. "Tell me, how did this happened? How did the Juro enter our mountains?"

Nandin hated the role he played in the devastation that had befallen on them, but he couldn't change it now; he could only own up to it. "I...I showed Hanna's friends how to get to the northern pass and told them a safe place to make camp while they waited for me to bring her back to them — that was the condition of my release from the Citadel and why they gave me permission to bring Hanna to the valley."

Mateo was surprised at this revelation — Nandin didn't keep secrets. "Then how did they find their way to the summit? Surely that would have taken weeks by trial and error. Unless...is it possible they've been scouting our mountains without us knowing?"

Nandin hung his head. He didn't want to reveal the truth as he had no desire to tarnish his friend's reputation, especially since he was now dead and couldn't defend or redeem himself. "I told them how to get there," he mumbled, "Karn was an old friend of ours and a friend of Hanna's...he asked to see the valley. We didn't know he had a Vaktare force nearby and the Juro army following."

"An old acquaintance asked to see the valley and you just showed them? You didn't even consider what that might mean?" Mateo snapped as he reached out and clutched Nandin's arm.

"Karn wasn't just an old acquaintance," Nandin retorted, "Jon practically hero-worshipped the guy. He was a star pupil, top of his class, the best at...everything. When he told Jon he thought his sacrifice to help the Kameil was admirable, he was finally able to let go of the guilt he'd had ever since coming here. Karn agreed with my decision to bring Hanna to you when she lost consciousness...I thought I could convince him that the Kameil were worth saving. I hoped when he saw the peaceful community going about their daily lives it would help our cause and he could convince Master Juro not to attack."

As Nandin spoke, Mateo read his Essence and learned that,

even though Nandin was taking the blame, Jon had been the one to show Karn and his companions the way. It was rare that Mateo ever had to read Nandin's mind, as he usually spoke the truth, but too much had happened lately for Nandin to be unchanged. The fact that he lied now in order to preserve his friends reputation made Mateo admire him all the more.

"This Karn sounds like an interesting Jagare; I would have you tell me more about him at some other time," Mateo said, sitting back and easing his tone. "Tell me how it was you were able to get past our foes and return to the valley."

Nandin described his fear and anger when he saw the Juro and the contempt they had for the Kameil, and it fanned the rage he'd felt. He started pacing about the room as he described how he met up with the other Yaru and they planned to infiltrate the camp. It suddenly dawned on him that he had yet to learn of the their fate. He was so preoccupied with Mateo's recovery, rescuing the buried Kameil, and being consumed by Jon's death, that he'd forgotten to consider about the peril his brothers may still be in.

"I should go back," he said making his way across the room.

"No," Mateo said as he swung his legs around and attempted to stand. Still too shaky from his recent ordeal he fell back on his bed. Nandin rushed to his aid. "I'm fine, I'm fine. I just require food and a bit more rest. But you can't go — we need you here. There could be more Kameil in need of your help; some will be without homes. I need you to start work removing the debris from the roads and the bridge has to be repaired."

"I've already started those things," Nandin said, "The Yaru could still be in danger...and Hanna, she was going to delay the Juro; I have to find out what happened to her!"

"She was working for Master Juro, she'll be fine and the Yaru are survivors; they'll return." He held up his hands to stop Nandin from arguing. "Besides I'm not going to risk your life — not after everything you've been through. Stay here. Help the Kameil... but first, get some rest."

Nandin reluctantly agreed. He could use some sleep, but he doubted he would be able to quiet his mind enough to achieve it.

"I have a gift for you," Mateo said.

Nandin cast him a weary look. "This is hardly the time — "

"Trust me...it will help. See Hatooin before you go back down to the valley."

Nandin wasn't in the mood to sleep and his added anxiety over Hanna and the Yaru would make it impossible; the hard work required to move the rocks sounded like a better outlet for his anger than him tossing and turning in bed. He was covered in the stench of dirt, sweat and blood, so at the very least he would go get washed up and put on some clean clothes before he went back to work. He figured that should give Hatooin enough time to get Mateo's so-called gift.

CHAPTER FORTY

Work it Out

THE YARU RETURNED.

It was late in the evening when they emerged from the woods exhausted and battered. They could have made it back sooner if they didn't follow the Juro down the mountain; Nean insisted that they be escorted to ensure they were well on their way.

As per Nandin's request, the castles guards scanned the woods, constantly waiting for any sign of their return. When they entered the valley, Hatooin was notified; he made his way out of the castle and across the broken bridge to assist them.

A rope was secured to the bridge to span the gap where it had been crushed by the avalanche. Normally it would be sufficient for the Yaru to clamber up, but since he was unsure of their condition, Hatooin rallied the guards in case the Yaru needed assistance.

"Captain Nean!" Hatooin shouted as they picked their way through the field of rubble. He counted their numbers and quickly did the math. "Ten? We lost ten Yaru?" he said, his voice full of distress.

Nean shook his head. "Five. Two men are helping Aaron; he received a rather bad slash across his leg and can't walk very well. Thanlin and Plyral are making sure the Juro and Vaktare make it all the way down the mountain."

Aaron was one of Nean's team members. He knew Aaron had successfully disarmed his share of the Vaktare and knocked them out afterwards. Unfortunately, in the process of sending a blow to a man's head, another Vaktare slashed out — it was Aaron's quick reflexes that left him with a gash instead of a missing limb. Thanlin and Plyral were to ensure none of the Vaktare decided to stick around and scope out the place; if they did, Nean gave them permission to deal with the traitors as they saw fit.

"Mateo will be pleased you've returned; I'm sure he will want a report on what occurred up there."

"Of course...does he wish me to meet with him right away?"

Hatooin spoke in hushed tones as they made their way back to the castle.

"Master Mateo is unwell at the moment. It would be best if you were to write it down for now. I will bring you to him when he is ready."

The fact that Mateo had survived the wreckage was astonishing; that he was currently indisposed was not overly surprising, but it touched upon the concern Nean had over his friends.

"What happened to Nandin and Jon?" he whispered.

He was afraid to find out the answer and didn't want the dejected Yaru to hear anymore distressing news if it came to that.

"Nandin is physically fine, but these events have pushed him to the edge. I fear for his sanity. Jon didn't make it...neither did Sarah.

Nean was saddened by Jon's death and startled at the death of his wife-to-be. He had assumed she would be the first to learn of the danger and would have headed straight to safety.

"How did they..." he began to ask, not sure he wanted to know the answer.

"Sarah helped Jon and Nandin with the evacuation," Hatooin explained. "They were the last to leave the quarry."

Nean hung is head. "They died as heroes," he said softly. "And the Kameil? How many lives were lost?"

Hatooin shook his head. "We don't have exact numbers yet, Nandin's guessing around twenty. I'm afraid many of the bodies are difficult to identify; they're still searching for more."

Nean turned back towards the Yaru. "Go get something to eat and then come back to the valley; we've got work to do."

* * *

The sledgehammer crushed the boulders into smaller pieces. Again and again Nandin smashed it into the rocks, breaking them apart. Once he was surrounded with the more manageable size stones, he lifted them up and tossed them into the wagon sitting at the edge of the road.

Nandin had been at it since he left Mateo's side, pausing only long enough to ingest food or water when someone pressed it into his hand. He worked all day, resting against the rubble whenever exhaustion took over. The gift Hatooin had supplied him with was a mask that Mateo had created and had yet to test out. It filtered out the Essence so a Yaru could stay in the valley for extended periods of time. Nandin was taking full advantage of it — he had to. Crushing the stones was the only thing preventing his grief from consuming him. Finding the occasional body was what prevented him from rushing back up the mountain; he hadn't given up hope of finding survivors. He tried to reassure himself that Mateo was right; that the Yaru would make it through whatever had transpired — Hanna was a different matter.

He had no idea what the Juro would do to her when she tried to stop them. And he knew she'd try to stop them: she would have seen that the quarry hadn't been cleared of all the Kameil; there was no way she'd have stood by and let them send destruction down upon them. Did they cast her out as a traitor? Arrest her? Or did they knock her down to prevent her from interfering? He just couldn't imagine a scenario that went well.

Currently, Nandin worked by himself as the Kameil took a break for their evening meal; they didn't have the endurance to keep at it non-stop like the Commander did.

Nean picked his way up to the top of the mound Nandin was working on. "I brought you a drink," Nean said handing Nandin a flask.

"Nean?" Nandin said sounding muffled. He squinted in an attempt to make out Nean's features. He hadn't noticed that it had gotten so dark.

"Yes, it's me. Let's take a seat."

Nandin removed his mask as he accepted the flask, took a swig and then found a boulder to sit on.

"When did you get back?" Nandin asked, relief evident in his voice.

"Just now. I sent the boys to go eat; they'll be down to help shortly."

"Good, I could use it. What happened up there?"

Nean went on to explain the ambush and Blades' need to kill as many Vaktare as possible.

"Was he successful?" Nandin demanded in a way that worried Nean.

"He took out his share; I'm not sure what he would have done if he had caught Hanna."

Nandin leaned forward. "Hanna? He went after her?"

"Yes,"

"And?"

"And I stopped him." A torrent of emotions crossed Nandin's face. Nean knew he needed to hear the whole truth. "I shot him with a blow dart and it hit him in the neck, here," Nean dragged his finger across the main artery in his neck. "He bled to death in a matter of minutes."

"*You* shot him?" Nandin wasn't sure he had heard correctly.

"Yes. I did. Then I ordered the attack to cease and for the Yaru to stand down — enough men had already died."

"What did the Yaru say?"

"Nothing. Everyone stopped…and then we rushed to see the avalanche."

"I mean, what did they say about you shooting Blades?"

Nean sighed. "They don't know; no one does. Except that Jagare, Karn and now you."

"Karn knew?"

"Yes. He thanked me. Thanked me for helping Hanna get away."

"Away where? Where was she going?"

"Home."

Nandin abruptly stood up and teetered on the spot. "What do you mean *home*?"

"Master Juro told me that when the Qual was released a portal opened, Hanna could feel it. While she had the chance, she took off to find it."

The relevance about the Qual being released hadn't registered with Nandin, at the moment he was too concerned about Hanna. "Did anyone see her go? Do we know if she made it?"

Nean shrugged. "Master Juro seems to think she did; he checked out the tear sight as we left."

Nandin sank back down and held his head in his hands. Once he left her on the mountain, he didn't know if he would ever see her again, but now he knew he wouldn't. Pain welled up inside him, threatening to overwhelm him. It was like losing Jon all over again.

"Come on, Nandin," Nean said offering his hand, "we should go and get something to eat."

"I'm not hungry and I've got work to do."

"Not tonight; I think you've done enough. Hatooin said you were out here every few hours all last night and since he gave you the mask, you haven't stopped. The boys and I will take a shift. Once you get a proper meal and had a decent sleep you can work some more."

Reluctantly Nandin rose again swaying for a second. The mask he'd been wearing had prevented him from breathing in the Essence, but working in the midst of the Essence was still having an effect. He lifted the sledgehammer and crashed it into the stones one more time before following Nean back towards the broken bridge.

CHAPTER FORTY-ONE

Sense of Purpose

NANDIN FELT HOLLOW.

Standing on his balcony, leaning against the railing, he stared out into the night. He allowed Nean to usher him back to the castle, but refused to join the others in the great hall for dinner. He had no appetite or wish to see anyone. When the knock came on his door, he ignored it.

Someone entered and he heard dishes being placed on his table. He didn't bother looking to see who it was.

"Your dinner is getting cold," Mateo said softly as he stepped through the doorway to join Nandin outside.

"That's fine. I'll eat it later. I'm glad you've recovered," he said unable to pull his gaze away from the darkness.

Mateo studied the man before him. Behind the dirt and stubble of the last few days there was something that had changed about Nandin. The fatigue, stress and sorrow he had endured caused the youthful, charismatic individual to wither way to be replaced by an angry, fractured man. He could relate only too well as he too had tasted the cold reality of defeat. He leaned on the rail as he peered into the night. He could barely make out the outline of the mountain where Nandin had taken Hanna.

He placed his hand on Nandin's shoulder. "Nean tells me she left," Mateo said reading Nandin's thoughts.

Nandin's jaw tightened, but he didn't reply.

"Said she ran through the clearing, jumping over things and dodging men. That's remarkable for someone who just had the treatment a few days ago."

Nandin tilted his head to glance at Mateo who continued to stare straight ahead.

"She was pretty remarkable," Nandin said.

"Was she?" Mateo asked. "In what way?"

"She…she had this way of seeing things — I don't mean the sight." He paused to carefully choose his words. "The questions she asked and the way she saw people. It was like…she never saw race, just the person."

"Sounds like a good quality to have. I know she meant a lot to you; I'm glad she recovered okay."

Nandin turned and leaned back on the railing, crossing his arms as he continued to stare ahead without seeing.

"More than okay," he said.

"What do you mean?" Mateo asked trying to keep the excitement out of his voice.

Nandin had planned not to tell Mateo anything about Hanna's recovery for fear he would seek her out, test her or force her into his service. But now she was gone — not even on Galenia. There was nothing Mateo could do to her now.

"She was awake just hours after the procedure; I mean, *really* awake. When I took her out of the castle she was mad at me for not letting her walk. In the woods she had the need to run. And she could see in the dark."

"She could see in the dark?"

Nandin smiled broadly. "Yes. She said she could see the Essence and that it glowed. Can you do that?"

Mateo shook his head. "No, I can't," he replied, taken aback.

"What about the Juro, can they?"

271

"Not that I'm aware of."

"Hmm. The mystery that is Hanna," Nandin smiled as he recalled her words. He hesitated as he remembered their flight up the mountain. "She could really run. I bet she was faster than Jon, but she didn't get a chance to go full out. Then there was the draka — " His smile broadened at the memory.

"Draka?"

"She actually rode it!" He explained the draka attack, how she jumped on it and stabbed it. "She'd never even seen one before, yet she climbed right up on its neck and stabbed it where Jon told her it was vulnerable. When I saw it dropping I thought she was done for. I called to her and reached out my hand. And she caught it! It was like we planned it. It was…amazing. I thought it horrible luck that it went for her, but in the end, it turned out to be its downfall not ours."

"It wasn't random that it chose Hanna."

"What do you mean?"

"The draka are attracted to the Essence, and Hanna had more than any Yaru I've made. It only made sense that it attacked her."

"Really?"

"Really."

"Master Juro did claim she is of all three races. She is like you, I guess, and Hanna said you burned the brightest." Still, she was gone. "I hope she's okay…at least she got what she wanted," Nandin said dejectedly.

"What was that?" Mateo replied calmly, suppressing the sudden delight he felt at this latest revelation.

"To go back home."

"How do you know she went home?"

"Well, apparently a portal opened and she went back through it — at least Master Juro thinks she did."

"But even if she did Nandin, we don't know where the portals go. It could have taken her to another world. She said she came to Galenia from a portal by Kayu. What proof do we have they all lead to the same place?"

Nandin's grief of losing Hanna forever was replaced by a sudden anxiety for her safety. "Is there a way we can find out?"

"I'm not sure…we could try reopening the portal. If we did, then we'd be able to confirm where it goes."

"But the portals…the tears, are destructive. The Juro brought down a mountain on us to prevent you from causing them."

"True. But let's think this through. A portal opened when the Qual was released, but then the Juro forced it all back. Which means there was no Qual being drained from anywhere."

"Are you suggesting that if you removed the Qual and put it back, no damage would occur?"

"Right. I could extract the Qual to create a portal to find out if Hanna made it home…and then replace the Qual. I just need to find a way to get it. Re-digging the quarry would take too long and is far too risky — I don't want another mountain being brought down on us." He paused as he thought it through. "It would have to be a quick and precise method, clean and unobtrusive. I'll need to go to the previous tear sights to see what I can learn, then come up with a plan to get the Qual. It'll take time…these things often do."

Nandin didn't know why Mateo would go through all the trouble of opening a portal to find out if Hanna was okay; he hardly seemed concerned of the possible consequences of giving her the treatment. He suspected Mateo had his own motivation. But Nandin didn't care. He needed to make sure Hanna was safe; after that, he'd ensure Mateo didn't continue creating portals. He had a sneaking suspicion Mateo really wanted to bring Hanna back. Nandin wanted it too, but he wasn't ready to admit it.

"What do you need me to do?" Nandin asked.

"Be the Commander. I've been complacent over the years...I let this happen, not you. I should have had sentries in the mountain and by the rivers. The Masters hadn't bothered coming out this way in over a century, but I should have known that one day they would return. I need you to improve our defences while I figure out these portals. Arrange the removal of the rubble, keep training the Kameil to hunt, give out the Essence tablets, protect the farms...and make them strong, Nandin." He scratched his chin as he thought it through. "Maybe, that's where I went wrong. I created the Yaru to be their protectors, but maybe I should have trained them...this valley made them vulnerable. They had no way to protect themselves from the Vaktare, no defence against the Juro as they watched their homes crumble before them. Everything fell on the shoulders of a few men — great men, but your numbers are too few. What will the Kameil do when the Juro return? And you know they will, this was only the beginning."

He gave Nandin a chance to absorb what he was saying. Remembering the fear the Juro expressed when gazing upon the valley, Nandin knew — Mateo was right.

"The Kameil are hardier than you know," Nandin said, "given the training and the tools they could defend the valley. But I don't know if I'm the man for the job. You may have forgotten my failure at the camp. Add to that, leading our enemies into the mountain...I don't think I've earned the right to do the job your asking of me."

"I need you to do this. You won't be doing it alone, you'll need to delegate, but I need you to command. I know it's a lot to take on. There are numerous, critical decisions to be made. But I trust you. You're a good man, Nandin. I know you'll do what's best for our people. Learn from your mistakes; don't quit because of them. The people need a leader; they will follow you."

Nandin straightened. He would be in charge. No more games. No more half-truths. The decisions would be his. And it's exactly what Jon would have done.

"Will you do it?" Mateo asked.

Nandin turned to study the valley below: a city full of people, dependent on Mateo and a few Yaru for their survival. It was time someone taught them to defend themselves. If he didn't do it, who would Mateo turn to? Who would he trust with that kind of power? Nandin didn't like the choices.

With new determination, he pushed back the grief that had taken hold of him and the guilt that threatened to bury him. "I'll do it," he said as he made his way back into his room. "Now... let's eat, I'm famished."

CHAPTER FORTY-TWO

Mind Over Matter

MATEO DELIBERATED.

After returning to his study, he sat down at his desk and pulled out his journal. The black leather book was lacking many entries from the past few days and he needed to get his thoughts down while they were still fresh in his mind. It was risky keeping the journals, as few would like what they found there. Unfortunately, it was the only way he'd found to keep his ideas clear and solidify his plans. Hatooin had his uses, but Mateo didn't believe in any one person knowing all of his intentions and concerns. At the end of the day, the only one he could truly rely on was himself.

Year 1105

Day 172

The devastation the Juro brought down on the quarry was absolute. They have completely blocked all access to the Qual and destroyed all of the machines. It is unfathomable that they broke from their routines long enough to come to the valley. That is typically the type of errand for their Jagare puppets. It was unpredictable that they realized only an army of Juro could stop me.

My use of the Essence to block their attack was a calculated risk. As the Essence coursed through me freely it was the first time I truly knew its raw power. It was extremely dangerous to channel the Essence as I did. Teaching

277

Hatooin how to purge my system proved, once again, to have been a wise choice.

Nevertheless, the valley is now in shambles; the quarry utterly destroyed. I'll have to devise a new, more effective way to reach the Qual. I came so close to collecting it and it's taking all my willpower to refrain from punishing those responsible. I can feel my control slipping; it's time to visit The Vault once again. The last thing Nandin needs right now is to be exposed to my unchecked emotions.

Hanna warrants further study. Her disappearance from Galenia was unfortunate, but has brought me closer to determining how to create the portals, as she called them. If releasing Qual does create them, then I will open one again, though I doubt it will be simple. I'll need to test my theory with caution — the Juro cannot know what I'm doing. How to proceed has yet to be determined. If I remove the Qual, it will cause damage, which they will discover sooner or later. I told Nandin I would return the Qual to the ground, but if I do I will no longer be able to create liquid Essence and consequently, no new Yaru.

If I can open a portal to Earth, perhaps I can bring more people like Hanna here and use the Qual to create a new race with Juro-like abilities. If I had a group of individuals like that I could hold off any attack on the valley.

I'll need to investigate the tear sights and see what they have in common. Hanna claimed there was no Essence in the area afterwards, but why? What prevented more Qual from filling the void I created? Does this mean portals open anywhere deplete of Qual?

There's too much I don't know — too many variables at the moment and no guarantee of success. The portals could lead to random places or Hanna could be one of a kind — it's possible the treatment wouldn't work on more of her people. It is an unreliable course of action.

I will proceed with my original plan, despite the fact it's proving more difficult to guide Nandin. Since he met

Hanna, my influence over him has weakened and the Yaru will follow his lead. Even without having the ability to manipulate their Essence, he can sway them and I know he would not approve of my plan.

If only Blades had survived, he wouldn't hesitate to take on any mission. Thanlin doesn't have the skills to lead the Yaru in this as of yet. I'll have to work with him. It's a setback, but I am determined to see this through.

Without creating more Yaru, it will fall to the Kameil to defend the valley if I succeed. Nandin will prepare them. Nean could do it, but I don't trust him. After all these years, I still haven't been able to discover his motives. The Kameil will rally to Nandin because of their discontent of me. He must surpass the odds; for when the time comes, it will take an army to protect the valley.

ABOUT THE AUTHOR

Born in Alberta, Canada, LAURA L. COMFORT is a freelance writer whose works include fantasy novels, script writing and educational resources such as Gamed Academy – Minecraft School. She has been a guest speaker at schools, youth groups and Literacy Day Events. She enjoys working with today's youth in writing workshops and mentoring future novelists. Her passions include writing, creating digital artwork and teaching. Always exploring and trying new things, some of her adventures include skydiving, caving, and climbing Mayan ruins, which have provided lots of material to help create her fantasy world.

Join the Galenia Wikia:
http://galenia.wikia.com/wiki/Galenia_Wiki

47858913R00176

Made in the USA
Charleston, SC
19 October 2015